John Edwin Nixon

Parallel Extracts Arranged for Translation into English and Latin

John Edwin Nixon

Parallel Extracts Arranged for Translation into English and Latin

ISBN/EAN: 9783337405120

Printed in Europe, USA, Canada, Australia, Japan

Cover: Foto ©Andreas Hilbeck / pixelio.de

More available books at **www.hansebooks.com**

PARALLEL EXTRACTS

ARRANGED FOR

TRANSLATION
INTO ENGLISH AND LATIN,

WITH

𝔑𝔬𝔱𝔢𝔰 𝔬𝔫 𝔍𝔡𝔦𝔬𝔪𝔰.

BY

J. E. NIXON, M.A.

FELLOW AND CLASSICAL LECTURER OF KING'S COLLEGE, CAMBRIDGE.

PART I.—HISTORICAL AND EPISTOLARY

NEW EDITION.

London:
MACMILLAN AND CO.
1879

PREFACE TO FIRST EDITION.

In lecturing on Latin Composition I had often felt a want of some collection of English and Latin passages, to put into the hands of my pupils, that I could refer to for illustration, and some summary of general rules to which I might refer the peculiarities of idiom in any passage that I discussed with them. I have tried to supply this want, and at the same time to provide passages suitable for translation from and into English, selected and arranged as parallels to some extent in subject or in style—in a few cases almost exact translations—and so as to be interesting as well as useful.

It is hoped that the small numerals in the extracts (which refer to the Notes on Idioms, and represent my own method of helping my pupils) will rouse the student to observe and classify for himself other peculiarities of diction besides those referred to, and encourage thought more effectually than foot-notes or adaptations; and that generally the book may help the teacher to teach directly and systematically much that students are often left to absorb unconsciously by a process of saturation or infiltration in writing out 'fair copies.'

I feel much indebted to Mr Potts' admirable little book (*Hints on Latin Composition*), and also to Mr E. A. Abbott's on *Latin Prose through English Idioms*. They satisfy a real want that has long been felt. Both I have made use of, though my line and method of teaching had been adopted before I saw either, and part of the book was in print before I saw the latter.

I am also much indebted to Professor J. B. Mayor and other friends for valuable hints and corrections in the proof-sheets.

N.   *b*

The Second Part will contain a selection of Oratorical, Philosophical and Miscellaneous Passages: and I hope to be able shortly to provide a selection of easy passages for Greek Prose Composition arranged on the same principle.

Suggestions and corrections will be gratefully received.

J. E. NIXON.

KING'S COLLEGE, CAMBRIDGE,
Jan. 1874.

PREFACE TO SECOND EDITION.

IN the Second Edition some corrections and additions have been made in the Notes on Idioms, and some easier pieces—translations, or adaptations of letters (in one or two cases borrowed from Melmoth's Pliny)—added at the end, with a general Index. A few references have also been added to Nägelsbach's *Stilistik*, a book invaluable for its copious examples, which I have lately compared throughout, and regret that I did not consult it for my first edition. It can and should be used even by those who have little or no knowledge of German, for the purposes of illustration. The numeration of the Notes, the numerical references, the numbering and paging of the Extracts have been left unaltered, to avoid confusion in the case of classes using both editions. It is hoped that the improved side-summaries of the notes will help to make the small numerical references more practically useful.

KING'S COLLEGE, CAMBRIDGE.
May, 1876.

Translations of some of the passages have been printed in such a way as to be readily distributable to a class. Application for these should be made direct to the Author.

CONTENTS OF NOTES ON IDIOMS.

ABLE OF HISTORICAL AND EPISTOLARY EXTRACTS.

(*Cicero, Pliny, Pope, Swift, Lamb, Sidney Smith, Cowper,
Leigh Hunt, &c.*)

Numbers in brackets are used for the purpose of reference to distinguish the English from the Latin Extracts.

The Extracts which will be found most easy for translation with the help of their parallels are Nos. (1—7), (13), (25), (55—60), and also such simple letters as (28), (31), (37), (38).

The Passages most useful for practice of *Oratio Obliqua* are Nos. (4), (6—8), (10—12); and (14), (16a), (25), (37a, b), (47a), may also conveniently be adapted for the same purpose.

NOTES ON IDIOMS[1].

The small figures in the Extracts refer to these Notes: the references in the Notes to the number and line of the Extracts.

§ 1. THE natural order of a Latin sentence is (i) subject, (ii) predicate, or (i) subject, (ii) object, (iii) verb, each with its own qualifying clauses closely attached.

§ 1.
Order and connexion of ideas.
§§ 1—9.

When the subject is contained in the verb, the verb will generally precede the object; e.g. *Dixit te aegrotare; dedi litteras Kal. Jun.;* but *Kal. Jun. Cicero litteras dedit; cf.* 29, 1; 31, 1; 37, 51—54.

Verb containing subject precedes.

Where this order is changed, as it constantly is, it is changed purposely for

Emphasis.
cf. §§ 4, 5 β, γ, 8.

α. emphasis, as in 3, 1; 22, 15, 19; 29, 26, so as to throw the subject, verb, or object into light or shade.

β. connexion of ideas, as 1, 22; 4, 2; 9, 1; 20, 22; 21, 27; so that particles signifying sequence of thought or time stand first; a few, like *quidem, autem, vero,* and other quasi-enclitics, take the second place.

Connecting particles.
cf. §§ 9 α, 34, 47, 50, γ.

γ. antithesis, as 1, 12; 17, 2; 25, 26; 39, 4, 6. esp. in chiasmus, *cf.* 23, 14, 17, 20; 39, 4, 8, 14.

Antithesis.

δ. euphony, rhythm, or variety, 1, 23; 3, 6, 12; 7, 38; 11, 17; 19, 29; 22, 28; 24, 1, 19, 26.

Euphony.

Mark well these changes in Latin, and emphasize accordingly in English translation; accustom your ear to catch the emphasis in English and reproduce it by the

---

[1] The rules given refer mainly to Latin, but may often be read conversely for English prose.

order in Latin. It will be found useful to accentuate English passages accordingly before translation ; e.g. 'I' am the man;' 'I am not' the man;' 'he will' go;' 'they may' come,' &c.; and even the feet of some rhythmical clauses may be marked as if verse, e.g. (1) 26; (2) 22; 36, 4, &c. ; 37, 21, &c.

§ 2.
Arrangement of compound terms,

§ 2. *a.* When two words form one combined idea (as adjective + substantive, or substantive + governed genitive) the most emphatic or prominent idea comes first in Latin, e. g. 3, 1, 2 ; 26, 34, 36 ; except when euphony (as in the case of monosyllables coming last) or other reasons (§ 1) forbid it, e.g. 26, 39.

attributes.

Accordingly, mere attributive *adjuncts* of a word or idea follow, essential modifications precede. In English attributes generally precede.

'The senator Cicero' becomes then '*Cicero senator,*' i.e. 'Cicero who was also a senator.' '*Senator Cicero*' would mean rather 'a senator, viz. Cicero.' *Cf.* 43, 4.

Cf. 6, 6, 14, 20; 19, 23 ; 23, 2; 24, 29; 25, 1; 26, 25 ; 53, 3.

β. Where more than two words are thus combined in one idea, enclose those that are less obviously connected between those that are more so; e.g. *tua in me pietas, populi ob haec facta indignatio.* See § 3 *β.*

Cf. 37, 21; 49, 23, &c.

§ 3.
Qualifying words and clauses.

§ 3. *a.* Qualifying words or clauses in Latin (especially adverbs and negatives) are placed near (and mostly before) what they qualify; when qualifying a clause they precede the clause[1]; when only a word, they precede the word ; e.g. *recte haec scribis, haec recte scribis; non haec timeo, haec non timeo; ne quod timeat quidem habet.*

Cf. 9, 3; 20, 27; 26, 29, &c.

---

[1] Similarly *quidem* (*ne—quidem*) and other enclitics follow closely the word *or the clause* that they qualify. *Cf.* 8, 15; 22, 6; 39, 27; 45, 7 ; 54, 18.

§ 3. β. Such qualifying words and clauses as would otherwise naturally drift to the main verb, must often in Latin be tied down to other members of the sentence to which they belong, by artificial collocation (as in § 2 β), or by the use of a participle or relative clause, —where in Greek the article would be used; e.g. *milites qui in urbe erant* (not *in urbe* alone) *manserunt—Vox e templo missa revocavit. Cf.* § 58.

Cf. 1, 5 ; 2, 5 ; 13, 30 ; 14, 11, 13 ; 16, 11 ; 24, 2, 3.

For exceptions (not uncommon) *cf.* Nägelsbach, pp. 22 and 204. §§ 3 and 75.

§ 4. a. Search out the *real* subject and bring it forward, whether in the nominative or oblique cases; e.g. *Marcum nihil horum fefellit.*

§ 4. Emphatic position of subject. cf. § 8.

Cf. 3, 1 ; 5, 1 ; 12, 1 ; 23, 13.

β. Find the real predicate and state it directly, not allusively or subordinately, or in a relative clause as often happens in English (see § 5 ε. and § 8); as, *sedens legebam*, I was seated reading.

Put real predicate in main verb.

Cf. (3) 19 ; (10) 9, 12 ; (26) 3 ; (29) 32 ; (31) 4.

γ. Mark and emphasize antithetical ideas, by change of order, so as to reproduce the force of the Greek μὲν and δὲ, or of our 'on the one hand,' 'on the other,' 'while,' 'respectively,' &c., whether you add or omit *quidem, autem, vero,* &c. *Cf.* 2, 1 ; 4, 14, &c.; 25, 16. On Chiasmus *cf.* Potts' "Hints," p. 46.

Antithetical order with or without emphatic particles.

δ. We often use 'actually,' 'indeed,' or some such word to emphasize, when the emphasis of order suffices in Latin. *Cf.* 7, 26 ; 43, 14 ; (43) 8.

ε. Arrange clauses in Latin chronologically ; e. g. put the aim before the action, the cause before the effect. *Cf.* § 9 γ.

Chronological arrangement. cf. 9 γ.

N.   c

§ 5.
Relatives,
and relative
clauses,
their place
and usage.

§ 5. *a.* The relative in Latin will come at the beginning of its clause, the antecedent as near it as possible, before or after, *as if the relative clause were an adjective.*

As connecting links
they come
first,

The Latin relative (as subject or object) often stands first in a sentence to connect it with a previous sentence, where we use a demonstrative or personal pronoun with or without the copula ; e.g. *Tum milites vocat; quos quum monuisset, &c.*

Cf. 25, 17 ; 37, 4 ; 45, 5 ; 48, 2.

as emphatic
also with
antecedent
attracted,

β. The antecedent is often attracted into the relative clause, often repeated in it—to prevent ambiguity (as in § 3 *β*) or to emphasize by repetition ; e.g. *quae urbs te unice coluit hanc urbem deles.*

Cf. 5, 15 ; 23, 4 ; 36, 2.

in apposition,

γ. Relative clauses (or their equivalents) in apposition to another idea will usually come first in Latin, last in English ; except where fact follows on hypothesis, or realization on conception : *metuens ne veniret—id quod factum est.*

Cf. 6, 5 ; 14, 8 ; 22, 9 ; 26, 16.

in antithesis.

So, too, in comparisons (*quo fortior eo felicior*, cf. 12, 12), where we invert the order : and generally.

Relatives
used in
Latin where
they are not
in English.

δ. Relatives (e.g. *that*) omitted in English must be expressed in Latin, *cf.* (10) 9, 12 ; (32) 12 ; (37) 49 ; (49) 9 ; and prepositional or adverbial clauses (e.g. 'the scene before us,' 'the house close by') often be replaced by relative clauses. For converse *cf.* § 9 *δ.*

Cf. 5, 11 ; (10) 15 ; 24, 2.

Where in English (as in Greek with the article) the participle is used substantivally for a class, the relative with clause must be used in Latin as a rule, except where, as in § 25, the *plural* present participle is used.

§ 5. ε. Relative clauses in Latin are essentially ad- Relative
junets, whether adjectival, adverbial, or co-ordinate, and clauses
must not be
must not stand for the main predicate. In English they used for
main predi-
often do so, some conventional or subordinate idea oc- cate.
cupying the main place (*cf.* § 4 β); e. g. *clades nova
afflixit urbem,* 'a fresh blow came that crushed the city.'

Cf. (13) 34; (24) 3.

ζ. Where you have two relative clauses consecutively, Consecut've
rel.itives.
do not join them, as is often done in English, by a copula
(except where they refer to different antecedents; e. g.
1, 15; 3, 18); but either make one relative serve for both
clauses, or change the latter clause into a co-ordinate
clause and the relative into a demonstrative or personal
pronoun; e. g. *quod ego probo, tu autem non* [*id*] *improbas.*

Cic. however, Leg. II. 2, has *patria pro qua mori, et
cui nos totos dedere et in qua nostra omnia ponere debemus*
by way of an accumulative intensive (*polysyndeton*).

Cf. (23) 2; (36) 19; (53) 6.

η. Double relatives in the same clause are common Double
relatives.
in Latin, rare in English; e. g. *quod qui dat,* &c.

§ 6. Do not unnecessarily change the nominative § 6.
Unneces-
case of co-ordinate and successive clauses as is often done sary change
of subject.
in English. To avoid this you may use the ablative abso- *cf.* § 9 β.
lute, subordinate clauses, active for passive, participles, &c.

Cf. (3) 1—5; (22) 5, 6; (31) 1.

§ 7. a. The passive occurs oftener in English than § 7.
Passives re-
in Latin, except in the past participle: *cf.* 3, 1; 9, 1; placed by
Actives.
(11) 8. The Latin passives are more cumbrous, less (But *cf* §§
25, 26.)
needed (*cf.* § 4 and § 8), less suited on the whole to the
objective simplicity and directness of the language.

It is especially perhaps in cases where we make things, Esp. to give
prominence
that are virtually objects, subjects of a (passive) verb, to living
agents.
and the *agents* subordinate, that they use the active

instead, with the agents as subjects and things subordinate. The so-called impersonal verbs, *tædet, &c.* occur frequently, but as a rule they shrank from personifying things or ideas as subjects or agents, where not necessary.

Cf. (11) 14; (17) 12, &c.

§ 8. *Te rogo.* 'It is you that I ask.' In English to emphasize an *object* we make it the subject of an auxiliary clause, or of a passive, that it may precede the verb. In Latin the object may be placed first. So, generally, position in Latin answers the effect of our underlining (with voice or pen), our auxiliaries 'do,' &c., or other tricks of emphasis; and therefore auxiliary verbs and relatives (English) will often be suppressed in translation.

Cf. § 5. ε. 7, 28; (7) 7; (8) 6; 10, 13; (10) 12; 39, 3, 8.

§ 9. *a.* The simple copula is oftener omitted than in English, e.g. *redit juvenis, rem narrat, implorat opem* (cf. 1, 2—9; (1) 2—9), and is often replaced by the relative; sometimes by adversative antithetical particles, *autem, vero, &c.*

Cf. § 5; 43, 11; 45, 5.

But a loose aggregation of sentences as in English is avoided, and clauses must (*cf.* § 47) be connected by emphasis of repetition, or particles, &c., *cf.* §§ 34, *a*; 47.

β. Co-ordinate (English) sentences must constantly be replaced by (Latin) subordinate clauses (the frequent repetition of 'and' being thereby avoided); the ablative absolute, deponent and passive past participles, relative, temporal, and other clauses will be used instead.

Cf. 2, 5; (2) 25; 4, 3, 5; (7) 44; 11, 11; 25, 11, 18.

These clauses will as far as possible keep the same subject and object, so that our repetition of pronouns ('him,' 'it,' &c.) will be avoided; e.g. *Tunc convocatos quum breviter admonuisset, paullisper moratus secum eduxit.*

Cf. § 6; (4) 5, 28; (6) 4, 7; (7) 25, &c.

Side notes: § 8. Emphasis in English requires use of passives or auxiliary clauses. § 9. cf. § 5. Connection of clauses. Omission of simple copula. Co-ordinate sentences replaced by subordinate, keeping the same subject and object. cf. § 6.

§ 9. γ. They will be grouped (subordinately to the main idea or action) in *natural logical* order of time, aim, cause and effect, connected by relatives, or antithetically by position alone, *autem, quidem, vero* often coming in where we use 'and' or 'while.' Cause, object, qualification or manner (causal, final, modal clauses) generally *precede* the main action, consecutive clauses follow, comparative follow or precede; except where the order is changed for emphasis or connexion of ideas, or where the object of an action is identical with or suggests its consequent result; e.g. *faces admovit ut aedem accenderet.*

And by the period, in natural, logical, chronological order. cf. § 4 ε.

Cf. § 4 ε; 3, 8—11; 5, 16—20; 15, 1—5; 17, 4—7.

Long sentences thus grouped, with the main verb reserved till the close, are called periods, and are commoner in history than in oratory or letters. *Cf.* Livy I. 6 and I. 16, &c.

The period.

δ. In parenthetical clauses, where we use a relative clause, or a clause in apposition without a verb [e.g. one of them named (or who was named) Manus; &c., *Unus ex his, Manus ei nomen erat*], a co-ordinate sentence without or with a copula is often found in Latin. *Cf.* 3, 1, 4; 7, 30; 24, 15; 25, 28; 33, 10; 34, 12; 39, 23. For other parentheses *cf.* 14, 5; 24, 5, 27; 43, 17; 44, 23; 48, 8; 54, 14. For converse *cf.* § 5 δ.

Parentheses by relatives or apposition in English: distinct co-ordinates in Latin.

§ 10. A proper name, as subject or object, is oftener repeated in English than in Latin. We often vary the repetition by a periphrasis, 'the old man,' 'the general,' &c. In both cases *is, ille* (if anything is wanted) will be found generally sufficient in Latin.

§ 10. Substantives, §§ 10—14. Repetition of subject.

Cf. (4) 30; (25) 4, 22, 26; (45) 19.

Where the proper name is so used in Latin it generally comes first, and is emphatic or distinctive.

Proper name repeated for emphasis only, in Latin.

Cf. 1, 14; 4, 11; 15, 1; 18, 17.

Descriptive Nominatives omitted. So too when, in English, descriptive nominatives are tacked on to relative clauses, the relative alone will be used in Latin. 'The sailors who had jumped down' = *qui desiluerant*. *Cf.* 13, 21, 31.

And the same rule holds in the case of other subjects and objects repeated in English to round the sentence, or balance it antithetically.

Cf. (2) 12, 15, 17, 25, 29; (3) 8, 17, 22; (15) 9; (16) 23.

Allusive periphrase expressed by separate clause. When however, as in § 18, a new idea is thus thrown in allusively, it may be expressed in Latin, but directly, by a separate clause; e.g. 'the veteran general was not to be deceived so easily:' *cf.* (14) 7.

§ 11. Substantival pleonasms. Double phrases. § 11. *a.* Double phrases to express single ideas are often used in English, single terms in Latin. 'A feeling of shame' = *pudor quidam*.

Cf. (2) 8; (9) 21, 25; (10) 2; (16) 23; (22) 34, 35, 39.

English conventional periphrases. *β.* Effete metaphors, needless synonyms and repetitions, and conventional periphrases (English) will be replaced in Latin by the simplest terms, or omitted.

As instances may be given the words *object, point, feature, circumstance, instance, capacity, relation, terms, person, expression, elements, incident, purport, idea, substance, theory, step, view, department, sphere, contingency, emergency, consideration, issue.*

Latin stock phrases. A few stock terms or phrases are found in Latin: the various meanings of *ars, res, locus, studium, genus, ratio, vis, sententia*, may be compared. *Cf.* Näg. § 8. The frequency of them in English is due partly to the want of genders in adjectives, which necessitates the use of neuter substantives, partly to the love of variety, partly to the composite elements of the language, which provide synonyms in abundance.

The want of such synonyms in Latin often makes it impossible to reproduce some of our finer shades of thought and expression; and words like *res, ratio*, &c., become too vague and indefinite.

Cf. 2, 1, 12, 22; (2) 2, 14, 24; (4) 3, 16; (6) 4, 6; (7) 48; (11) 2, 7, 17, &c.

§ 11. γ. The repetition, in comparisons and other connexions, of the substantive or its equivalent, or of the word 'one,' 'ones,' is unnecessary in Latin ; e. g. *magnae majora sunt vitia quam parvæ urbis;* such substantive when referring to two adjectives, &c., generally comes after the second, in the singular if the two ideas are singular and separate, in the plural if they are joined as a plural idea ; *cf.* 16, 15. *Repetition of nouns and equivalents avoided.*

Cf. § 16 ε. 5, 12; 25, 30; 26, 41, 62; 44, 3.

§ 12. Substantives are not used so much in Latin as by us, and must often in translation be (α) taken into the verb, replaced by (β) adverb, (γ) adjective, (δ) participle, (ε) gerundive, relative or other verbal clauses. *§ 12. Less frequent use of substantives in Latin.*

In such cases the qualifying adjective will often become an adverb. *Cf.* (2) 9; (11) 17; (25) 6.

α. *Facta quae imperavit. Cf.* 1, 26; 7, 19; 9, 22.

β. *Haec saepius dicta,* 'the frequent repetition of these remarks.' *Cf.* (2) 27; (3) 7; 7, 37.

γ. *Trepidi coeunt,* 'in alarm.'

Cf. (4) 3; (6) 3; 7, 9; 8, 9.

δ. *Pauca locutus,* 'after a few words.'

Cf. (1) 10; (5) 26; 7, 11; 8, 26.

ε. *Nescis quid possint, quid sit agendum,* 'their power,' 'line of action;' *quanti esset, emerit,* 'value,' 'purchase-money.' *Cf.* Näg. §§ 36—9.

So also the 'site,' 'scene' = *qua;* 'the question' = *-ne, num;* 'the reason for' = *cur;* 'amount' = *quantum;* 'time' = *quum;* 'limit,' 'maximum' = *quo ne longius, pluris,* &c. or *quoad* with verb.

Cf. (6) 2; (12) 15; 23, 8.

It should be specially noticed that the English substantive is used for definite *times* of action without expressing it, where a *tense* form must therefore be used in Latin: e. g. 'non-payment' may be *quod non solvitur, solvebatur* &c., *ne solvatur* &c. in any tense.

§ 13.
Abstract
replaced by
concrete
nouns.

§ 13. In Latin substitute the concrete reality for the abstract idea; the thing or person (qualified or not) for the quality or characteristic of it; e.g. *aperte adulantem nemo non odit*, 'open flattery all hate,' and, generally, matter-of-fact phrases for idealisms or mental conceptions: as the 'top of the mountain,' *summus mons;* 'the capture of the city,' *capta urbs;* 'the rest of the booty,' *reliqua præda;* 'all of us,' 'three hundred of us,' *nos omnes, nos trecenti;* 'city of Rome,' *urbs Roma;* 'Rome,' *Romani;* 'the hour of nine,' *hora nona;* sometimes on the contrary we find *vox voluptatis*, 'the word pleasure,' &c., but rarely; *cf.* Madvig, § 286.

Cf. (2) 10, 23; (4) 12; (5) 3; (6) 11; (7) 53.

Person pre-
ferred to
thing as
subject.
cf. §§ 7, 14.

The nominative case will often have to be changed to avoid making an idea the subject; cf. § 7.

Cf. (3) 10; (17) 19; (19) 9; (25) 9.

Cf. Näg. §§ 9—19, on the usage of the *Species* for the *Genus.*

Realism of
Latin.

§ 14. The same tendency to realism and matter of fact is shown in such direct personification of ideas as *aures* for 'ear,' *oculi* the 'eye,' *corpus* for 'self.' *Cf. scribere sua manu*, 'to write one's self.'

Cf. 2, 11; 15, 12; 17, 13; 26, 53; 52, 10.

cf. § 13.

Write *Marcus fertur dixisse*, rather than *fertur Marcum dixisse*, thereby making a person rather than a sentence or idea the subject. *Cf.* 8, 9; 17, 7; 20, 26.

Substan-
tival prepo-
sitions
rarer in
Latin.
cf. § 50.

The (English) tendency to the use of substantives appears in prepositional terms: in spite of, *tamen, nihilominus;* in consequence of, *ob, ex, propter;* in the midst of, *inter;* in accordance with, *ex, secundum;* in return for, *pro;* on condition that, *ita ut;* in proportion as, *prout;* by the side of, *propter;* as we often use present participles also (e.g. 'owing to,' 'respecting,' 'pending,' 'touching,' 'according to') as prepositions, *cf.* § 25 β.

§ 15. a. The so-called indefinite article 'an' (*un*, *ein*, *uno*) is sometimes expressed by *unus* in early Latin; often by *quidam;* sometimes by *aliquis*, or *is* (*a* man) *qui;* mostly it is left unexpressed; e.g. *inest hominibus vis quaedam* ('*a* power'). *Cf.* 21, 11; 31, 14, 24.

§ 15.
Articles and
pronouns,
§§ 15—17.
'an,' *qui-
dam,* &c.

β. The English 'one' (except as numeral, cf. 3, 4) is rarely *unus*, but *quidam*, (*is*) *qui*, *quis*, *aliquis*, sometimes *alius—alius;* in some senses *tu*, or rather the verb in the 2nd person; and it is often left untranslated as in § 11 γ, as also the indefinite 'some;' e.g. *is erat qui*, 'he was one of those men who;' *sunt qui*, &c.; *Dama ex servis* (*quidam*), 'one of his slaves.'

Indefinite
'one,'<br>'some.'

Cf. 3, 16; 9, 24.

γ. The = that (cf. *le*, *la*, *il*, *lo*, *le* from *ille*) is a weak demonstrative, omitted in Latin where the definiteness is otherwise expressed; or translated by *hic*, *ille*, *is*, *iste*, or the relative. *Cf.* 1, 15, 18; 25, 28; 32, 12.

'The'=*hic
ille.* &c. or
omitted.

§ 16. a. *Is* takes up the subject of a previous sentence where we repeat a proper name (§ 10); often = *a*, *the*, *such as*, *such*. *Cf.* 1, 7; 9, 21; 29, 27; 31, 26.

§ 16.
Is for proper
name.
cf. § 10.
'*Is*'='such.'

β. *Ille* points to a new or different subject; and so *illud* generally = τόδε (or ἐκεῖνο), that which follows. It is often used also of celebrities of the *distant* past, of the ancients (esp. in oratory), as *hic* of the moderns.

Ille.

Cf. 39, 19; 45, 26; 54, 4; 55, 8.

γ. With *hic*, *ille* means generally the *more remote*, i.e. the former, *hic* the nearer, the last or latter. *Ilic*, in the sense of 'this last,' often takes up the subject of a preceding sentence, like *is*. *Cf.* 5, 4; 31, 5, 18.

Hic, ille.

Ilic is used frequently in Cicero of Rome—the Roman world, as if 'this that you see before your eyes;' just as we say 'our government,' 'our army.' *Cf.* Cic. *Cat.* IV. 4. 7; *Att.* XII. 19. 1; *p. Cæl.* VI. 14, &c.; Näg. § 44.

Iste.

δ. *Iste* refers to the second person, as *ille* to third, and *hic* (this near me) to the first.

Omission of
'that,'
'them,' 'it,'
&c.

ε. 'That' is omitted (*cf.* § 11 γ) in sentences like 'my wish and that of Cicero,' or the substantive is repeated as in 1, 24. So also the personal pronouns 'them,' 'it,' when mere repetitions of an object before expressed; cf. § 9 β, § 10 ; but not always.

Cf. 13, 14, 19; (15) 10; 21, 17 ; (36) 13.

§ 17.
Personal
pronouns,
when ex-
pressed.

§ 17. *a.* Pronouns in Latin when emphasized or contrasted must be expressed, and then sufficiently represent our additions of 'for my part,' 'on the one hand,' &c. Sometimes *quidem, vero,* &c. are added. *Cf.* § 47, &c.

Cf. 26, 31; (26) 47 ; 45, 8, 21.

Idem;
ipse.

β. *Idem* will often express our 'all the same,' 'on the other hand,' 'at once,' 'again,' 'very,' &c.; and *ipse,* our 'very,' 'the fact of,' 'of itself,' with numerals 'exactly :' e.g. *hoc ipsum terret, triginta dies erant ipsi, hunc ipsum, tum ipsum.*

Cf. 21, 10; 30, 3; 32, 7; 34, 15.

Nemo; quis-
quam; nul-
lus; ullus.

γ. *Nemo* and *quisquam* are substantival, the latter being used in negative sentences, or questions implying negation. *Nullus* and *ullus* are generally used for their genitive and ablative; e.g. *nullo cogente; nullius te miseret; nullius avari; nec prohibente ullo* (Livy), not *quoquam; est ne quisquam?* Otherwise *nullus* and *ullus* are adjectival and used in the same kind of sentences.

Nemo and *quisquam* are also used adjectivally with *homo, vir, parens, mulier,* and other appellatives.

Aliquis;
quis; qui-
dam, &c.

δ. *aliquis, aliquid*, substantival   { = 'at least some' but undefined, may be called *aliqui, aliquod*, adjectival   { defined, may be called definite indefinites.

So *nonnullus* also and *nescio quis.*

quidam, substantival and adjectival, is definite.

quivis, adjectival and substantival,
quilibet, adjectival,
quis, substantival, *qui,* adjectival, after
si, ne, or relatives ;
} indefinite,

alius = ἄλλος, other and different, of many.

alter = ἕτερος, other, second, of two, as *neuter, uter, uterque;* so *quisque* of many, *uterque* of two.

§ 17. **ε.** The suffix *que* (orig. *quei, indefinite* ablative from *qui*) seems to give the force of 'soever,' otherwise given by repetition; as *ubiubi* = *ubicunque* = *ubique; utut* = *utcunque* = *utique,* 'howsoever;' so *quisquis* = *quicunque* = *quisque* (cf. Tacitus for this usage of *quisque*), the adjunct being enclitic and indefinite.

The force then of *primus quisque* is not '*each* first,' but '*the* first whoever he be,' and so 'all the first ;' *primo quoque tempore,* 'the first opportunity whatever it be;' cf. 13, 6; 26, 53; 43, 16.

The usage of *quisquis* and *quicunque* for 'every" is noticeable in phrases such as *quidquid progredior,* 'at every step ;' *quidquid increpat,* 'at every noise ;' cf. Näg. § 36.

§ 18. **α.** In English, adjectives or participles (or other words) are prefixed to substantives for pure word-painting, as attributives, or to suggest allusively class, quality, cause, condition, &c.   In Latin either omit them or express the cause, condition, &c., separately and directly, by participle, adjective, or verbal clause, placed after the substantive; e.g. 'the disappointed adventurers murmured,' *milites elusi fremere.* The participle is also omitted in such expressions as 'a man named Cotta,' *Cotta quidam.* Adjectives, &c.,§§18—24. Attributives or epithets, when superfluous.

β. Where in English they are artificial or metaphorical, simplify. Simplified in Latin.

Cf. (9) 18; (15) 2, 8, 11; (16) 23;   (25) 15, 18, 20;   (42) 2.

γ. The English participial adjective must be expressed by a simple adjective ; or treated separately as a verbal predicate, as above ; or expressed by a relative Participial adjectives, rarer in Latin.

clause. There are but few participial adjectives in
Latin, as *prudens, sapiens, amans, potens, tutus, doctus,
expeditus* (found with comparative and superlative forms
and adjectival usage). In English most participles (present act. and past pass.) are used as adjectives; e. g. 'a
lost cause,' 'a dazzling sight.' For instances of Lat. adjectival participles, *cf.* Näg. § 72.

Cf. (2) 11, 27, 29; (3) 7; (31) 1; (32) 5; (48) 15.

§ 19.
Adjectival
pleonasms.
§ 19. a. The practice, common in many English
authors, of giving each substantive its epithet, or group-
ing substantives, adjectives, or verbs in couples, (*cf.* § 28
β.) must generally be avoided in Latin, though occasionally it occurs, especially in ornate oratory; *cf.* 32,
5—15; (32) 4—16.

Antithetical
repetitions.
β. So too antithetical repetitions of synonyms to
balance clauses. *Cf.* §§ 11 γ; 28 β.

Cf. (2) 10—13, 23, 29; (9) 12; (10) 6; (12) 13, 15, 18; (17) 8.

Double ad-
jectives, &c.
γ. Where (in English) several adjectives are prefixed
to substantives without *copula*, connect them (in Latin)
and place them after their substantives; e.g. *oculos habuit
claros ac nitidos*, but also *nigris vegetisque oculis*, 20, 27;
21, 41.

Cf. (9) 3; (13) 8; (18) 6, 22, 2; (32) 1.

§ 20.
Adjectives
as clauses:
§ 20. a. The (Latin) adjective or participle, as in
English, may often represent a minor clause by itself, as
the Greek adjective with ὤν, especially in Tacitus (where
it often stands for a main clause); e.g. *inops ac desertus
quid poterat facere?*

Cf. 2, 1, 10; 4, 22; 5, 12; 11, 7, 17; 13, 14; 24, 36; 49, 38.

replaced by
verbal
clause.
β. However the relative or some other verbal clause
will often have to be used instead; e. g. 'naturally cruel
and passionate he now gave full play to his passions,'
*quum (ut qui) natura sævus et impotens esset, libidi-
nibus se totum dedidit.*

§ 21. The adjective or participle in one language often replaces the adverb in the other; e. g. *Invitus veni,* 'I came unwillingly;' *sero veni,* 'I was late in coming.'

Simple Latin adjectives, especially those in *-osus,* are used for English substantival expressions; e.g. *difficilis, periculosus,* &c., 'attended with difficulty, danger,' &c.; *saevum,* 'marked with cruelty;' *cruentus,* 'stained with blood.'

Cf. (4) 24; 8, 9; 36, 25, 27.

§ 21. Latin adjectives replaced by adverbs, or substantives.

§ 22. Many (English) adjectives, like 'useless,' 'possible,' 'impracticable,' 'usual,' have to be rendered by verbal clauses; e. g. *qua soles lima,* 'with your usual criticism;' *rem et posse et debere fieri,* 'that the measure was both practicable and expedient;' and Latin adjectives, also, by English substantival or verbal clauses; e.g. *impotens, capax,* &c.

So also English participles when equivalent to clauses; *Cf.* § 18. § 25. (49) 32.

Cf. (14) 20, 21; (20) 4, 15; (22) 7.

§ 22. English adjectives by verbs, or substantives.

As also participles.

§ 23. The adjective is constantly used as the main predicate with verbs in Latin; e.g. *Primus abiit; novissima exuitur laudis cupido.*

§ 23. Latin Adjectives as predicates.

§ 24. *a.* Superlatives in one language replace comparatives in the other;

e.g. *Uter horum doctior?* 'Which of these is the cleverest?' *Prior ego,* 'I was first to speak.'

quo nihil iniquius, 'a most unfair course.'

Cf. 3, 16; (6) 5; (32) 2; 36, 2.

§ 24. Superlatives, comparatives, and positives interchanged.

β. The Latin comparative is often rendered by our 'too,' as in 'too great,' *majus quam quod fieri possit;* 'too great for lightning,' *majores fulguribus,* or *quam fulgura,* (26, 27); often by our 'rather' or 'so:' or by a simple positive; e.g. in the Latin, *fortior quam felicior.*

Cf. 7, 13; 19, 32; 22, 2, 16; 33, 14; 36, 2; 45, 26; 51, 15.

Lat. comparative rendered by 'too,' 'rather,' 'so,' &c.,

superlative by positive,

§ 24. γ. The positive replaces the superlative, especially in English, our superlative being often awkward in form, and less used; *Cato vir justissimus*, 'That just man Cato.'

Cf. 21, 8—11; 33, 3; 37, 49; 38, 16.

or by intensives.
cf. § 35.

δ. Latin superlatives mean not only 'most' but 'very;' *optimus* = 'best,' 'one of the best,' 'very good,' or simply 'good.'

Cf. 36, 1; 43, 4; 45, 23; 48, 9.

Comparisons.

ε. Comparisons are made in Latin usually by simple co-ordinate clauses, the copula or copulative relative replacing our 'as,' 'than,' &c.; *tantus ille quantus ego* means strictly 'he is *so great, and* I am *so great;*' *ille æque atque ego*, 'he equally, and I equally.'

§ 25.
Present
Participles
—when not
used in
Latin.

§ 25. a. The Latin present participle active is not so freely used as in English, *cf.* §§ 18, 22, 31; the English participle being often replaced (i) by the infinitive; e.g. (26) 39, cf. 26, 23; or by (ii) the historic imperfect or infinitive, as in descriptions, cf. (26) 15, and 26, 40; (iii) or by prepositions, *cf.* § 14; or (iv) by a co-ordinate clause, as in 31, 19;

e.g. (i) *mutari omnia videmus*, 'we see all things changing.'

(ii) *pars arma capere, alii fugere, plerique metu torpebant*, 'some seizing arms, others running away, most standing paralyzed with fear.'

(iii) *ob hæc, de hoc*, 'owing to this, concerning this.'

(iv) *caelum est mitissimum: oleas et vites profert;* 'the climate is mild, producing both the vine and olive.'

Present
participle—
strictly present.
cf. § 20 a.

β. The Lat. pres. part. is strictly present and marks *simultaneous* action; loose English participles, present in form only, must be translated by past participle, *quum* with past subjunctive, *postquam* with indicative, &c.;

e.g. 'so saying, he left the house,' *quum haec dixisset
e domo exiit.*

Cf. 2, 1, 6, 14; 3, 19, 21; 8, 5, 13, &c.

'Pendent' impersonal participles, like 'considering,' § 25.
'excepting,' 'counting,' and even strictly present parti- 'pendent'
ciples, may have to be translated by *dum* (mostly with pres. part.
pres. indic.), *si* (mostly with fut. perfect), *quum* and a verb,
past. part., ablative absolute, &c. *Cf.* 24, 40, 41; 31, 3.

§ 25.　γ. Subject to these rules the pres. part. may Lat. pres.
be used in temporal, causal, conditional, modal, concessive part.
when used,
senses.

Cf. 2, 14, 24; 3, 4, 22; 7, 29; 8, 21; 13, 14, 39; 20, 35; 22,
31—6; 24, 35, 40; 29, 30; 47, 2.

δ. It is frequently used in oblique cases where we esp. in
oblique
use verbal clauses, *cogitanti saepe occurrit.* cases,

Cf. 3, 9; 38, 30; 39, 15.

ε. It is constantly used in oblique cases (rarely in and for
classes of
the nominative), especially in the genitive plural (as in men or
things.
Greek with the article), for classes of men or things.
Cf. §§ 41 ε, 42 *a.* *Cf.* Näg. § 29.

Cf. 2, 15; 7, 20; 9, 4; 24, 47; 26, 36; 33, 14; 34, 8; 48, 9.

ζ. The present participle passive is wanting in Latin, Pres. part.
passive
and is replaced by verbal clause or the past participle wanting in
Latin.
passive in some cases, e.g. 'the besieged' *qui obsidentur,*
(*qui obsidebantur*). *Cf.* Näg. § 28.

Cf. 3, 10; 5, 7; 7, 31; 13, 34.

η. The present participle of English neuter verbs Eng. pres.
part.
will often have to be replaced by the past participle neuter.
passive; e.g. *Inde ad suos conversus.* *Cf.* 7, 8; 13, 9.

§ 26.　*a.* The past participle active, being wanting in § 26.
Past Parti-
Latin except in deponents, is generally expressed by ciples
active want-
quum, ut qui, &c., with the subjunctive, *ubi, postquam,* ing in Latin.
with the indicative, ablative absolute, or simple adjective,

or by past participle passive in agreement with object; e.g. *vinctos* (or *quum vinxisset*) *eduxit*.

Cf. § 25 β; 11, 1; 14, 1, &c.

English past part. pass. for Lat. preposition.

§ 26.　β. The past participle passive is often translated by prepositions or the ablative of a noun ('prompted by' = *ex*, *propter*), or omitted altogether.　*Cf.* § 28 ε.

Cf. (24), 23; (25) 24.

Lat. past part.

γ. The Latin past participle, from want of an article, cannot be so often used as in Greek for a substantive; though occasionally so used (as the present § 25 ε); cf. Näg. § 28.

δ. nor for an adjective.　*Cf.* § 18 γ.

§ 27. Verbs, §§ 27 —29. Tenses— Present, &c., inexact use in English. cf. 25 β.

§ 27.　a. The vague English present tense must often be replaced by future, *futurum exactum*, perfect or present subjunctive; and the perfect similarly by the pluperfect; the future by the *futurum exactum;* e.g. *scribes si quid habebis*, 47, 10; *quae formaveram dicto*, 34, 10.

cf. § 29 a.

β. The English perfect, e.g. 'is written, &c.,' *scriptum est*, must be carefully distinguished from the present of the same form, *scribitur*.

Cf. 29, 33; 34, 2; (36) 10; (38) 5, 15, 19, 24, 26; (42) 3; (46) 16; (49) 12, 21; 52, 5; (53) 12.

Verbal pleonasms and periphrases in English.

§ 28.　a. In verbs as in nouns, (English) conventional periphrastic expressions and obsolete metaphors must be replaced by simpler and more direct terms.

'He observed, remarked, replied, continued' = *inquit* (often omitted) 'I repeat,' *inquam;* and so *ago, capio, esse, habere, ire, posse, facere*, will often translate more artificial terms like 'manage,' 'discuss,' 'embrace,' 'exist,' 'constitute,' 'deliver,' &c. The verbs 'to avail one's self,' 'assure,' 'represent,' 'allude,' 'qualify,' 'convey,' 'communicate,' 'enhance,' will furnish other instances in some of their uses.

Cf. 6, 1; 12, 21; 14, 3, 9; 15, 11; 25, 19; 31, 17; 35, 5; and
(1) 26; (2) 2; (4) 6: (5) 10; (6) 13; (7) 31; (9) 24; (22) 25, 30,
34, 39.

§ 28. β. Antithetical repetitions of the verb (or of its equivalent) are mostly suppressed in Latin where unemphatic, one verb serving for two or more clauses. Cumulative repetitions however are common in oratory.

§ 28 Verbal pleonasms, and antithetical repetitions. cf. § 19 β.

Cf. (2) 13, 29; 7, 21.

γ. Where the Latin verb *is* repeated, we, in English, use a synonym for variety, or the auxiliaries 'did,' 'had,' &c., to represent the verb; but cf. 10, 15; 21, 16, 17; (24) 47.

English synonyms or auxiliaries replace verb.

δ. Many verbs disappear altogether in translation, as 'succeeded in,' 'managed to,' 'failed to,' 'refrain,' 'continued to,' 'ended in,' 'keep,' 'cease,' 'begin,' 'get,' 'find,' &c. (*cf.* § 29 γ), or are only represented by adverbs, or the negative. § 36.

Quasi-auxiliary verbs (English) disappear;

Cf. (15) 19 ; 23, 3, 14; (23) 16; (26) 4, 13, 35, 75; 44, 9.

ε. So also participles, '*marked* with cruelty,' '*attended* by circumstances,' &c.; 'a slave *called* Dama,' *Dama quidam.*

so too participles.

Cf. § 21; 23, 3, 14; (24) 8.

§ 29. α. Tenses (Latin) keep their strict time; use therefore for continued incomplete actions the imperfect, for single complete acts the aorist perfect (where we use the same tense for both); and the pluperfect where the action has preceded that of the perfect or imperfect, as you use the perfect when the action has preceded that of a present.

§ 29. Strict use of tenses in Latin (cf. §§ 25 β, 27 β) imperfect, &c.;

β. Remember that *scripsi* is εγραψα, γεγραφα, γραψας εχω, (*scriptum habeo*); that *erat* is not the same as *fuit* which (as *vixit*) conveys an idea of completed (sometimes terminated) existence, and is less often used; *erat* standing as an aorist instead, owing to the intrinsic idea of verbs of existence. *Cf.* (24) 51.

perfect and aorist.

N.   *d*

Latin imperf. paraphrased in English.

§ 29. γ. The Latin imperfect is often best translated by the periphrastic 'proceed' 'keep,' 'continue,' 'get,' &c., when the auxiliary 'was' (speaking, &c.) is not sufficient; or by adverbs like 'constantly,' 'often,' 'still,' 'gradually;' generally by our loose aorist.

Cf. 7, 33—6; 25, 3, 5, 15, &c. (25) 4, 21, &c.; (26), 13.

§ 30. Subjunctive and indicative: their one leading idea.

All mere conceptions belong to subjunctive.

§ 30. a. Wherever a fact is stated directly, or referred to objectively, the indicative must be used; where it is alluded to merely as an idea of the mind, or stated indirectly as in *oratio obliqua*, the subjunctive. All mere conceptions, then, belong to the subjunctive, and a mental conception is implied in all its uses. Aims and objects are conceptions: so also causes not realized as facts: and wishes, and conditions—(though a condition may form such an obvious fact that it is expressed as such. e.g. *si lucet, lucet*). *Cf.* 1, 20; 3, 6; 27, 8, 15; 37, 40; 46, 5.

So-called pure conjunctives gen. elliptical and mere conception.

Of the six so-called pure uses of the conjunctive (Potential[1], Conditional, Concessive, Optative, Dubitative, Hortative, *cf.* the Primer, p. 141), five are strictly elliptical, dependent on verbs (as *fac ut, suadeo ut,* &c.) suppressed: such dependent clauses as mere conceptions naturally belong to the subjunctive. The 'conditional pure use' (as in 19, 14; 26, 38) is of course also a conception (*vellem ire*) dependent on a condition often unexpressed. *Cf.* 19, 14; 40, 1, 4, 33; 44, 10; 53, 19.

In what sense the future indic. is or is not conception.

β. The future too it may be said is strictly pure conception, and should belong to the subjunctive. It may be seen indeed that etymologically it is closely connected with the subjunctive; both the future and fut.

---

[1] The subjunctive has never the sense of possibility or potentiality. 'What can I do?' is only an inexact interchange of idiom for *quid faciam?* '*Petunt ut eant*' no more proves a latent idea of *licet* or *potest* in the subj. than '*placet ire*,' '*censeo esse*,' shew a latent *d here* in the infinitive.

perf. indic. are often almost identical in form with the pres. and perf. subj., and might almost as well be classed with the subj. tenses[1], which they often replace, or are replaced by; but it is also true that the future may be stated as a fact (just as much as the past, though belonging to the region of fact, may be treated as a conception or hypothesis); though, even then, the ideality or uncertainty of the future often leads to the use of the subjunctive, the certainty of the past even in hypothesis to that of the indicative; e.g. *si velis* for *si voles; manebo donec redeat (redierit); ausim; haud facile dixerim; fecit si potuit,* cf. 27, 14.

§ 30.   γ. Frequency (with temporal conjunctions, or *si*, or relatives), *as an indefinite conception,* may reasonably take the subjunctive, and does so generally in Livy and Tacitus. See Madvig, § 359.

§ 30 γ. 'Frequency:' an indefinite conception.

Cf. 9, 5; 16, 33; 17, 13; 21, 10; 22, 25.

δ. Conjunctions have no inborn predilection for indicative or subjunctive. We shall find that most may be used with either, and there are good reasons for the exceptions. We must not take then for our guide arbitrary rules, that they rejoice in this or that, but examine the idea of the sentence, and see whether it is a conception or fact stated. The facts about their usage may be summarized as follows: reasons for the usage are added below: of course all (except sometimes *dum*) are found with subjunctive in *oratio obliqua* or dependent sentences.

Conjunctions used with either mood, according as fact or conception is expressed.

[1] It must not be forgotten that, chronologically, tense-forms precede the existence of moods: that in fact moods and the classification of tenses under them are arbitrary though useful fictions of grammarians, and though in the main based on truth, are still open in some details to question and possibly to subsequent revision.

Conjunctions.	Sometimes or always found with Subjunctive.	Generally with Indicative (but also with Subjunctive).
(i) Causal.	*Quum.*	*Quod, quia, quoniam, quandoquidem, siquidem.*
(ii) Temporal.	*Quum, antequam, priusquam.*	*Quum, quando, ut, quoties, ante (prius-) quam, postquam, simul, dum, donec, quoad.*
(iii) Final, implying object.	*Ut, ne* (=*utne*[1]), *quo, quin, quominus.*	None.
(iv) Concessive, implying attendant circumstances.	*Licet, quamvis, ut.*	*Quanquam, ut ut, si, nisi, etsi, etiamsi.*
(v) Conditional, implying hypothetical qualifications.	*Dum, modo, dummodo. Si.*	*Si.*
(vi) Consecutive, implying result.	*Ut.*	None.
(vii) Comparative.	*Tanquam, velut, ut, quasi.*	*Ut,* &c.

Moods used with causal conjunctions.   i. Cause, as a statement of fact, is generally expressed by the indicative; causal conjunctions then are mostly found with the indicative—compounds of *quidem* (which means '*in fact,*' e.g. *siquidem, quandoquidem;* cf. Roby, §§ 1747, 1988,) nearly always; but cause *in your own mind or the mind of another* is conception, not fact, and takes the subjunctive with *quum* (a kind of temporal conception implying sequence and so cause), or with any of the causal conjunctions given above. It should be remarked that *si,* like *quando, quum,* only incidentally expresses cause, and that *siquidem* is generally purely hypothetical not causal; cf. *pro Mil.* XVIII. 48. *Cf.* 7, 7, 15, 41; 22, 3, &c.

with temporal,   ii. All temporal conjunctions are found both with indicative and subjunctive. Simple juxtaposition of facts co-ordinately ar-

---

[1] *Ne* is used to negative final, imperative, optative, and some conditional clauses; *non* all other clauses, and all subordinate parts or fractions even of imperative clauses. Zumpt's (p. 861), Madvig's (§ 456, obs. 2), and Heindorf's (Horace, *Sat.* II. 5, 91) instances to the contrary from the poets are only apparent exceptions. It is not till Quintilian's time that instances occur like *non dixeris, non perdamus.*

ranged requires the indicative; therefore use *quum, postquam* with
the indicative where you wish to state two facts in some temporal
connexion; but as soon as you get to pure conception (as often of
a fact never realized, e. g. *priusquam rex veniret abiit*) or inchoate
and incomplete actions, these particles take a subjunctive ; *postquam* very rarely, because it refers mainly to complete past
actions.

Cf. 3, 6 ; 7, 33, 34 ; 9, 24 ; 16, 14 ; 23, 7, 35, &c.

N.B. Notice that *dum* is found mostly with the pres. indic. §30.
even in oblique narration (as vividly descriptive); *ante quam, prius-* with *dum,
postquam,*
quam* (if with the indicative), and *postquam,* with the perfect rather *quum,*
than pluperfect ; e.g. *postquam venit* = after he *had* come; the point
of time to mark (after which the other event happened) is *venit*
not *venerat*. Where we wish to mark strongly a previously completed fact, and not merely to use it as a point of time, the pluperfect is found, e. g. *postquam occiderat;* 'after he had first killed.'
Cf. 24, 40 ; 47, 2, 7; 51, 16.

Quum however (as marking chronological sequence with causal
connexion more or less implied, or as stating facts allusively and
not directly) takes the subjunctive in connexion with historic tenses.

iii. An aim must be a conception, and these particles are only with final,
found with subjunctives. Cf. 3, 6 ; 9, 4, &c.

iv. Concessive, as conceding either a fact or a hypothesis, will with concessive,
take accordingly indicatives or subjunctives. Elliptical forms like
licet (ut)—(*fac) ut*, really introduce dependent sentences which
come under another rule, and are only apparent exceptions.
Quamvis and *quantumvis* are, strictly, not conjunctions but adverbs
qualifying an elliptical dependent clause, e. g. *quamvis sit, &c.,*
be it as much as you like, &c. Cf. 29, 19 ; 47, 9.

In Tacitus *quamvis* is usually found with indicative, *quamquam*
with subjunctive, as also sometimes in Livy.

v. You may take either a certain fact or a conception as a with conditional,
condition. These particles therefore are found with both moods.
Cf. 37, 21, 24, 39 ; 52, 6, 24, 28.

vi. Consecutive clauses are found invariably in the subjunc- with consecutive,
tive, as merely qualifying preceding statements and not stating
(otherwise than allusively) a fresh fact. (The Greeks often seem
to treat their ὥστε as a mere copula = *itaque*.) Cf. 7, 20; 20, 4.

vii. Comparison also takes indicative or subjunctive accord- with comparative.
ingly as you compare conceptions or facts.

Cf. 7, 50; 28, 3; 39, 27.

§ 30.
Final or consecutive
with *ne* or
non, e.g.
fit ut, &c.

Subjunctives, preceded by *ut*, often stand alone parenthetically, or as subjects apparently of *fit, abest, accidit, restat,* &c.
(Madv. § 373), where a substantival infinitive could often be used.
They doubtless are, or were originally, either *final* or *consecutive*
classes, and take for their negative *ne* or *non* accordingly: so that
the negative may be used as a test; e.g. *ne plura dicam, restat ut
ne taceam, tantum abest ut non taceam,* &c. Cf. 15, 9; 27, 14;
37, 40. They may be used (as *quod* with indic.) with any tense—
e.g. *accedit quod faciam, ut facturus sim, quod facturus essem.* Cf.
Cic. *p. Rosc. Amer.* §§ 83, 104.

Subjunctive
Tenses.

§ 30. ε. The tenses in the subjunctive follow the
rules laid down in § 27, § 29, but differ slightly from the
indicative.

They are constantly used in a relatively or absolutely
future sense, or where you would expect futures, no doubt
from the connexion[1] in character and etymology of this
mood with the future; e.g. *metuo ne veniat ; gratulerne
tibi an timeam ? dubito an faciam.* Cf. 17, 11 ; 19, 11 ;
37, 60 ; 38, 4, 8, 14.

Even the past tenses (imperf. and pluperf.) seem to
have a future sense in wishes and conditions, but they
always imply at the same time something past and impossible. An act of the past, *existing only in hypothesis,*
is hopelessly unreal[2], as the past is unalterable; e.g. *si
venisset, utinam adisset, veniret si posset.* In final sen-

---

[1] The pres. and perf. subj. (just as their counterpart the
Greek subj. resembles the primary tenses of the indicative) are
in form like the indic. futures, and are used of future conceptions
or contemplated possibilities: the imperf. and pluperf. of past
events, sometimes real, sometimes hypothetical and therefore
unalterable impossibilities, being more akin to the past tenses of
the indicative (just as the Greek optative implying less reality
than the subjunc. approximates in form to the historic tenses of
indicative, which are used also for unrealities or unalterable impossibilities).

[2] Beginners cannot be too often cautioned that the imperfect
subj. cannot be used of future ideas (except futures from a *past*
standing point), and has nothing to do with probability or possibility except incidentally.

tences (*haec monui ut veniret*) the past is used after the past : because if the action is past, the preceding aim of it must be also, even though future with respect to the action. *Cf.* Madv. § 378.

§ 30. ζ. In *oratio obliqua* the pres. subj. is constantly used for the future : *scribet si quid habebit* frequently becomes *dicit se scripturum si quid habeat ;* but where it is necessary to express at once the future or conditional as well as the conceptive or dependent meaning of a clause, the subjunctive cannot *do double duty*[1] (*cf.* Madvig on pluperf. § 381 sub fin.) without leading to ambiguity, and the future or conditional meaning has to be marked more fully and distinctly ; e. g. (*scribat*) *scriberet si quid* (*habeat*) *haberet*, but *accedit ut scripturus* (*sit*) *esset si quid* (*habeat*) *haberet :* not *ut scriberet*, which would mean 'that he wrote.' The protasis, it will be noticed, remains unchanged (*cf.* 40, 23), and the pluperfect (*si quid habuisset*) would only be used in a different sense, of a definite uncontinuing time of action.

§ 30. Dependent conditional futures.

The change may be expressed in a tabular form thus :—

(1)   (Fact.)   (Fact subord.)

Scribebat ⎫   *Accedit ut scriberet si quid*
Scripturus erat ⎬ *si quid*   *haberet*
fuit ⎭ *habebat.*   ...*ut scripturus esset* ⎫ *si quid*
                                                    fuerit ⎬ *haberet.*

(2)   (Hypoth.)   (Hypoth. subord.)

Scriberet ⎫   *Accedit ut scripturus*
Scripsisset ⎬ ⎫ *si quid*   *esset* ⎫ *si quid haberet.*
Scripturus esset ⎬⎨ *haberet.*   *fuisset* ⎬
fuisset ⎭⎭

(3)   (Fact + Hypoth.)   (Fact + Hypoth. subord.)

Scripturus fuit ⎫ *si quid*   *Accedit ut scripturus fuerit*[2],
erat ⎬ *haberet.*   *si quid haberet.*

---

[1] I am indebted for this expression originally to Mr H. Jackson, (Trin. Coll.), as also for several other suggestions.

[2] Madvig (§ 381) seems to confuse cases (2) and (3).

§ 30.
Sequence of
Tenses.

§ 30. η. In the sequence of subordinate clauses the present and perfect of a main clause are followed by the present and perfect subj., the imperfect or the aoristic past-perfect by the imperfect and pluperfect subj. In these clauses the imperfect of the subjunctive is also aoristic in sense : while the perfect is less so than in its indicative (being used mostly of completed perfect actions); though in consecutive clauses, aoristic also.

e.g. i. *ut veniat dat (dedit) talentum.*

ii. *ut veniret* (or *quum venisset), dabat (dederat) dedit* (aorist) *talentum.*

iii. *tam stultus erat ut veniret* (consecutive), or *ut venerit,* of one completed or definite action.

Cf. 3, 10; 6, 7; 20, 4, 8, 36, 41; 41, 22.

Future
Perfect
Subjunc-
tive.

θ. The *futurum exactum* subjunctive, both in the active and passive, seems to have the same form as the perfect subjunctive, *not* that of the *futurum exactum* indicative ; e.g. *polliceor me venturum, si potuerim ; tam segnis est ut futurum sit ut jam redierim ante quam profectus sit*[1]. *Cf.* Madvig. 379, and see β. But it would be more correct to say that in such cases the perf. subj. is used loosely for the future; or that the so-called perf. subj. in *-erim* is strictly the subj. from the fut. perf. *-ero*, which however (as the pres. subj.) loses its future meaning generally, except in hypothetical, final and absolute clauses. *Cf.* 41, 13; 43, 9. *Cf.* also Cic. *Rosc. Am.* XLIV. 128 : *ad Att.* VII. 7, 7, and VII. 8, 4 ; in *ad Fam.* VI. 12, 3 (*confecta futura sit*) we have the full form of a future perf. subj. (*Cf.* Draeger, § 141.)

Fut. subj.
Active and
Passive.

ι. The simple future is periphrastic, *amaturus sim :* for the passive some periphrasis, as *non dubium est quin*

---

[1] Both the two tenses must be looked upon therefore as identical, sometimes future in meaning, sometimes past ; this confusion being due to the fact that the whole mood is used doubly, now to express the idea of the Gk. subj., now that of the optative.

futurum sit (or *in eo futurus sim*) *ut amer*, will have to
be used, if the active cannot be used. The periphrastic
forms are found with all tenses of *sum*, with *foret* as
well as *esset;* more rarely however with *fuero, fore.*

§ 30. κ. This last periphrasis *fore, futurum esse ut* Periphrastic
future of
amem, amer, is often found for the future active and Infinitive
with *fore*
passive infinitive, especially where the simple future forms
would be awkward or do not exist. Forms like *debellatum
fore, absolutum fore*, occur in Cic., Liv., &c.; as also *dicto
audientes fore, habendum fore.*

§ 31. a. The infinitive often replaces our present par- § 31.
The Latin
ticiple, *vidi ruere*, 'I saw it falling,' (or 'fall'); but *vidi* Infinitive
for Eng.
ruentem, 'I saw it while it was falling.' part.;

Cf. 26, 11; 23; 36, 21; 38, 22.

So in our 'ceased (began) speaking,' 'went on consuming,' &c.

β. The infinitive of surprise ('To think that,' &c.) is of surprise.
found in Latin, generally with the enclitic *ne;* e.g. *Te
ne nescire! At te Romæ non fore!* But we find also
a direct interrogative with or without *ne*, and an ellipse
of the verb; e.g. *Ita ne Brutus? Cf.* 45, 2; (45) 7.

The accusative of exclamation, with adjectives and
participles, is more common, and may sometimes be used
instead. *Cf.* 36, 16; 38, 3; 54, 9.

γ. The English (or Greek) epexegetic infinitive must Epexegetic
Infinitive.
be replaced by the supine or gerund, by *ut* or relative
with subjunctive, or by some substantival periphrasis;
'to say the truth,' *ut vera dicam;* sometimes it may be
made the main verb of the sentence. *Cf.* § 4 β, 28 δ,
'I shall be glad to come,' *laetus veniam.*

Cf. 28, 3; 30, 2; 47, 12; 49, 12, 18, 26; 50, 15.

The final infinitive is expressed by *ut* or *qui* with Final Infinitive.
subj. or by the part. in *-rus. Cf.* 8, 11, 13, &c.

§ 32. *a.* The Latin infinitive though substantival cannot be used with prepositions (as our verbal in '*ing*,' or the Greek infinitive); the gerund may be, but with some only.

β. When you come to an expression like 'without doing,' you must settle by the context whether it is past, present, or future, consequence, mode, or condition, and translate accordingly, e. g. *re infecta, nullo obstante, non coactus abiit; nihil facientem miserum est morari; nisi feceris; vix haec facies, ut non facias et illa; abiit neque fecit.* *Cf.* 33, 17; 36, 16.

(Marginal note: § 32. Lat. Infin. not used with prepositions as our verbal or Lat. Gerund. Manifold time and sense of verbal in -ing.)

§ 33. Generally the English verbal in -*ing* may be rendered:

i. In the nominative or accusative by the Latin infinitive or *quod* with indicative; e. g. *quod abes aberas, &c. (te abesse) tamdiu, mirum est* (or *miror*).

ii. In the other cases by the finite verb with *ex (ob, &c.), eo (id) quod;* e. g. *ex eo quod abes aberas, &c.* 'from your being away.'

iii. Or by the gerunds with and without prepositions; e. g. *certus eundi; ad eundum paratus.*

iv. Or by the gerundive and noun, with or without prepositions; e. g. *ex (de, &c.) re agenda;* sometimes even with pronoun, *offerendi mei.* Cic. *c. Rull.* II. 5, 12.

v. Or by verbal clauses with *quum, ubi,* &c.; or participial clauses as above, § 32 *β*; or by adverbs; e.g. *inscienter,* 'without knowing.'

Cf. 6, 20; (14) 10; 15, 10; 29, 5, 30; 49, 9, 12, 33, 41.

In all cases the *time* of the verbal must be expressed; if the action be past or present, then use *quod* &c. with past or present indic.; if future or final, use *ut, ne, quo minus,* &c. with subjunct. past or present (*cf.* § 30 *η*). *Cf.* Näg. § 37.

(Marginal note: § 33. Verbals in 'ing,' how translated)

§ 34. In its use of particles, connecting and others, Latin is more simple and realistic than English; and un-

(Marginal note: § 34. Particles, when omitted.)

necessary particles must be omitted in translation, especially when used for emphasis, where position alone suffices in Latin.

Cf. §§ 4, 8, 17; 49, 26, 58; 53, 20; 56, 20.

no sooner—than; scarcely—when; just as	sometimes are rendered by *et—et, simul —simul*, or the past participle passive, *captum statim occidit;* sometimes by *vix...quum; (dixerat)...quum.*	§ 34. Particles, connecting, qualifying, &c.
while—yet; on the one hand— on the other;	*ut—ita; quum—tum.*	

'not you *but* I,' *ego non tu;*

'by this time,' *jam;* 'from the first,' *jam tum;*

'at once,' *idem* or *et—et (et bonus et strenuus);*

'at all events,' 'at least,' 'in any case,' *certe, omnino;*

'positively,' 'actually,' *quidem*, or unexpressed; e.g. *facere voluit et fecit (quidem); quamvis sit felix sicut est;*

'quite,' *omnino, valde, plane;*

'of course,' *quidem, vero, sane; profecto.*

'good,' 'very well,' *optime, esto;*

'yes,' *etiam, maxime, aio, sic, ita, immo* (with or without *vero*);

'no,' *non, minime, nego;*

'not,' *ne,* of a purpose, *non* otherwise; *minus (sin quo &c minus).*

Both English and Latin particles have widely different meanings according to position and the accents of the sentence, which must be carefully marked ; *Ambiguous particles.*

e.g. 'still' = (i) *nihilominus, tamen,* (ii) *adhuc,* (iii) *usque;*

'indeed' = (i) *sane quam (dolui),* (ii) *sane, quidem*

(μεν) answered by *sed* (δε), &c., (iii) *ita ne ?*
(iv) (*minime*) *vero*, (v) *re vera ;*

'well' = (i) *bene*, (ii) *quid igitur ?* (iii) *at, atqui,*
(iv) *jam, jam vero*, resumptive, (v) often left
unexpressed.

Quidem, vero, tamen, enim sometimes *enimvero,*
-nam, -dum are enclitics.

Unconnected sentences are not so frequent in Latin
as in writers like Macaulay ; *jam, tum, inde, &c.,* often
have to be introduced. But very often they are connected not by particles, but by some word brought em-
phatically forward which serves as a connecting idea ; or
by the relative. At other times *quod, quod contra, quod si,*
quanquam, ergo, itaque, quare, proinde, autem, nempe,
scilicet, porro, jam vero, quid ? quid quod, &c., will be used.

In descriptive clauses, like 'It was *now* getting
dark,' the 'now' will disappear or be replaced by *tunc*,
as our descriptive 'here' is by *ibi, illic*, 'hence,' by *inde*.
Adhuc, similarly, is used less frequently of the past time,
though found in that sense occasionally, as also *nunc*
tunc, &c. *Ibi, ibidem* are also used for *hic* in its strict
sense to avoid repetition of *hic*, or to intensify it : *cf. hic*
ibidem. Cic. *Rosc. Am.* 13.

Cf. (1) and (8); (10) 1; (11) 12; (25) 13, 22; **and** 15, 18; 25,
23, 28; 26, 3, 19, 33; 45, 1—16; 46, 1—6.

§ 35. English writers use for effect 'such,' 'so,' 'so
great,' oftener than is done in Latin. Translate by the
superlative, comparative, or simple positive; often also
by *adeo, tam, tantus, &c.* (not *sic* or *ita*), sometimes by
the relative ; e.g. *qua munditia homines ! quae est tua*
bonitas. Yet we often find *tantus* where the 'so' would
be dropped in English, and *toties* for 'over and over
again.' Cic. *c. Rull.* II. 7, 17.

Cf. (7) 14; (26) 21; (36) 2; (37) 4, 5, 20; 37, 21; 44, 6; 49, 9;
51, 22.

'This' 'that', often prefixed similarly for effect in English—*cf.* (10) 5, 13—may often be omitted in translation. Intensives. &c., omitted.

§ 36. *a.* Adverbs (or adverbial phrases, as *ex occulto*) in Latin are constantly used where we use substantives (especially of time and space), or adjectives, or verbs; e.g. *diu, procul, inscienter; haud dubie aderit*, 'he is sure to be there,' &c. For instances of the converse, *cf.* Näg. § 83. § 36. Adverbs.

On the other hand they use verbs where we use adverbs, substantives, or adjectives, (*cf.* § 22); e.g. *qua soles cura; ut erat miti ingenio; quae est tua facilitas; solet (videtur) ire*, 'he usually (apparently) goes.'

Cf. 3, 2; 19, 31; (20) 29; 42, 2; 48, 16; 54, 6, 19.

§ 37. In letters the precision of Latin appears in the use of '*scribere*' for our colloquial 'say' (*quod scribis*), *litteras accipere*, for 'hear;' and the constant insertion of such verbs where we omit them ; e.g. 'In my last letter,' &c., 'In your note of the 24th inst,' *in ea epistola quam dederas, &c.* § 37. Epistolary idioms, §§ 37—39.

Where we quote from a letter without preface, they prefix *scribis*, &c.; and mention facts directly instead of alluding to them as we do.

Cf. 45, 6; 42, 1 and (12) 2; 44, 1 and (44) 2 ; 47, 12 and (47) 16, 21; 55, 1.

§ 38. Another instance of this precision is the use of the epistolary imperfect and pluperfect *dabam*, &c., which should be used (as in our phrases 'I am writing this,' 'I send this,' 'I have written so far,') where especial attention is called to the time of the letter-writing. § 38. Epistolary imperfect.

The perfect is similarly used where we use the present. *Cf.* 47, 2, 13; 54, 4, &c.

Cf. 37, 47; 41, 27—31; 44, 20; 47, 2, 3, 10, 18, 19; 49, 35; 56. 2.

§ 39.
Epistolary
phrases.

§ 39. Some familiar and idiomatic terms, mainly
nom letters, are here given :—

'Remember me,' &c., *salutare, salutem dicere, dare,
mittere;*

'post,' 'postman,' *tabellarius;*

'to send, deliver, a letter,' *dare, perferre, litteras;*

'my dear Cicero,' *mi Cicero;*

'Cicero sends his love,' *salvebis a Cicerone;*

'write and give my love,' *jubebis valere litteris;*

'let me know,' *fac me certiorem;*

'good bye, God bless you,' *ama nos et vale, vale et
salve;*

'so believe me, yours,' &c., *ergo bene vale;*

'mind you come,' *fac (cura ut) venias;*

'*Do* please come,' *veni si me amas;*

'believe me,' 'be assured,' *sic habeto, scito;*

'greet *for me*,' &c., *saluta nostris verbis;*

'positively,' &c., *moriar ni, ita vivam;*

'much obliged,' *amo te, amavi te, amabo te;*

'please,' 'pray,' parenthetically, *amabo, si me amas,*
44, 33;

'you must know,' *scito;*

'he gave me *express* instructions *from you*,' *me tuis
verbis admonuit;*

'letters of the same purport, contents, tenor,' *eodem
exemplo epistolae;*

'let me tell you,' 'I assure you,' *narro tibi;*

'that same night,' *nocte proxima, nocte quae secuta est*
or *nocte eadem;*

'the eve of,' *nocte quae—pridie erat.*

Colloquial-
isms in
Letters.

Of course in letters the colloquialisms of every-day
life are to be found oftener than in other prose;

quid agis? ecquid fit? 'how are you?' 'is anything
going on?'—*ago* and *facio* being used very freely;

cf. *actum est de eo ; bene actum cum eo ; quid eo factum,'* &c.

quid quaeris, 'enough,' 'in short;'

Di immortales, obsecro te, 'good heavens ;'

ais ne (tu, vero)? quid ais? 'What?'

noli, fac, &c., 'don't,' ' do.'

Titles and names are used only in the superscription, rarely elsewhere. Sometimes we find *Heus tu,* for 'What do you mean, Sir?' 'I say, Sir;' and *mi amice* or the name of a friend in the middle of a letter. A termination of a letter like ours will be found 37. 50. They end as a rule abruptly, with and without a *'Vale,'* or the date of time or place. (*Datum, dedi.*) They begin sometimes (after the salutation) with S.V.B.E.V., &c. *Cf.* 30, 4. Postscripts are found. *Cf.* 47 *a,* 49 *β.*

Cf. 38, 11, 16, 17, 27; 44, 23; 47, 8, 20; 52, 12-11, 20-2.

§ 40. The order of sentences in letters is much more easy and natural than in other prose. The period or anything like it would be out of place. The style will also be sometimes very elliptical ; verbs (e.g. *ire, agere, facere, esse, ferre, venire, videre*) being frequently omitted as in § 42 γ. The familiar courteous future e.g. *dices* (cf. λέγοις ἄν) is used for the imperative sometimes, as also *noli dicere, ne dixeris, &c.,* to avoid a direct command.

§ 40. Epistolary idioms, order, ellipse, &c.

Cf. 45, 9, 22; 47, 3, 4, 10, 20; 52, 17, 22.

§ 41. The chief peculiarities of idiom in Latin historical and descriptive writing are :

§ 41. Historical idioms, §§ 41, 42

a. The use of the historic present as aorist, as in 15, 3, &c. In sequence of tenses dependent on this, the present is sometimes treated as a present, sometimes as an aorist (especially in *oratio obliqua* and where the

Historic present.

dependent clauses come before the present, as in 9, 24);
sometimes the two ideas are confused, and presents and
imperfects follow intermixed, as in 10, 2—11; 17, 16.

§ 41.
with *dum*

The use of *dum* with the present (cf. § 30) arises
similarly from this kind of vivid narration.

Cf. 1, 2; 4, 10; 12, 6, &c.; 25, 11, &c.

Hist. Inf.

§ 41. β. The use of the historic infinitive as a main
verb to express rapid sequence or vivid description;
where we use the hist. pres. or the verbs 'began to,'
'proceeded to,' &c., and often the participle or the verbal
substantive in *-ing*.

Cf. §§ 28, 8, 31; and (1) 21; 2, 15; (4) 18; 7, 9, 27; 12, 1—4;
26, 28.

Omission of
sum, &c.

γ. The omission of the verb, mostly of *est*, *sunt*, and
esse, or *inquit*, &c. (very rarely the subj. of *sum*, cf. 2, 3;
4, 9); and in cases (Madv. § 478) where the present
participle of *sum* might be used if it existed.

Cf. §§ 28, 40; and 17, 24; 21, 30—3; 24, 18; 25, 28; 31, 14.

Verb used
for part.

δ. Use of imperfect indic. (26, 40) or *quum* with
subjunctive (7, 33) where we use a kind of ablative
absolute, or *pendent* participle. Cf. § 25 (ii).

Part. as
subst.

ε. The use of the present participle as substantive.
Cf. § 25 ε, § 42 a.

Abl. Abs.
for co-ordi-
nate clause.

ζ. The ablative absolute, with or without participle,
at the end of a sentence where we use a co-ordinate clause.
Cf. § 9, § 42 δ.

§ 42.
Tacitean
idioms.

§ 42. Tacitean idioms :—

Pres. part.
frequent.

a. Frequent use of present participle, as § 41 ε, § 25 ε,
both for clauses (temporal, conditional, &c.), and also for
persons, and classes, or for abstract substantives : and of
the passive participle similarly.

Adeo furentes infirmitate retinentis accendebat. *Hist.*
I. 9. *Nec deerant sermones increpantium.* *II.* I. 7.

Cf. 2, 15, 19; 8, 19; 19, 9, 32; 24, 47.

§ 42. β. Similar use of adjective, as participle, or as
if ὤν were omitted; *pronus ad novas res scelere insuper*
agitatur.

§ 42.
Adj. for
Part.

Cf. § 20, and 8, 9, 11; 18, 9; 24, 31.

γ. Omission of copula-verb, especially with adjectives; omission of other common verbs readily supplied.
Especially in the favourite parenthetical use of *incertum*
an (dolo), or *sive—sive*. *Sive verum istud sive ex in-*
genio principis fictum. *Cf.* 24, 49.

Omission
of copula-
verb, &c.

Cf. 2, 3, 9, 12; 4, 9, 13; 11, 17.

δ. Frequent use of ablative absolute both before
and, more frequently, after the main verb, as co-ordinate
clause (stating a fresh fact), or as attendant circumstance, &c.; e.g. *lubrico statu, attritis opibus, II.* I. 10;
of the gerund in *do*, 24, 35, similarly; of the gerundive
(e.g. *An.* XI. 32, *dissimulando metu digreditur*) in modal
or final sense, *cf.* 22, 12; of the ablat. absol. used im-
personally, e.g. *explorato, nuntiato, cf.* 4, 3. But *cf.* Tac.
An. XV. 24, 28 with *An.* XI. 32.

Abl. Abs.
for co-ordi-
nate.

Cf. 2, 6; 4, 12; 11, 12, 17.

ε. Use of *quamquam* with subjunctive, and with participles, *An.* XI. 32; XVI. 15 (and *quamvis* with indicative);
more frequent use of the subjunctive generally, wherever
a fact can be stated subjectively or where the indefinite
idea of frequency justifies its use; on the other hand,
occasional interpolation of the indicative in *obliqua oratio*,
and frequent use of the construction, *circumveniebatur*
ni...se opposuissent.

Subj. for
Ind.

Cf. 2, 3, 18; 4, 22; 8, 20; 16, 14, 33.'

N.   *e*

Asyndeton.

§ 42. ζ. Omission of conjunctive and disjunctive copulas.

Cf. 11, 7, 15, 17.

Zeugma, &c.

η. Union or confusion of incongruous ideas and constructions.

Cf. 2, 10; 8, 10, 16; 9, 7; 10, 14; 11, 10—12; 16, 5, 37; 18, 17; 22, 27.

Infinitives substantivally, epexegetically.

θ. Free use of infinitives (i) as substantives both as subject and object (as in Greek with the article), (ii) epexegetically as in Greek; (iii) with ellipse of verb, to express habit, inception, &c., even after *quum, ubi;* e.g. *legionibus cum damno labor, et fodere rivos. An.* xi. 20. *auferre, trucidare, rapere, falsis nominibus imperium... appellant. Agr.* 30.

Tacitean imitations of Greek and poet. forms.

ι. Imitation of Greek and of poetical forms, as in the use of the genitive (for ablative), of the objective genitive, of the subjective dative for ablative; of adjectives or participles for substantives and for adverbs: in the use of the positive for the comparative; in the variety of periphrases for common ideas (as death, suicide, &c.): e.g. *volgus mutabile subitis; adrogans minoribus; sermonis nimius; vehementius quam caute, &c.*

Cf. 2, 2; 22, 11, 14, 23; 23, 28.

Brevity: Ellipse:

κ. General tendency to brevity, condensation, and ellipse of prepositions and nouns as well as verbs (as in γ); frequent usage of verbs in peculiar senses, e.g.

verbs in special sense.

agere, to continue, live, stay; *tendere,* to encamp; *imputare, expedire, &c.;* or with peculiar constructions, e.g. *fungor, potior,* with accusative.

Cf. 4, 14; 10, 8; 11, 2, 11; 22, 4.

Generally it will be seen that most of the peculiarities involve, either imitation of Greek—often as if the (Greek) article or participle ὤν were understood—or an affectation of brevity, or a preference for a subjective turn of thought suggestive rather than explicit, or, lastly, a desire for singularity or variety of expression.

§ 43. *a.* In English we often follow the train of thought in another's mind, his reasonings, or statements, and state them directly with or without a prefatory 'he said,' 'he advised,' &c. This is our *oratio obliqua*, marked only by the use of the past for the present, pluperfect for perfect (would, could, &c., for will, can). Ambiguities often occur in consequence. *[margin: § 43. English oratio obliqua.]*

Cf. (6) 12; (7) 10; (8) 15; (11) 5, &c.; (15) 7, 17.

β. In Latin the verb cannot be thus left in the indicative mood, but is thrown into the infinitive or subjunctive. The subject becomes an accusative, the verb an infinitive, both in the main and in the co-ordinate clauses; while subordinate or dependent verbs become or remain subjunctives, in present or past tenses accordingly as the original main verb is present, past, or historic present. § 30 γ, vi. § 41 *a.* *[margin: Latin oratio obliqua.]*

Cf. 4, 10—19; 6, 5—21; 11, 3—7; 12, 15.

γ. Words introducing this *oratio obliqua*, 'urging,' 'saying,' 'he exclaimed,' 'he continued,' are omitted generally; *dixit, respondit, videbatur, apparebat, ferebatur, &c.*, are sometimes used. *[margin: Ellipse of verbs.]*

Commands and exhortations, dependent on *monet, monuit ut, &c.* suppressed, are put in the present or imperfect subjunctive.

Cf. 1, 6; 8, 15; 11, 3, 14; 12, 15; 24, 20.

δ. Independent questions when put in *oratio obliqua, as other main clauses,* are expressed by the accusative with the infinitive (being dependent on *dicit, &c.* not on *rogat, &c.*), e.g. *Quem non videre?* except where the second person of the *oratio recta* has to be expressed, when to avoid confusion the subjunctive is mostly used, as if it were a dependent clause. So *nonne vides* *[margin: Questions in oratio obliqua.]*

becomes *nonne videret;* but *nonne video, videmus?* become•
nonne (se) videre? and *nonne videt, vident? nonne videre•
eos? &c.* See Madvig, § 405. *Cf.* 6, 11; 10, 3, 4; *cf.*
also Cic. *p. Rosc. Am.* 23. 64.

§ 43.
Indirect
interroga-
tive.

The indirect interrogative however approximates to a
simple dependent clause (when attached to a main verb
expressed), and is treated as such (see β); *quaerit ubi esset
Cato, ubi tu esses, ubi ipse esset.*

Questions
orig. in subj.
subordina-
ted.

§ 43. ε. Questions originally in the subjunctive (like
other dependent clauses) when put in *oratio obliqua* remain in the subjunctive with a change of tense according
to β, or § 30 ζ; e.g. *utri pareum ?* becomes *utri pareret ?*
or *utri parendum esset ?* in *oratio obliqua;* in both cases
equally a main governing verb or a condition being
suppressed.

Here, as in § 30 ζ, the rule holds good that the subjunctive
cannot do double duty. Quid faceres ? (conditional) becomes
quid facturus esset ?

Qui copula-
tive with in-
fin.

ζ. The relative *qui* is often treated as a copula
(= *et is*) and followed by the infinitive mood, the relative
sentences being then co-ordinate and not dependent.
However the subjunctive is oftener found, so that the
sentence becomes a qualifying clause. See Madvig, § 402.
E.g. *esse illi pecuniam et eloquentiam queis multos an-
teiret* (or *anteire*).

§ 44.
Speeches in
oratio
obliqua.

§ 44. Short speeches in English are generally expressed in *oratio recta;* in Latin by *oratio obliqua:* but
not always: e.g. 26, 35; (15) 18; 30, 2. As a rule
oratio obliqua is oftener used in Latin than in English
for all speeches.

Cf. (1) 26; (7) 37; (10) 4; 16, 26; (28) 7; (30) 1.

§ 45.
Metaphors:

§ 45. *a.* Metaphors are less frequent in Latin than

English, and where used are used more consciously and consistently[1]. *Cf.* 3, 15; (4) 18; (9) 23, &c.

§ 45. β. English is thickly strewn with buried metaphors—fossils of bygone ages, Greek, Roman, Saxon, Norman; they need not be reproduced in Latin, if dead and unmeaning in the English, and will otherwise often require simplifying; e.g. 'agony,' 'afflicted,' 'redundant,' 'redound,' 'affluence,' 'inured,' 'despond,' 'astonished.' *Cf.* § 11 β. On the other hand, their Latin originals can often no longer be expressed in English by such effete derivatives, but will require the substitution of other words and more lively metaphors.

§ 45. When not reproduced:

γ. Metaphors may often in translation be shifted from the verb or adjective to the noun, or *vice versa;* e.g. *magna vis telorum volabat; defluxit salutatio; signa non fucata sed domesticis inusta notis veritatis.*

Shifted from verb to noun, &c.

The most ordinary Lat. metaphors it will be noticed come from the ideas of gushing and flowing, burning, flame or heat. In attempting to translate a metaphor first grasp the main leading idea of it, whether *extent, swiftness, rest, development,* &c., discarding at first incidentals. Then choose an *essential* equivalent suiting the idiom of the language, afterwards working in the incidentals harmoniously.

Sources of and

Rule for translating metaphors.

δ. Where we use similes taken from nautical (as in Greek) or commercial matters, or our old national pursuits, as archery, the Romans take theirs from legal or military matters, and from their own peculiar habits,

Metaphors from national habits, pursuits:

---

[1] Not always however: *cf.* Cic. *in Catilin.* IV. 3, 6. *Latius opinione disseminatum est hoc malum; manavit non solum per Italiam, verum etiam transcendit Alpes; et obscure serpens multas provincias occupavit. Id opprimi sustentando et prolatando nullo pacto potest.*

pursuits, and institutions; they will often use similes where we do not, and *vice versa;* e. g. *Epicuri castra ; tirocinium ; in ordinem cogi ; vita mancipio nulli datur ; columen reipublicae;* 'two strings to one's bow ;' 'to hit, miss, overshoot, &c., the mark ;' 'to draw the long bow,' &c., 'mainstay,' 'to launch a scheme,' 'to tack,' 'to weather,' 'to draw upon the imagination,' 'to endorse,' 'to credit with,' &c.

more material in Lat. § 45. ε. English similes and figurative expressions are more idealistic, Latin more material and matter-of-fact : e.g. *cedant arma togae ; nervi reipublicae ; succus et sanguis oratorum.*

See Cic. *de Oratore,* III. 38, 153 sqq.; Quintil. *Inst. Orat.* Bk. VIII.

Cf. 6, 7; (10) 9, 15 ; (14) 14; (15) 10, 19; (22) 4; (32) 5, 7; (35) 16; (36) 10; (39) 9, 16; and 14, 6; 22, 7; 26, 34, 56, 72; 37, 36, 60; 46, 12; 49, 14—19; 53, 7; 55, 5, 11.

§ 46. Repetitions of verb in Latin instead of equivalent. cf. § 28 β. § 46. *Jubes me venire; veniam,* 'you ask me to come ; I will' (*cf.* § 28), is a difference of idiom due to the use of auxiliaries in English and not in Latin, and to our love of variety. We seldom repeat the same verb ; sometimes we say 'I will *do* so,' to avoid the repetition ; and in Latin *faciam* can be similarly used, though not so frequently. Cf. *id quod fit, factum est,* 'as it does, did.' In Latin the verb is sometimes omitted altogether. *Cf.* 55, 18.

Cf. 11, 13 ; (38) 23 ; 43, 5, 7, 14, 16 ; 52, 24; 56, 9.

§ 47. Abruptness of English. § 47. A story is often introduced by *ferunt* in Latin, where in English it begins abruptly : *cf.* 39, 20 ; (39) 18.

Connecting links in Latin *accidit ut, adde quod,* &c. Sometimes *factum est ut, accidit, accedit, evenit, ut,* will be found useful in introducing incidents, or results, *forte* being often added, or beginning the story. So *adde quod, accedit quod,* with indicative, in all tenses.

Similarly the English imperative is sometimes too § 47.
fac, cura,
&c.
abrupt for Latin : and *fac, cura, vide, noli,* or the simple
future or fut. perfect may have to be used: e.g. *fac
scribas ; scribes ; ne scripseris; noli scribere.*

Cf. 13, 36; 30, 6; 38, 8, 14; 40, 22.

So also sentences really inferential will be introduced *autem,sane,*
vero, &c.;
cf. §§ 9 a and
34 sub. fin.
by *igitur,* &c., adversative and antithetical, by *autem,*
vero, &c.; concessive, by *sane, profecto, quidem;* epexegetic,
by *et quidem, etiam porro,* &c.   *Cf.* 7, 12, 14 ; 14, 20 ;
18, 16; 24, 41; 42, 8; 45, 7; (46) 6, 9; (47) 2, 13;
(49) 2, 12; (51) 10, 15.

§ 48.   Ambiguities arise in the use of common words § 48.
Ambiguous
use of words.
from the fact that they do not cover exactly the same
ground in both languages.

a.   Omnis is not only 'all,' 'the whole' (as *totus*), *Omnis.*
'every' (but not in sense of *quisque*), but also is constantly equivalent to our 'any;' cf. *omnino,* 'in any
case;' in expressions like *omnium cum dolore,* it may
often be translated 'general,' 'universal.'   *Cf.* 22, 31; 25,
19.

β.   Once—or 'on *one* (i.e. an) occasion'—is simply *Once.*
expressed by *quum* if that can be introduced, at other
times *forte* may express it, or it is left untranslated; 'once,'
'on a former occasion,' 'formerly,' *quondam, olim* (once on
a time) ; or, more indefinitely, 'at least once,' 'before
now,' *aliquando;* 'once' numerically, and similarly 'once
for all,' *semel;* e.g. *forte ludebam quum, &c.; quondam
ludebam ; aliquando lusi ; semel lusi.*

γ.   'No,' where meaning 'not,' and in expressions No, not,
nullus.
like 'no sun, no moon,' will often be translated by *non,*
not by *nullus.*   On the other hand *nullus* is occasionally
found in the sense of 'not at all,' e.g. *is non modo
nullus venit sed,* &c.   *Nullus* with ablative is used for

'without,' e. g. *nullo ordine, cf.* (13) 17, without the *cum* that usually marks attendant circumstance. *Cf.* § 50, Näg. § 82, and Madv. § 257. *Cf.* 2, 23 ; 11, 10 ; (22) 2 : (53) 14.

'Tell.' δ. So 'tell' may have to be translated by *dicere, nuntiare, scribere, jubere, certiorem facere;* 'ever' by *unquam, semper, aliquando, quando;* 'as' by *quum, ut, sicut, quam,* &c.

§ 49. 'May,' 'might,' &c. as auxiliaries. § 49. Care must be taken to distinguish between 'might,' 'would,' 'could,' 'should,' used as auxiliaries in subjunctive clauses, and the same used as perfects of 'may,' 'will,' 'can,' 'shall.' These (like 'ought' from 'owe') are coupled with a past or perfect subordinate tense in English (necessary only because their own past or perfect sense has got obscured), e.g. might, &c., *have done, have been doing;* but in Latin the present must be used: *licuit, voluit, potuit, debuit (debebat, debuerat,* &c.), *facere.*

Cf. 12, 2, 15, 19; 26, 38; 32, 5; (37) 10; 37, 33; (45) 16; 48, 21.

Latin perf. infin. with 'may,' 'might,' &c. rare. The Latin perfect infinitive is sometimes used after these verbs to mark a completed action, but never to mark the past time of the power or duty, &c., of doing it, as in English ; e.g. *potuerat fecisse,* 'he might have done it already.'

'May,' 'will,' &c., as main verbs. Similarly 'may,' 'will,' 'shall,' are not always auxiliaries, but main verbs with an infinitive following.

Such words vary in meaning according to their accent, and may have to be expressed as above by *posse,* &c., or by the fut. in *-rus;* by the gerund; *statuo; opus est,* &c.

'Must,' 'ought,' &c. 'Must,' like 'ought,' is properly a past tense, but is used in a present and future sense, as 'ought' also.

'Would,' 'should.' 'Would' is also used in a frequentative sense, e.g. 'he would often say,' *solebat dicere, dicebat.* The con-

ditional use of 'would,' 'should,' must be carefully distinguished from their use as futures; e. g. *veniret si posset;
dixit se venturum.*

Where the above are used as auxiliaries to mark the
subjunctive mood it is due to their 'future' meaning, and
the quasi-future sense of subjunctive conceptions.

§ 50. *a.* Before translating English prepositions para-
phrase their meaning; sometimes the substantive will
disappear; if not, distinguish first the *case* to which the
idea belongs (accusative of motion, limitation, extension,
&c., dative of recipient, &c., ablative of manner, cause,
&c.), and then, if necessary, prefix the preposition most
suitable.

§ 50.
Preposi-
tions.

E. g. 'of' may be translated by the simple genitive of origin, 'Of.'
possession, quality, part, without preposition; by the ablative of
quality, of locality, of subject, of material, of distance; *vir magna
virtute, Turnus (ex) ab Aricia, de te, (e) saxo murus: intra mille
passuum ab hoste aberant.*

'From' may mean source (*ex*); beginning, distance, departure, 'From.'
absence (*ab*); sequence, time (*ab, ex*); cause, *ex, prae,* with ablative,
or *ob, propter,* with accusative. Sometimes a possessive pronoun
may be used, *sine tuis litteris,* 'letters from you.'

'With' may mean the manner, instrument (*vi, gladio, per-* 'With.'
cussus); quality (*senex promissa barba*) of the simple ablative; or
the attendant circumstance (or person), generally requiring *cum*
with the ablative, e. g. *tecum, cum gaudio,* but also *magno studio;*
see Madv. § 257; also 'at the house of,' *apud.*

'Without' is sometimes expressed by *absque, sine;* by *nullus,* 'Without.'
§ 48 γ; by adj., or verb, *expers, careo, vaco,* &c.; by phrase, as in § 33.

'For' may mean the simple dative of recipient or advantage, &c.; 'For.'
the simple ablative or genitive of price, *Quanti emptum? tribus
assibus;* or the objective genitive, e. g. *amor patris;* or the simple
accusative of duration of time, without or with *in* (*tres menses, in
aevum*); or the ablative of amount of time, e. g. *novem annis,* cf. 37,
53; or the ablative (originally local) with *pro, pro te;* or 'as,' 'in
place of'=*vice, pro,* e. g. *vice consulis, pro praetore;* or purpose,
tendency, destination (*in* or *ad* with accusative); or *causa,* &c. with

gen., e.g. *honoris causa;* or *prae* expressing a preventive cause, e. g. *prae lacrumis.*

'In.' 'In' (when not used loosely for 'into') is confined to the ablative, but will not be translated by *in* except in strictly local senses, but by the simple ablative.

'To.' 'To' may mean the dative; the ablative of attendant circumstance (*cum omnium gaudio*); but will usually be expressed by the accusative; *ad* will give the further idea of '*up* to;' *in* of 'into;' *versus* of 'towards;' 'up to,' *tenus.*

'Under.' 'Under' may mean place (*sub, subter*); inferiority of age, rank, number (*minor*); subjection (substantive or adjective); condition, 'under these circumstances' (ablative or phrase).

'By.' 'By' may mean proximity (accusative with *apud, juxta, prope, ad, propter*); or motion near or past (*trans, praeter* with accusative); or the agent or instrument, *ab, per;* or the instrumental or modal ablative; or distribution, e.g. *in dies,* day by day.

'On.' 'On' is used of place, with motion (*in, super* with accusative); of rest (*in, super* with ablative, and *supra* with accusative); of direction, *ab ortu, ab sinistra;* of time (ablative), *Kal. Juniis;* or in sense of 'after' (*ex* with ablative, *post* with accusative).

'Through.' 'Through' may mean agency (*per*); instrumentality (ablative); motion (*per, trans, super* with accusative).

'At,' &c. 'At,' *ad, apud,* of place, or the locative (*Romae*) &c.; or 'against,' *in;* or gen. or ablat. of price.

Similarly 'after,' 'before,' 'near,' 'about,' &c., have various meanings that must be carefully distinguished. They must not be confused with adverbs and conjunctions of the same form.

Prepositions repeated in Latin. § 50. β. Prepositions in Latin must be repeated with succeeding substantives, except where these latter form one idea; 'in peace and war,' *in bello et in pace.* Nor can two prepositions be as a rule used with the same substantive as in English; e.g. 'with or without thee,' *vel tecum vel sine te.*

Cf. 3, 21, 23 ; 15, 8, 18; 21, 14, 21; 35, 14, 18 ; 36, 22.

Position of prepositions. γ. Prepositions immediately precede the substantive or substantival phrase that they belong to; except where emphasis requires part of the latter to come first, *multis de causis, ad recte faciendum.*

This is the case even with relatives. However, both with relatives and other pronouns, some (as *cum, contra,* *inter, propter*) follow occasionally; *tenus* and *versus* regu- larly; e. g. *quos inter; te propter; hactenus,* &c.

As regards enclitics like *enim, quidem, que,* that come as the second word of the clause, the substantive or phrase is generally regarded as one word with its prepo- sition when the latter is a monosyllable (cf. the fact that in Greek some monosyllabic prepositions have no accent); e. g. *de te enim; per me quidem, in reque tanta,* though sometimes *inque re tanta.*

§ 50.   δ. Carefully distinguish when the preposition belongs to the verb and when to the substantive.   In phrases like 'the book I asked for,' the preposition may belong to a verb governing a suppressed relative; in 'the friend I went with,' to the relative suppressed.   The meaning will often depend on the accent.

Cf. (10) 15; (35) 9—17, &c.

ε.   Prepositions with verbals where the gerund and gerundive are not used are replaced by the conjunction and verb, *ut, quin, &c.,* e. g. 'kept from falling,' &c.; *cf.* § 33.

§ 51.   a.   The arrangement of compound numerals is the same in Latin as in English: seventeen is *sep-* *tem decim* (occasionally *decem et septem*); *viginti septem,* twenty-seven, or *septem et viginti,* seven *and* twenty; and so with the *Latin* ordinals, *vicesimus primus,* or *primus et vicesimus* (where English is different).   After 100 the larger number precedes, with or without *et* in Latin, with 'and' in English.   Numbers beyond 100,000 are expressed as multiples of that number by the adverbs *bis, ter, decies,* &c. (*centena millia*). *Cf.* 'This property of six millions of sesterces,' *haec bona sexagies.* Cic. *Rosc. Am.* 21.

§ 51.
Mille.

N.B. *Mille* in the singular is indeclinable and either substantival or adjectival : *millia* is declinable and substantival ; e.g. *duo millia hostium caesa.*

Cf. 16, 7, 15, 28 ; 17, 27 ; 24, 7, 24 ; 26, 7 ; 33, 21 ; 37, 53 ; 39, 21.

Distribu-
tive nume-
rals.

§ 51. β. Distributive numerals, *singuli, bini, septeni, &c.*, mean ' 1, 2, 7 a-piece;' except when joined with plural noun-forms of singular meaning, when they give simply a plural meaning, *binae litterae, trina castra;* but *unae litterae*, not *singulae*. In compound numerals, as *ter deni, vicies centena*, they are used without a distributive sense.

Per-centage.

These distributives may be used to translate per-centage ; e.g. *terni in millia aeris.* Livy XXXIX. 44.

But per-centage of interest on money is expressed as a fraction of the principal.

E.g. *unciarium fenus* $= \frac{1}{12}$, i.e. $8\frac{1}{3}$ per cent. per year of 10 months, which is for our year of 12 months "10 per cent."

Semunciarium = " 5 per cent."

Usurae centesimae $= \frac{1}{100}$ per month = " 12 per cent."

So *binae centesimae* = 24 per cent.

Usurae quincunces $= \frac{5}{12}$ of the centesimae, i.e. 5 per cent.

Usurae deunces = 11 per cent.

Unciarium fenus = " 1 per cent."

Cf. 1, 5 ; 10, 12 ; 29, 2 ; 43, 17.

Particles
qualifying
numerals,
plus.
minus.

γ. *Amplius, plus, minus* may be prefixed to numerals (whatever case they are in or are joined with), *quam* being omitted ; e.g. *umbram non amplius* VIII *pedes longam.* Similarly we find (Livy XXXVIII. 38) *obsides ne minores octonum denum annorum neu maiores quinum quadragenum;* *quam* being omitted. ' Under thirty' may be translated by *minus triginta annos natus, minor triginta annis, minor triginta annos natus, minor triginta annorum.*

Ad (about) is found prefixed to numerals *with all* § 51.
Ad: ipse,
admodum,
fere, &c. *cases* adverbially, *ad duo millia et trecenti occisi*, Liv. X. 17.; but not in Cicero. The following are also found added or prefixed to numerals; *admodum,* 'about,' or 'quite;' *ipse,* 'exactly;' *numero,* 'in all,' or unexpressed in English; *minimum* (*quum minimum,* Plin.) 'at least;' and *si* (*quum*) *maxime, fere, ut plurimum,* &c.

§ 51. δ. Multiplicatives (*duplex, triplex, &c.*) are used Multiplica-
tives. with *quam; pars mea duplex quam tua ;* forms in *-plus* are also used, *quadruplus, duplus,* and their neuters as substantives. But generally (*sex*) *partibus major, minor,* is found for our '(six) times as great;' e.g. *sol amplius duodeviginti partibus maior quam terra* (Cic. *Acad.*); *duabus partibus* or (*duplo*) *amplius* (Cic. *Verr.*); '18 times greater or as great,' 'twice as much:' where notice, that the XVIII *partibus* is the full measure of the thing that exceeds, *not of the excess* as might have been expected. This may be compared with their inclusive method of reckoning.

ε. Fractions are expressed by use of the 12 divisions Fractions. of the *as* (especially for land, inheritance, interest); or of the numerals (cardinal, ordinal, and distributive) with *partes* or *pars.* Often the fraction is split into two. *Heres ex besse* ($\frac{2}{3}$), *ex deunce et semuncia* ($\frac{2}{3}\frac{3}{4}$); *duae partes* ($\frac{2}{3}$), *tres partes* ($\frac{3}{4}$) (as in Greek); or *duae tertiae* ($\frac{2}{3}$), *tres septimae* ($\frac{3}{7}$); *tres cum semisse* ($3\frac{1}{2}$); *tertia pars et octava paulo amplius,* 'a little more than $\frac{11}{24}$ths'; *Sicilicus* $\frac{1}{48}$th (of *as,* or $\frac{1}{4}$th of *uncia*); *scrupulus* $\frac{1}{24}$ of *uncia* $= \frac{1}{288}$th of *jugerum.*

Cf. 17, 21; 20, 19.

ζ. Though *momentum* (like *punctum* and *articulus*) Fractions of
time. is used for a small portion of time (*horae momento nullo, momentis horarum,* Plin. *N. H.* VII. 161, 172; *momento*

temporis, Liv. XXI. 33 ; *parvo momento,* Caes.), yet our
divisions of the hour were unknown to the Romans,
and must be expressed by fractions, as in the following,
(mainly taken from Pliny *N. H.*) ; *dimidia hora ; dodrans
horae ; quintae partes horae tres ; bis quinta pars horae ;
semuncia horae* ($= 2\frac{1}{2}$ minutes); *dodrans semuncia horae,*
$47\frac{1}{2}$ min. ; *partes octo unius horae ; sesquihora* ($1\frac{1}{2}$ hr.);
*horae quattuordecim et dimidia cum triyesima parte unius
horae* ($14\frac{16}{30}$ hrs.). This last will form a useful model;
as of course *sexagesima pars* could be used similarly.
Cf. 9, 22 ; 48, 15. We find also *scrupulus* (in inscrip-
tions) for $\frac{1}{24}$th of hour $= 2\frac{1}{2}$ minutes; *sicilicus* for $\frac{1}{48}$th
of hour $= 1\frac{1}{4}$ minute.

§ 52. To mark the hour of the day, write *prima,
secunda, &c.,* from 7.0 A.M. to 6.0 P.M., adding *noctis*
from 7.0 P.M. to 6.0 A.M. inclusive ; but remember that
prima (the line *one* on the dial) marks both the period
6.0 to 7.0, and the conclusion of the same, i.e. 7.0.
[Cf. our 'in his 20th year' with ' 20 years old.']

    Cf. 33, 10, 19 ; 34, 3, 11 ; 41, 21, 27, 30 ; 56, 1.

Hora (like ὥρα, of the year only, till about 150 B.C.) meant
merely a division of the day. As they divided their *as* into
12 parts, they divided their day, and eventually their night also,
into 12 hours. At first the *hora* was $\frac{1}{12}$th of a natural day or
night, and varied in length from $1\frac{1}{4}$ hr. to $\frac{3}{4}$ hr. It must soon
however have been found expedient to make *hora* a fixed time,
$\frac{1}{12}$th of what Pliny calls an equinoctial day ; still the fact of his
distinguishing them in his calculations (*horae nunc aequinoctiales,
non cuiuscunque diei significantur,* XVIII. 221) shows that the old
meaning of *hora* was in use then (probably side by side with
the new, and both marked on dials). His remark in *N. H.* II. 79
is worth quoting. '*Ipsum diem alii aliter observavere. Babylonii
inter duos Solis exortus; Athenienses inter duos occasus: Umbri
a meridie in meridiem : vulgus omne a luce ad tenebras : sacerdotes
Romani et qui diem diffiniere civilem, item Ægyptii et Hipparchus
a media nocte in mediam.*'

Horae sometimes was used for the dial itself, *horologium.* Dials. *Videt iudicem oscitantem mittentem ad horas,* Cic. *Brut.* 54. *Moveri horas videmus,* Cic. *N. D.* II. 38.   And often for the quarters of the heavens corresponding with the sun's position at certain hours (cf. *meridies*). Plin. *N. II.* VI. 32, 37 ; XVII. 11, 16.

Remember that the Romans, not having our minute accurate Divisions of divisions of the hour, marked time less exactly.   The following day and hour. are common expressions: *mane, bene mane, multo mane, hodie mane, cras mane, postridie mane, hesterno die mane* (or *vesperi* similarly): *sexta hora diei,* Pl. *N. II.* II. 180, or *meridies; hora diei inter septimam et octavam; inter horam diei decimam et undecimam; noctis tertia hora; prima, secunda, tertia, quarta, vigilia; nocte concubia, media, intempesta: diluculo,* &c.

The following passages also may be of use as illustrations:
Ut illum Di perdant primus qui horas reperit
Quique adeo primus statuit hic solarium.
Plaut. ap. Gell. III. 3. 5.

Tunc Scipio Nasica primus aqua divisit horas aeque noctium et dierum, idque horologium dicavit anno urbis DXCV.
Plin. *N. H.* VII. 60. *cf.* II. 78.

Quinta dum linea tangitur umbra.   Pers. III. 4.

Quum post horam primam noctis occisus esset, primo diluculo nuntius hic Ameriam venit: *decem horis nocturnis,* sex et quinquaginta millia passuum cisiis pervolavit. Cic. *Rosc. Am.* VII. 19.

Cf. Martial IV. 2, and Becker's *Gallus.*

§ 53.   We cannot mark the day of the week in Latin. § 53. We can the days of the month by expressing the date as so Days and months, &c. many days (*reckoning inclusively*) before the Nones (the 5th or 7th[1]), the Ides (the 13th or 15th), or the Kalends; e.g. a.d. VI. *Kal. Jun.* (May 27th), or *ante diem sextum Kal.;* or the original form, *sexto* (*die ante*), or VI. *Kal. Pridie, postridie Kal.,* are also found.

We may express the year in modern dates, either The year.

---

[1] In March, July, October, May,
The Nones are on the seventh day.

simply as A.D.; or as A.U.C., in this case adding on the year A.D. to the date of the building of Rome, 753.

The period of a week may be marked roughly by *nundinae, nundinum,* 'market-day' = eight days ; *trinum nundinum, trinundinum* (i. e. 17 days, or from the first to the third market-day), and *biduum, triduum, quatriduum,* may also be found useful.

Cf. 23, 11; 29, 17; 41, 3, 30; 44, 21; 46, 14.

PARALLEL EXTRACTS.

HISTORICAL AND EPISTOLARY.

C. Plinius Fusco Suo S.—Quaeris quemadmodum in secessu, quo jam diu frueris, putem te studere oportere. Utile in primis, et multi praecipiunt, vel ex Graeco in Latinum vel ex Latino vertere in Graecum : quo genere exercitationis proprietas splendorque verborum, copia figurarum, vis explicandi, paratur : simul quae legentem fefellissent transferentem fugere non possunt. Intellegentia ex hoc et judicium adquiritur. Nihil offuerit quae legeris hactenus ut rem argumentumque teneas quasi aemulum scribere lectisque conferre, ac sedulo pensitare quid tu, quid ille commodius. Poteris et quae dixeris post oblivionem retractare, multa retinere, plura transire, alia interscribere, alia rescribere. Laboriosum istud et taedio plenum sed difficultate ipsa fructuosum, recalescere ex integro et resumere impetum fractum omissumque, postremo nova velut membra peracto corpori intexere nec tamen priora turbare. Scio nunc tibi esse praecipuum studium orandi ; sed non ideo semper pugnacem hunc et quasi bellatorium stilum suaserim. Ut enim terrae variis mutatisque seminibus, ita ingenia nostra nunc hac nunc illa meditatione recoluntur. Volo interdum aliquem ex historia locum adprehendas, volo epistulam diligentius scribas. Nam saepe in orationes quoque non historica modo sed prope poetica descriptionum necessitas incidit, et pressus sermo purusque ex epistulis petitur. Habes plura etiam fortasse quam requirebas, unum tamen omisi ; non enim dixi quae legenda arbitrarer : quamquam dixi, cum dicerem quae scribenda. Tu memineris sui cujusque generis auctores diligenter eligere. Aiunt enim multum legendum esse, non multa. Qui sint hi adeo notum probatumque est ut demonstratione non egeat ; et alioqui tam immodice epistulam extendi ut, dum tibi quemadmodum studere debeas suadeo, studendi tempus abstulerim. Quin ergo pugillares resumis et aliquid ex his vel istud ipsum quod coeperas scribis ? Vale.

Pliny.

1. CINCINNATUS. Postero die dictator cum magistro equitum in concionem venit[41], justitium edicit, claudi tabernas tota urbe jubet, vetat quemquam privatae quicquam rei agere; tum, quicunque aetate militari essent, armati cum cibariis in dies 5 quinque[3] coctis vallisque duodenis ante solis occasum [Martio] in campo adessent[43]; quibus aetas ad militandum gravior esset, vicino militi, dum is arma pararet vallumque peteret[30], cibaria coquere jussit. Sic juventus discurrit ad vallum petendum. Sumpsere, unde cuique proximum fuit; prohibitus nemo est; 10 impigreque omnes ad edictum dictatoris praesto fuere. Inde composito agmine legiones ipse dictator, magister equitum suos equites ducit. Media nocte in Algidum perveniunt et, ut sensere, se jam prope hostes esse, signa constituunt[13]. Ibi dictator, quantum nocte prospici poterat, equo circumvectus 15 contemplatusque, qui[5] tractus castrorum quaeque forma esset, tribunis militum imperavit, ut sarcinas in unum coniici jubeant, militem cum armis valloque redire in ordines suos. Facta, quae imperavit[12]. Tum, quo fuerant ordine[6] in via, exercitum omnem longo agmine circumdat hostium castris et, 20 ubi[33] signum datum sit[30], clamorem omnes tollere jubet; clamore sublato, ante se quemque ducere fossam et jacere vallum[9]. Edito imperio, signum secutum est. Jussa miles exsequitur; clamor hostes[11] circumsonat. Superat inde castra hostium et in castra consulis venit; alibi pavorem, alibi gaudium ingens 25 facit[35]. Romani, civilem esse clamorem atque auxilium adesse[43], inter se gratulantes[12], ultro[28] ex stationibus ac vigiliis territant hostem. LIVY, III. 27.

2. ARMINIUS. Nox per diversa[11] inquies, cum[25] barbari festis epulis, laeto cantu aut truci sonore subjecta vallium ac resultantis saltus complerent, apud Romanos[34] invalidi ignes, interruptae voces[42] atque ipsi passim adjacerent vallo, oberrarent tentoriis, 5 insomnes magis quam pervigiles. coepta luce missae[9] in latera legiones, metu an contumacia, locum deseruere, capto[25] propere campo umentia ultra. neque tamen Arminius quamquam libero incursu statim prorupit: sed ut haesere caeno fossisque impedimenta, turbati circum milites, incertus signorum ordo, 10 utque tali in tempore sibi quisque properus et lentae adversum imperia aures[46], inrumpere[12] Germanos jubet, clamitans 'en Varus eodemque iterum fato vinctae legiones!' simul haec[34] et cum delectis scindit agmen equisque maxime vulnera ingerit, illi sanguine suo et lubrico paludum lapsantes excussis[25] recto-

(1.) STORY OF CINCINNATUS. Then the Master of the people and the Master of the horse went[41] together into the forum, and bade every man to shut up his booth, and stopped all causes at law, and ordered that every man who was[30] of an age to go out to battle should be ready in the Field of Mars[5] 5 before sunset, and[9] should have with him victuals for five days, and twelve stakes; and the older men dressed the victuals for the soldiers, whilst the soldiers went about everywhere to get their stakes; and they cut them where they would[49], without[32] any hindrance[12]. So the army[10] was ready in the Field of 10 Mars at the time appointed, and they set forth from the city, and[9] made such haste, that ere the night was half spent[20] they came[41] to Algidus; and when they perceived that they were near the enemy, they made a halt[13]. Then Lucius rode on[9], and saw how the camp of the enemy lay[28]; and he ordered his 15 soldiers to throw down all their baggage into one place, but to keep each man his arms and his twelve stakes. Then they set out again in their order of march as[5] they had come from Rome, and they spread themselves round the camp of the enemy on every side. When this[9] was done, upon a signal 20 given they raised a great shout, and directly every man began[41] to dig a ditch just where he stood, and to set in his stakes. The[34] shout ran through the camp of the enemy, and filled them with fear; and it sounded even to the camp of the Romans who were shut up in the valley, and[9] the consul's men 25 said one to another, "Rescue is surely at hand, for that is the shout of the Romans[44]." ARNOLD.

(2.) DEFEAT OF VARUS. Fatigue and discouragement now began to betray[28] themselves in the Roman ranks[11]. Their line became less steady; baggage-waggons were abandoned from the impossibility[12] of forcing them along; and[9] as this happened, many soldiers left[41] their ranks and crowded round 5 the waggons to secure the most valuable portions of their property[11]; each busy about his own affairs[11], and purposely slow in hearing the word[11] of command from[50] his officers. Arminius now gave the signal for a general[18] attack[12]. The fierce shouts of the Germans pealed through the gloom[13] of the 10 forests[6], and in thronging multitudes they assailed the flanks of the invaders[10], pouring[25] in clouds[45] of darts on the encumbered legionaries, as they struggled up the glens or floundered[25] in the morasses. Arminius, with a chosen band of personal[11]

1—2

15 ribus disicere obvios, proterere iacentes[41]. plurimus circa aquilas
labor[11], quae[9] neque ferri adversum ingruentia tela neque figi
limosa humo poterant. Caecina dum sustentat[33] aciem, suffosso
equo[9] delapsus circumveniebatur, ni prima legio sese opposuisset.
juvit[7] hostium aviditas, omissa caede praedam sectantium[42] ;
20 enisaeque legiones vesperascente die in aperta et solida[11]. neque
is miseriarum finis. struendum vallum, petendus agger, amissa
magna ex parte per quae[11] egeritur humus aut exciditur
caespes ; non[48] tentoria manipulis, non[48] fomenta sauciis ; in-
fectos[9] caeno aut cruore cibos dividentes[25] funestas[13] tenebras et
25 tot hominum milibus unum iam reliquum diem lamentabantur[29].

TACITUS, *Ann.* I. 65.

3. Liberas aedes[7] conjurati (et omnes forte militabant)
imminentes viae augustae, qua descendere ad forum rex solebat[36],
sumpserunt. Ibi quum instructi armatique ceteri transitum
expectantes starent[25], uni ex eis (Dinomeni fuit nomen), quia
5 custos corporis erat, partes datae sunt, ut, quum appropin-
quaret[30] ianuae rex, per causam aliquam in angustiis sustineret
ab tergo agmen. Ita, ut convenerat, factum est. Tanquam[11]
laxaret elatum pedem ab stricto nodo, moratus turbam Dino-
menes tantum intervalli fecit, ut, quum in praetereuntem sine
10 armatis regem impetus fieret[25], confoderetur[30] aliquot prius
vulneribus, quam succurri posset. Fuga satellitum, ut ia-
centem videre regem, facta est ; interfectores pars in forum
ad multitudinem laetam libertate[11], pars Syracusas pergunt
ad praeoccupanda Andranodori regiorumque aliorum consilia.
15 Ceterum praevenerat non fama solum qua[9] nihil in talibus
rebus est celerius[24], sed nuntius etiam ex[15] regiis servis.
Itaque Andranodorus et Insulam et arcem et alia[11], quae
poterat quaeque opportuna erant, praesidiis firmarat. Hexapylo
Theodotus ac Sosis post solis occasum iam obscura luce invecti,
20 quum cruentam regiam vestem atque insigne capitis ostenta-
rent[25], travecti[25] per Tycham[9] simul ad libertatem, simul ad
arma vocantes[25], in Achradinam convenire jubent. Multitudo
pars procurrit in vias, pars in vestibulis stat, pars ex tectis
fenestrisque prospectant et, quid rei sit, rogitant. Omnia[11]
25 luminibus collucent strepituque vario complentur. In Insula
inter cetera Andranodorus praesidiis firmarat horrea publica,
Locus saxo quadrato saeptus atque arcis in modum emunitus
capitur[41] ab iuventute[11] quae praesidio eius loci attributa erat ;
mittuntque nuntios in Achradinam, horrea frumentumque in
30 senatus potestate esse. LIVY, XXIV. 7, 21.

retainers round him, cheered[9] on his countrymen by voice and [15]
example. He and his men aimed their weapons particularly
at the horses of the Roman cavalry[10]. The wounded animals[10],
slipping about in the mire and their own blood, threw[9] their
riders, and plunged among the ranks of the legions, disordering[25] all round[5] them[4]. [20]

The bulk of the Roman army fought[29] steadily and stub-
bornly, frequently repelling[25] the masses of the assailants, but
gradually losing the compactness[13] of their array. At last, in
a series[11] of desperate attacks the column was pierced[9] through
and through, two of the eagles captured[9], and the Roman host, [25]
which on the yester morning[52] had marched forth in such[35]
pride[12] and might, now broken up into confused fragments[12],
either fell fighting beneath the overpowering[18] numbers[13] of the
enemy, or perished in the swamps and woods in unavailing
efforts[12] at flight. CREASY. [30]

(3.) INSURRECTION AT SYRACUSE. An empty house in
this street had[7] been occupied by the conspirators: when[9] the
king came opposite to it, one of their number[11], who was one
of the king's guards, and close to his person[14], stopped just
behind him, as if something had caught his foot; and whilst [5]
he seemed trying to get free, he checked the advance[13] of the
following multitude, and left[26] the king to go on a few steps
unattended. At that moment the conspirators rushed out of
the house[9] and murdered him. So sudden was[9] the act[11], that
his guards could not save him: seeing[25] him dead, they were [10]
seized with a panic and dispersed. The murderers hastened,
some into the market-place of Leontini, to raise the cry[12] of
liberty there, and others to Syracuse, to anticipate the king's
friends, and secure the city for themselves and the Romans.
Their tidings however had flown[45] before them; and Andrano- [15]
dorus, the king's uncle, had already secured the island[13] of
Ortygia, in which was the citadel. The assassins[10] arrived[9] just
at nightfall[13], displaying[25] the bloody robe of Hieronymus, and
the diadem which they had torn from his head, and calling[4]
the people to rise in the name of liberty. This call[10] was [20]
obeyed: all the city, except the island, was presently in their
power; and in the island itself a strong building[6], which was[29]
used as a great corn magazine for the supply[11] of the whole
city, was no sooner[34] seized by those whom Andranodorus had
sent to occupy it, than they offered to deliver it up to the [25]
opposite party. ARNOLD.

4. ARMINIUS. Flumen Visurgis Romanos Cheruscosque interfluebat[29]. eius in ripa cum ceteris primoribus Arminius adstitit, quaesito[9]que an Caesar venisset, postquam adesse responsum est[9], ut liceret[12] cum fratre conloqui oravit. erat[10] is[16] in exercitu cognomento Flavus[9], insignis fide et amisso[13] per vulnus oculo paucis ante annis duce Tiberio. tum permissu * * progressusque salutatur ab Arminio; qui[9] amotis stipatoribus, ut sagittarii nostra pro ripa dispositi abscederent postulat[41], et postquam digressi, unde ea deformitas oris interrogat fratrem. illo locum et proelium referente[9], quodnam praemium recepisset exquirit[6]. Flavus aucta[13] stipendia, torquem et coronam aliaque militaria dona memorat, inridente[42] Arminio vilia servitii pretia. Exim diversi ordiuntur, hic[28] magnitudinem Romanam, opes Caesaris et victis[4] graves poenas, in deditionem venienti paratam clementiam; neque conjugem et filium eius hostiliter haberi[43]; ille fas[11] patriae, libertatem avitam, penetralis Germaniae deos, matrem[13] precum sociam; ne propinquorum et adfinium denique gentis suae desertor et proditor quam imperator esse mallet. paulatim inde ad iurgia prolapsi[9] quo minus pugnam consererent ne flumine quidem interiecto[13] cohibebantur, ni Stertinius adcurrens plenum irae armaque et equum poscentem[9] Flavum adtinuisset. cernebatur contra minitabundus Arminius proeliumque denuntians[25]; nam pleraque Latino sermone interiaciebat, ut qui Romanis in castris ductor popularium meruisset.

TACITUS. *Ann.* II. 9.

5. ARCHIMEDES. Achradinae murum, qui, ut ante dictum est, mari alluitur[5], sexaginta quinqueremibus Marcellus oppugnabat. Ex ceteris navibus sagittarii funditoresque, vix quemquam sine vulnere consistere in muro patiebantur; hi, quia spatio missilibus opus est, procul muro tenebant naves; iunctae[9] aliae binae quinqueremes, demptis interioribus remis, ut latus lateri applicaretur, quum exteriore ordine remorum velut una navis agerentur[25], turres contabulatas machinamentaque alia quatiendis muris portabant. Adversus hunc navalem apparatum Archimedes variae magnitudinis tormenta in muris disposuit. In eas, quae[5] procul erant, naves saxa ingenti pondere emittebat[29]; propiores levioribus eoque magis crebris petebat telis;

(4.) MEETING OF ARMINIUS AND HIS BROTHER. The brother
of Arminius had assumed[28] the Roman name of Flavius, and had
gained considerable distinction[12] in the Roman service[11], in which
he had lost an eye from a wound in battle[9]. When the Roman
outposts approached the river Weser, Arminius called[9] out to 5
them from the opposite bank, and[9] expressed[28] a wish to see
his brother. Flavius stepped forward, and[9] Arminius ordered
his own followers to retire, and[9] requested that the archers
should be removed from the Roman bank of the river. This
was done[9]: and the brothers began[4] a conversation from the 10
opposite sides of the stream, in which[5] Arminius questioned
his brother respecting the loss[13] of his eye, and what battle
it had been lost in, and what reward he had received for his
wound[10]. Flavius[6] told[41] him how the eye was destroyed, and
mentioned[28] the increased pay that he had on account of its 15
loss[11], and showed the collar and other military decorations
that had been given him. Arminius mocked at these as
badges[45] of slavery; and then each began[41] to try to win the
other over: Flavius boasting[28] the power of Rome, and her
generosity to the submissive; Arminius appealing to him in 20
the name of their country's gods, of the mother that had borne
them, and by the holy names[11] of fatherland and freedom, not
to prefer being the betrayer to being the champion of his
country. They soon proceeded to mutual[21] taunts and menaces,
and[9] Flavius called aloud for his horse and his arms, that he 25
might dash across the river and attack his brother; nor would
he have been checked from doing so, had not the Roman
general[2], Stertinius, run up to him, and forcibly detained him.
Arminius stood[29] on the other bank, threatening the rene-
gade[10], and defying him to battle. CREASY. 30

(5.) SIEGE OF SYRACUSE. Marcellus brought up his ships
against the sea[5]-wall of Achradina, and endeavoured by a constant discharge[13] of stones and arrows to clear the walls of their
defenders, so that his men might apply their ladders, and mount
to the assault[12]. These ladders rested on two ships, lashed 5
together broadside to broadside, and worked as one by their
outside oars. But Archimedes had supplied the ramparts with
an artillery so powerful, that it overwhelmed the Romans before
they could get[30] within the range[11] which their missiles could
reach[20]: and when they came closer, they found[28] that all the 10
lower part of the wall was loopholed; and their men were

postremo, ut sui vulnere intacti tela in hostem ingererent, murum
ab imo ad summum crebris cubitalibus fere cavis aperuit[12], per
15 quae[5] cava pars sagittis, pars scorpionibus modicis ex occulto[36],
petebant hostem.   Quia propius quaedam subibant naves, quo
interiores ictibus[11] tormentorum essent, in eas tollenone super
murum eminente ferrea manus firmae catenae illigata quum
iniecta prorae esset[9] gravique libramento plumbi recelleret ad
20 solum, suspensa prora navem in puppim statuebat; dein re-
missa.[9] subito velut ex muro cadentem navem cum[50] ingenti
trepidatione nautarum ita undae affligebat, ut, etiamsi recta
reciderat, aliquantum aquae acciperet.   Ita maritima oppugnatio
est elusa, omnisque spes eo versa, ut totis viribus terra aggrede-
25 rentur[33].   Sed ea quoque pars eodem omni apparatu tormentorum instructa erat.   Ita consilio habito[9], quoniam omnis conatus
ludibrio esset, absistere oppugnatione atque obsidendo[12] tantum
arcere terra marique commeatibus hostem placuit.

LIVY, XXIV. 34.

6.   Romae haud minus terroris ac tumultus erat[28], quam
fuerat triennio ante, quum castra Punica obiecta Romanis[12]
moenibus portisque fuerant.   Neque satis constabat animis, tam
audax[13] iter consulis laudarent vituperarentne.   Apparebat[28]
5 (quo[5] nihil iniquius[24] est) ex eventu famam habiturum. "Castra
prope Hannibalem hostem[18] relicta sine duce cum exercitu, cui
detractum[7] foret omne, quod roboris, quod floris fuerit; et
consulem in Lucanos ostendisse iter, quum Picenum et Galliam
peteret, castra relinquentem[25] nulla alia re tutiora, quam errore
10 hostis, qui ducem inde atque exercitus partem abesse ignoraret[30].
Quid futurum, si id palam fiat?" Veteres eius belli clades, duo
consules proximo anno interfecti[13] terrebant[7].   Et[43] ea omnia ac-
cidisse, quum unus imperator, unus exercitus hostium in Italia
esset: nunc duo bella Punica facta, duos ingentes exercitus,
15 duos prope Hannibales in Italia esse.   Quippe et Hasdru-
balem, patre eodem[2] Hamilcare genitum, aeque impigrum ducem,
per tot in Hispania annos Romano exercitatum bello, gemina
victoria insignem, duobus exercitibus cum clarissimis ducibus
deletis[13].   Nam itineris quidem celeritate ex Hispania et con-
20 citatis[33] ad arma Gallicis gentibus multo magis, quam Hannibalem ipsum, gloriari posse.   Omnia maiora etiam vero praesidia hostium, minora sua, metu interprete, semper in deteriora[11]
inclinato, ducebant[-9].

LIVY, XXVII. 44.

struck down[7] with fatal aim by an enemy whom they could not see, and who shot his arrows in perfect security[36]. If they still persevered[9], and attempted to fix their ladders, on a sudden enormous stones or huge masses of lead were dropped upon them, by which their ladders were crushed to pieces, and their ships were almost sunk. At other times machines like cranes were thrust out over the wall; and the end of the lever, with an iron grapple affixed to it, was[29] lowered upon the ships. As soon as the grapple had taken hold, the other end of the lever was lowered[9] by heavy weights, and the ship raised out of the water, till it was made[28] almost to stand upon its stern; then the grapple was suddenly let go[9], and the ship dropped into the sea with a violence which either upset it, or filled it with water. With equal power was the assault on the land side repelled, till Marcellus in despair[12] put a stop to his attacks; and it was resolved merely to blockade the town, and to wait for the effect of famine upon the crowded population[11] within.

ARNOLD.

(6.) BEFORE THE BATTLE OF METAURUS. Meanwhile, at Rome, the news[12] of Nero's expedition[13] had caused the greatest excitement and alarm. All men felt[29] the full audacity[13] of the enterprise[11], but hesitated[29] what epithet[11] to apply[28] to it. It was evident that Nero's conduct[13] would be judged of by the event, that[5] most[24] unfair criterion[11], as the Roman historian truly terms[28] it. People reasoned[28] on the perilous state in which Nero had left the rest[13] of his army, without a general, and deprived of the core[45] of its strength, in the vicinity[12] of the terrible[18] Hannibal. They talked[29] over the former disasters of the war, and the fall[13] of both the consuls of the last year. All these calamities[43] had come on them while they had only one Carthaginian general and army to deal[28] with in Italy. Now they had two Punic wars at a time. They had two Carthaginian armies; they had almost two Hannibals in Italy. Hasdrubal was sprung from the same father; trained up in the same hostility to Rome; equally practised in battle against their legions; and, if the comparative speed and success with which he had crossed the Alps was a fair test[12], he was even a better general than his brother. With fear for their interpreter of every rumour, they exaggerated the strength of their enemy's forces[4] in every quarter, and criticised and distrusted their own. CREASY.

7. BATTLE OF METAURUS. *a.* Romae neuter animi habitus
satis dici enarrarique potest, nec quo incerta exspectatione
eventus civitas fuerat, nec quo victoriae famam accepit. Nun-
quam per omnes dies, ex quo[11] Claudium consulem profectum[12]
5 fama attulit, ab orto[13] sole ad occidentem, aut senator quisquam
a curia atque ab magistratibus[11] abscessit, aut populus e foro.
Matronae, quia[25] nihil in ipsis opis erat, in preces obtestatio-
nesque versae[9], per omnia delubra vagae suppliciis votisque fati-
gare deos. Tam sollicitae[12] ac suspensae[12] civitati fama incerta
10 primo accidit, duos Narnienses equites in castra, quae in fau-
cibus Umbriae opposita[12] erant, venisse ex proelio, nuntiantes[25]
caesos[13] hostes. Et primo magis auribus, quam animis, id ac-
ceptum erat, ut[11] maius laetiusque[24], quam quod mente capere,
aut satis credere possent : et ipsa celeritas fidem impediebat,
15 quod biduo ante pugnatum dicebatur[29]. Literae deinde ab L.
Manlio Accidino missae ex castris afferuntur de Narniensium
equitum adventu. Eae litterae per forum ad tribunal praetoris
latae senatum curia exciverunt[29]; tantoque certamine ac tumultu populi ad fores curiae concursum[12] est, ut adire nuntius
20 non posset, *sed* traheretur a percontantibus[25] vociferantibusque,
ut in rostris prius quam in senatu litterae recitarentur. Tandem
summoti et coerciti a magistratibus, dispensarique laetitia inter
potentes eius animos potuit[28]. In senatu primum, deinde in
contione litterae recitatae sunt; et pro cuiusque ingenio aliis
25 iam certum gaudium, aliis nulla ante futura[28] fides erat, quam
legatos consulumve[50] litteras audissent.

b. Ipsos deinde appropinquare[12] legatos allatum[12] est.
Tum enimvero omnis aetas currere[41] obvii, primus[8] quisque
oculis auribusque haurire tantum gaudium cupientes. Ad
30 Mulvium usque pontem continens[11] agmen pervenit. Legati
(erant L. Veturius Philo, P. Licinius Varus, Q. *Caecilius*
Metellus) circumfusi omnis generis hominum frequentia in
forum pervenerunt, quum[25] alii ipsos, alii comites eorum, quae
acta essent, percontarentur; et ut quisque audierat[29], exer-
35 citum hostium imperatoremque occisum, legiones Romanas
incolumes, salvos consules esse, extemplo aliis porro[28] im-
pertiebant gaudium suum. Quum aegre in curiam perven-
tum esset, multo aegrius summota turba, ne patribus misceretur,
litterae in senatu recitatae sunt. Inde traducti in contionem
40 legati. L. Veturius, litteris recitatis[9], ipse planius omnia, quae
acta erant, exposuit cum[50] ingenti assensu, postremo etiam
clamore universae contionis, quum[25] vix gaudium animis cape-

(7.)   *a.* AFTER THE BATTLE. From the moment[11] that Nero's march[13] from the south had been heard of at Rome, intense anxiety possessed[20] the whole city. Every day the senate sat[29] from sunrise[13] to sunset; and not a senator was absent: every day the forum was crowded from morn- [5] ing till evening, as each hour might[49] bring some great tidings[12]; and every man wished to be[8] among the first to hear them[9]. A doubtful rumour arose, that a great battle[12] had been fought, and a great victory won only two days before: two horsemen of Narnia had[43] ridden off from the [10] field to carry the news[12] to their home; it had[43] been heard and published in the camp of the reserve[18] army, which was lying[88] at Narnia to cover the approach[13] to Rome. But men dared[29] not lightly believe what they so much wished to be true: and how, they said[43], could a battle fought in the ex- [15] tremity[13] of Umbria be heard of only two days after at Rome? Soon however it was known that a letter had arrived from L. Manlius Acidinus himself, who commanded the army at Narnia: the horsemen had[43] certainly arrived there from the field of battle, and brought tidings[12] of a glorious victory[11]. The [20] letter was read first in the senate, and then in the forum from the rostra; but some still refused to believe: fugitives[43] from a battle-field might[49] carry idle tales of victory to hide their own shame; till the account came directly from the consuls, it was rash to credit it[6]. [25]

     b. At last, word[11] was brought that officers of high rank[11] in the consul's army were on their way[12] to Rome ; that[9] they bore a despatch from Livius and Nero. Then the whole city poured out of the walls to meet them, eager[25] to anticipate the moment[11] which was to confirm all their hopes. For two miles, as far [30] as the Milvian bridge over the Tiber, the crowd formed[28] an uninterrupted mass; and when the officers appeared, they could scarcely make their way to the city, the multitude thronging[25] around them, and overwhelming them and their attendants with eager questions. As each man learnt[27] the [35] joyful answers[11], he made haste to tell them to others: "the enemy's army is destroyed[44]; the general slain; our own legions and both the consuls are safe." So the crowd re-entered the city; and the three officers, all men of noble names, L. Vetu- rius Philo, P. Licinius Varus, and Q. Metellus, still followed[7] [40] by the thronging[18] multitude, at last reached the senate-house.

rent. Discursum inde ab aliis circa templa deum, ut grates
agerent, ab aliis domos, ut coniugibus liberisque tam[35] laetum
45 nuntium impertirent. Senatus, quod M. Livius et C. Claudius
consules incolumi exercitu ducem hostium legionesque occidis-
sent[30], supplicationem in triduum decrevit. Eam supplicationem[7] C. Hostilius praetor edixit; celebrata a viris femi-
nisque est. Omnia templa per totum triduum aequalem turbam
50 habuere, quum[25] matronae amplissima veste cum liberis, perinde
ac si debellatum[12] foret, omni solutae metu deis immortalibus
grates agerent. Statum[7] quoque civitatis ea victoria *firmavit,*
ut iam inde haud secus quam in pace res inter se contrahere[28]
vendendo, argentum creditum solvendo, auderent.

LIVY, XXVII. 50, 51.

8.   Posito ubique bello magna pars senatus extremum dis-
crimen adiit[28], profecta[9] cum Othone ab urbe, dein Mutinae
relicta. illuc adverso de proelio adlatum[12]: sed milites ut
falsum rumorem aspernantes, quod infensum Othoni senatum
5 arbitrabantur[25], custodire[41] sermones, voltum habitumque tra-
here in deterius: conviciis postremo ac probris causam et initium caedis quaerebant, cum alius insuper metus senatoribus
instaret, ne praevalidis[20] iam Vitellii partibus cunctanter[36]
excepisse victoriam crederentur. ita trepidi[12] et utrimque anxii
10 coeunt, nemo privatim expedito consilio, inter multos[11] societate
culpae tutior[28]. rediere omnes Bononiam, rursus consiliaturi;
simul medio temporis plures nuntii sperabantur. Bononiae,
divisis[9] per itinera qui recentissimum[11] quemque percontarentur, interrogatus Othonis libertus causam digressus habere se
15 suprema eius mandata respondit; ipsum viventem quidem relictum, sed sola posteritatis cura et abruptis vitae blandimentis.
hinc admiratio et plura interrogandi pudor, atque omnium
animi in Vitellium inclinavere. intererat consiliis frater eius
L. Vitellius seque iam adulantibus[13] offerebat, cum repente
20 Coenus libertus Neronis atroci mendacio universos perculit[12],
adfirmans[25] superventu quartae decumae legionis, iunctis a Brix-
ello viribus, caesos victores, versam partium fortunam. causa
fingendi fuit, ut diplomata Othonis, quae neglegebantur, laetiore
nuntio revalescerent. et Coenus quidem rapide in urbem vectus
25 paucos post dies iussu Vitellii poenas luit: senatorum peri-
culum auctum credentibus[12] Othonianis militibus vera esse
quae[11] adferebantur[29]. nec ultra in commune congressi sibi[11]
quisque consuluere, donec missae a Fabio Valente epistulae
demerent[42] metum[30]. et mors Othonis quo laudabilior[5], eo velo-
30 cius audita.

TAC. *Hist.* II. 52.

The people pressed after them into the senate-house itself: but even at such a moment the senate forgot not its accustomed order[5]; the crowd was forced back; and the consul's despatch was first read to the senators alone. Immediately afterwards [45] the officers came out into the forum: there L. Veturius again read the despatch; and[9] as its contents[11] were short, he himself related the particulars[11] of what he had seen and done. The interest[18] of his hearers grew more intense with every word; till at last the whole multitude broke out into a universal[21] cheer, and [50] then rushed from the forum in all directions to carry the news to their wives and children at home, or ran to the temples to pour out their gratitude[13] to the gods. The senate ordered a thanksgiving of three days; the praetor announced it in the forum; and for three days every temple was crowded; and [55] the Roman wives and mothers, in their gayest dresses, took their children with them[9], and poured forth their thanks to all the gods for this great deliverance[12]. ARNOLD.

(8.) NEWS OF THE BATTLE OF THE BOYNE. Meanwhile Dublin[13] had been in violent commotion. On[9] the thirtieth of June[53] it was known that the armies were face to face[14] with the Boyne between them, and that a battle was almost inevitable[22]. The news[12] that William had been wounded [5] came that evening. The first report was[8] that the wound was mortal[9]. It was believed[9], and confidently repeated, that the usurper was no more[45]; and, before the truth was known, couriers started bearing the glad tidings of his death to the French ships which lay[29] in the ports of Munster. From day- [10] break[52] on the first of July[53] the streets of Dublin were filled with persons[11] eagerly asking[25] and telling news[42]. A thousand wild rumours wandered[28] to and fro among the crowd. A fleet of men of war under[50] the white flag had been seen from the hill of Howth[43]. An army commanded by a Marshal of France [15] had landed in Kent. There had been hard fighting[12] at the Boyne: but the Irish had won the day[45]: the English right wing had been routed[9]: the Prince of Orange was a prisoner[9]. While the Roman Catholics heard[41] and repeated these stories[11] in all the places of public resort, the few Protestants who[5] were [20] still out of prison, afraid of being[33] torn to pieces, shut themselves up in their inner chambers. But, towards five in the afternoon[52], a few runaways came straggling in with[5] evil tidings[12]. By six it was known that all was lost[45]. MACAULAY.

9. (*a*) JERUSALEM. Urbem[7] arduam situ opera molesque
firmaverant, quis vel plana[11] satis munirentur[12]. nam duos colles
in immensum[11] editos claudebant[29] muri per artem obliqui[12]
aut introrsus sinuati, ut latera obpugnantium ad ictus patesce-
5 rent. extrema[12] rupis abrupta ; et turres, ubi mons iuvisset[30],
in sexagenos pedes, inter devexa[11] in centenos vicenos[que] attol-
lebantur, mira specie ac procul intuentibus[13] pares. alia intus
moenia, regiae circumiecta[25], conspicuoque fastigio turris Antonia, in honorem M. Antonii ab Herode appellata. Templum
10 in modum arcis propriique muri, labore et opere ante alios ;
ipsae porticus, quis templum ambibatur[29], egregium propug-
naculum[41]. fons perennis aquae, cavati sub terra montes[13] et
piscinae cisternaeque servandis imbribus. TAC. *Hist.* v. 11.

(*b*) MARCELLUS AT SYRACUSE. Marcellus ut moenia in-
15 gressus[9] ex superioribus locis[11] urbem omnium ferme illa tem-
pestate pulcherrimam subiectam oculis[45] vidit, illacrimasse dicitur partim gaudio tantae perpetratae rei[11] partim vetusta gloria
urbis. Atheniensium classes demersae[13] et duo ingentes exercitus cum duobus clarissimis ducibus deleti[13] occurrebant[11] et tot
20 bella cum Carthaginiensibus tanto cum discrimine gesta, tot
tam opulenti tyranni regesque. Ea quum universa occurrerent
animo, subiretque cogitatio, iam illa momento horae arsura[12]
omnia et ad cineres reditura, priusquam signa Achradinam ad-
moveret[30], praemittit Syracusanos[15], qui intra praesidia Romana,
25 ut ante dictum est, fuerant, ut alloquio leni impellerent hostes
ad dedendam urbem. LIVY, xxv. 24.

10. Postremo promptis[20] iam et aliis seditionis ministris
velut contionabundus interrogabat[29], cur paucis centurionibus,
paucioribus tribunis in modum servorum oboedirent. quando
ausuros[43] exposcere remedia, nisi novum et nutantem adhuc
5 principem precibus vel armis adirent? satis per tot annos ig-
navia peccatum[12], quod tricena aut quadragena stipendia senes
et plerique truncato ex vulneribus corpore tolerent[33]. ne dimissis quidem finem esse militiae, sed apud vexillum ten-
dentes[42] alio vocabulo eosdem labores perferre[23]. ac si quis tot
10 casus vita superaverit[29], trahi adhuc diversas in terras, ubi per
nomen agrorum uligines paludum vel inculta montium acci-
piant. enimvero militiam ipsam gravem, infructuosam[12]; denis
in diem[3] assibus[8] animam et corpus aestimari: hinc vestem arma
tentoria, hinc saevitiam centurionum et vacationes munerum
15 redimi[28]. TAC. *Ann.* I. 17.

✓ (9.) Titus at Jerusalem. Jerusalem at this period[11] was[7] fortified[29] by three walls, in all those parts where it was not[7] surrounded by abrupt[19] and impassable ravines; there it had but one. The whole circuit of these walls was[7] guarded[29] with towers, built of the same solid masonry with the rest[13] of the walls. These were thirty-five feet broad, and thirty-five high; but above this height[19], were lofty chambers, and above those again upper rooms, and large tanks to receive the rain-water. The fortress Antonia stood[29] alone, on a precipitous rock near ninety feet high, at the north-west corner of the Temple. It was likewise a work of Herod. High above the whole city rose[28] the Temple, uniting[25] the commanding[11] strength of a citadel with the splendour of a sacred[19] edifice. Looking down[25] upon its marble courts, and on the Temple itself, it was impossible, even for a Roman, not to be struck[29] with wonder, or even for a Stoic, like Titus, not to betray[28] his emotion. Yet this was the city[8], which in a few months was to lie a heap of undistinguished ruins[12]; and the solid Temple itself, which seemed built for eternity[11], not "to have one stone left upon another." Surveying[25] all this, Titus, escorted[28] by a strong guard[11] of horse, rode slowly round the city; but if thoughts[11] of mercy occasionally entered into a heart, the natural humanity of which[5] seems to have been steeled[45] during the whole course[11] of the siege, the Jews were sure[28] to expel them again[6], by some new indication[12] of their obstinate ferocity.

MILMAN.

(10.) But no sooner[34] was the resolution[12] of the two captains made known, than a feeling[11] of discontent broke forth among their followers, especially those who were to remain with Pizarro on the island. "What![43]" they exclaimed[43], "were they to be dragged to that obscure[18] spot[11] to die[31] by hunger? The whole expedition had been a cheat[19] and a failure, from beginning to end. The golden countries, so much[35] vaunted, had seemed to fly before them as they advanced[25]; and the little gold[5] they had been fortunate enough to glean[33] had all been sent back to Panama to entice other fools to follow their example. What had they got in return for all their sufferings[12]? The only treasures they could boast[8] were their bows and arrows, and they were now to be left to die on this[35] dreary island, without[50] so much as a rood of consecrated ground[5] to lay their bones[45] in[50]!"

PRESCOTT.

11. Tunc contractos[9] in principia iussosque[25] dicta cum silentio accipere temporis ac necessitatis monet[41]. unam in armis salutem[43], sed ea consilio temperanda manendumque intra vallum, donec expugnandi hostes spe propius succederent ; mox 5 undique erumpendum[12]: illa eruptione ad Rhenum perveniri. quod si fugerent, pluris silvas[8], profundas magis paludes, saevitiam hostium superesse ; at victoribus[42] decus gloriam. quae domi cara[11], quae in castris honesta, memorat ; reticuit de adversis. equos dehinc, orsus a suis, legatorum tribunorumque 10 nulla[48] ambitione fortissimo cuique bellatori tradit, ut hi, mox pedes in hostem invaderent. Haud minus inquies[9] Germanus spe cupidine et diversis ducum sententiis agebat[29], Arminio[42] sinerent[43] egredi egressos[46]que rursum per umida et impedita circumvenirent suadente, atrociora[11] Inguiomero et laeta barbaris, 15 ut vallum armis ambirent : promptam expugnationem, plures captivos, incorruptam praedam fore[43]. igitur orta die proruunt fossas, iniciunt crates, summa valli prensant, raro[20] super milite et quasi ob metum defixo.

TAC. *Ann.* I. 67.

12. At imperitae multitudini[7] nunc indignatio[11], nunc pudor pectora versare[41] et ab intestinis avertere[11] malis : nolle[41] inultos hostes, nolle successum non patribus, non consulibus ; externa et domestica odia certare[11] in animis. Tandem superant ex- 5 terna ; adeo superbe[12] insolenterque hostis eludebat[20]. Frequentes in praetorium conveniunt[41] ; poscunt pugnam, postulant, ut signum[11] detur. Consules velut deliberabundi capita conferunt, diu colloquuntur. Pugnare cupiebant, sed retro revocanda et abdenda cupiditas erat, ut adversando remorandoque 10 incitato semel militi adderent impetum. Redditur responsum, immaturam rem[11] agi ; nondum tempus[11] pugnae esse ; castris se tenerent[43]. Ita dimissis, quo[5] minus consules velle[28] credunt, crescit ardor pugnandi. Accendunt[7] insuper hostes ferocius multo, ut statuisse non pugnare consules cognitum est : quippe 15 impune se insultaturos[43] ; non credi militi arma ; rem[11] ad ultimum seditionis errupturam, finemque venisse Romano imperio. His freti occursant portis, ingerunt probra ; aegre abstinent, quin castra oppugnent. Enimvero non ultra contumeliam pati Romanus posse[41] ; totis castris undique ad consules curritur ; 20 non iam sensim, ut ante, per centurionum principes postulant[12], sed passim omnes clamoribus agunt[28].

LIVY, II. 45.

(11.) He then summoned[41] a council of his officers to consider the plan of operations[11], or rather to propose to them the extraordinary[18] plan on which he had himself decided. This[8] was[9] to lay an ambuscade for the Inca, and[9] take him prisoner in the face[14] of his whole army! It was[43] a project[11] full of peril[4], bordering[25], as it might well seem, on desperation. But the circumstances[11] of the Spaniards were desperate[4]. Whichever way they turned, they were menaced[7] by the most appalling dangers; and[9] better was it bravely to confront the danger, than weakly to shrink from it, when there was no avenue[11] for escape.

To fly was now too late. Whither could they fly? At the first signal of retreat, the whole army of the Inca would be upon them. Their movements would be[7] anticipated by a foe far better acquainted with the intricacies of the sierra than themselves; the passes would be occupied, and[9] they would be hemmed in on all sides; while the mere fact of this retrograde movement[12] would diminish the confidence, and with it the effective[11] strength of his own men, while it doubled that[16] of his enemy. PRESCOTT'S *Peru.*

(12.) As soon[31] as this was known, the disappointed[18] adventurers[18] exclaimed[41] and threatened; the emissaries[12] of Cortes, mingling with them, inflamed their rage; the ferment[12] became general; the whole camp was almost in open mutiny; all demanding[25] with eagerness[36] to see their commander. Cortes[9] was not slow in appearing; when[9], with one voice, officers and soldiers expressed their astonishment and disappointment at the orders[12] which they had received. It was unworthy, they cried[43], of the Castilian courage[18] to be daunted at the first aspect[12] of danger, and infamous to fly before any enemy appeared[4]. For their parts[17], they were determined not to relinquish an enterprise[11], that had hitherto been successful, and which tended so visibly to advance[28] the glory and interest of their country. Happy[20] under his command[13], they would follow him with alacrity[36] through every danger, in quest[12] of those settlements and treasures which he had so long held out to their view[12]; but, if he chose rather to return to Cuba, and tamely give up all his hopes of distinction and opulence to an envious rival[18], they would instantly choose another general to conduct them in that path of glory, which he had not spirit to enter[43].

ROBERTSON.

13. (*a*) Tyre. Urbem a continenti quattuor stadiorum fretum dividit[7]: Africo[34] maxime obiectum crebros ex alto fluctus in litus evolvit. Nec accipiendo operi, quo Macedones continenti insulam iungere parabant, quicquam magis quam ille
5 ventus obstabat[12]. Quippe vix leni et tranquillo mari moles agi[28] possunt: Africus vero prima quaeque[17] congesta, pulsu illiso mari, subruit, nec ulla tam firma moles est, quam non exedant undae, et[34] per nexus operum manantes et, ubi acrior flatus extitit, summi operis fastigio superfusae[25]. Praeter hanc diffi-
10 cultatem haud minor alia erat: muros turresque urbis praealtum mare ambiebat[7]: non[46] tormenta nisi e navibus procul excussa mitti, non scalae moenibus applicari poterant: praeceps in salum murus[9] pedestre interceperat[7] iter; naves nec habebat[29] rex et, si admovisset[16], pendentes et instabiles missilibus arceri
15 poterant. urbem tamen obsidere statuit; sed ante iacienda moles erat quae continenti urbem committeret.

(*b*) Iamque[34] paulum moles aqua eminebat, et simul aggeris latitudo crescebat, urbique admovebatur: quum[34] Tyrii, magnitudine molis, cuius incrementum eos antea fefellerat,
20 conspecta[33], levibus navigiis nondum commissum opus circumire coeperunt, missilibus quoque eos[10], qui pro opere stabant incessere.

Inter haec Tyrii navem magnitudine eximia, saxis arenaque a puppi oneratam[9], ita ut multum prora emineret, bitumine ac
25 sulphure illitam[9] remis concitaverunt, et quum magnum vim venti vela quoque concepissent, celeriter ad molem successit: tum prora eius accensa, remiges desiluere in scaphas, quae ad hoc ipsum[11] praeparatae sequebantur[29]. Navis autem, igne concepto, latius fundere incendium coepit, quod, priusquam posset[30]
30 occurri, turres et cetera opera in capite molis posita[3] comprehendit. At qui[10] desiluerant in parva navigia, faces et quicquid alendo igni aptum erat in eadem opera ingerunt. Iamque[34] non modo Macedonum turres, sed etiam summa tabulata conceperant ignem: quum hi, qui in turribus erant, partim haurirentur
35 incendio, partim, armis omissis[25], in mare semet ipsi immitterent. Nec incendio[6] solum opera consumpta, sed forte eodem die vehementior ventus totum ex profundo mare illisit in molem, crebrisque fluctibus compages operis verberatae se laxavere, saxaque interfluens unda medium opus rupit. Prorutis igitur
40 lapidum cumulis, quibus iniecta[9] terra sustinebatur[29], praeceps in profundum ruit, tantae[3] que molis vix ulla vestigia invenit Arabia rediens[25] Alexander.   Curtius, iv. 3.

(13.) *a.* Tyre was situated on an islet nearly half a mile from the mainland; the channel between[3] the two being shallow towards the land, but reaching a depth[12] of eighteen feet in the part adjoining[5] the city[9]. The islet was[7] completely surrounded by prodigious walls, the loftiest portion[13] of which, 5 on the side fronting[5] the mainland, reached a height not less than 150 feet, with corresponding solidity[11] and base. Besides these external fortifications, there was a brave[18] and numerous population[11] within, aided[26] by a good stock of arms, machines, ships, provisions, and other things essential to defence. 10

It was not[8] without reason, therefore, that the Tyrians, when driven to their last resource, entertained[28] hopes of holding out even against the formidable arm[11] of Alexander; and against Alexander as he then stood, they might[49] have held out successfully; for he had as yet no fleet, and they could 15 defy[28] any attack made simply from land.

b. Alexander began the siege of Tyre without[43] any fleet; the Sidonian and Aradian ships not having yet come[4]. It was[8] his first task[11] to construct a solid mole two hundred feet broad, reaching[25] across the half mile[18] of channel between[3] the main- 20 land and the islet. But the work, though prosecuted with ardour and perseverance[36], was tedious and toilsome, even near the mainland, where the Tyrians could do little to impede it[16]; and[9] became far more tedious as it advanced into the sea, so as to be exposed to their obstruction[13], as well as to[34] damage from 25 winds and waves. The Tyrian triremes and small boats perpetually annoyed[29] the workmen, and destroyed parts of the work, in spite[14] of all the protection devised[7] by the Macedonians, who planted[27] two towers in front[14] of their advancing[25] mole, and discharged projectiles from engines provided for the 30 purpose[11]. At length, by unremitting[12] efforts the mole was pushed forward[58] until it came nearly across the channel to the city-wall; when suddenly, on a day[5] of strong wind, the Tyrians sent forth a fireship loaded with combustibles, which[5] they drove against the front of the mole[9] and set fire to the two 35 towers. At the same time, the full naval force[11] of the city, ships and little boats, was sent forth to land men at once on all parts of the mole. So successful[9] was this attack[11], that all the Macedonian engines were burnt, the outer wood-work which kept[29] the mole together was torn up in many places, and a 40 large part of the structure[11] came to pieces.   GROTE.

14. Quod[9] ubi egressus[25] Scipio in tumulum, quem[5] Mercurii vocant, animadvertit[25], multis partibus nudata defensoribus moenia esse, omnes e castris excitos[9] ire[26] ad oppugnandum[12] et ferre scalas iubet[41]. Ipse trium prae se iuvenum validorum
5 scutis oppositis[25] (ingens enim iam vis omnis generis telorum e muris volabat[43]) ad urbem succedit; hortatur, imperat, quae in rem sunt, quod[5]*que* plurimum ad accendendos militum animos intererat, testis spectatorque virtutis atque ignaviae cuiusque adest[28]. Itaque in vulnera[45] ac tela ruunt; neque illos[7] muri
10 neque superstantes armati arcere queunt, quin certatim adscendant. Et ab navibus[11] eodem tempore ea[15], quae mari alluitur, pars urbis oppugnari coepta est. Inter haec repleverat iam Poenus armatis muros, et vis magna ex ingenti copia congesta telorum suppeditabat; sed neque viri nec tela nec quicquam
15 aliud aeque quam moenia ipsa sese defendebant[12]. Rarae[23] enim scalae altitudini aequari poterant, et quo quaeque altiores, eo infirmiores erant. Itaque quum summus quisque evadere non posset[30], subirent tamen alii, onere ipso frangebantur[29]. Quidam, stantibus scalis, quum altitudo caliginem oculis offudisset[26], ad
20 terram delati sunt. Et quum passim homines scalaeque ruerent, et ipso successu audacia atque alacritas hostium cresceret, signum receptui datum est. LIVY, XXVI. 44.

15. BATTLE OF THRASYMENUS.—Consul, perculsis[12] omnibus[48], ipse satis, ut in *re*[11] trepida, impavidus[9] turbatos ordines, vertente se quoque ad dissonos clamores, instruit, ut tempus locusque patitur, et quacunque adire audirique potest, adhortatur ac stare[24]
5 ac pugnare iubet[41]: nec enim[43] inde votis[8] aut imploratione deum, sed vi ac virtute evadendum esse; per medias acies ferro viam fieri, et, quo timoris minus sit, eo minus ferme periculi esse[41]. Ceterum prae[19] strepitu ac tumultu nec consilium nec imperium accipi poterat, tantumque aberat, ut sua signa atque
10 ordines et locum noscerent[33], ut vix ad arma capienda aptandaque pugnae competeret animus. Et erat in tanta caligine maior usus aurium quam oculorum[14]. Ad gemitus vulnerum ictusque corporum aut armorum et mixtos strepentium[25] paventiumque clamores circumferebant ora oculosque. Alii fugi-
15 entes pugnantium[25] globo illati[9] haerebant[29]; alios redeuntes in pugnam avertebat[7] fugientium agmen. Deinde, ubi in omnes partes nequicquam impetus capti, apparuitque, nullam nisi in dextera ferroque salutis spem esse, tum sibi quisque dux adhortatorque factus ad rem[45] gerendam, et nova de integro
20 exorta pugna est. *Ib.* XXII. 5.

(14.) In the midst[14] of these untoward[13] dissensions, Went-worth, with the advice[12] of a council of officers, attempted to storm Fort San Lazaro. Twelve hundred men, headed by General Guise, cheerfully marched to the attack. There was no breach in the wall : the signal for the night attack (for such 5 had been designed) was protracted till nearly broad[45] day ; and the deserters who[5] undertook[27] to act as guides were afterwards found[23], either through ignorance or ill intention, to have led them to the very strongest part of the fortification[11]. Nay more, on reaching[33] the works, it was discovered, that from the 10 neglect of the officers, the scaling-ladders were partly too short, and partly left behind. Yet in spite of all these shameful[18] disadvantages[11], the soldiers fought[29] with stubborn[12] intre-pidity ; whole ranks were mowed[45] down by the enemy's can-non without[32] dispiriting the rest ; and one party had actually[34] 15 attained[34] the summit[11] of a rampart, when their leader, Colonel Grant, received a death-wound, and the men a repulse[12]. Still, however, the survivors remained[29] undaunted under the mur-derous[13] fire[11] of the fort, until half their number had fallen, and[9] until their officers, perceiving[25] valour to be useless[22], and 20 success impossible, suddenly gave the signal to withdraw.

MAHON.

(15.) BATTLE OF NIEUPORT, A.D. 1602. The[13] current[45] of the retreating and pursuing[25] hosts swept[41] by the spot where Maurice[4] sat on horseback, watching[25] and directing the battle. His bravest and best general, the veteran[18] Vere, had fallen[9] ; the whole army, the only army, of the States was 5 defeated, broken, panic-struck ; the Spanish[18] shouts of victory rang on every side. Plainly the day[45] was lost, and with it the republic. In the[24] blackest[18] hour that the Netherland common-wealth had ever known, the fortitude of the stadtholder did not desert him[16]. Immoveable as[3] a rock in the torrent he stemmed[41] 10 the flight[13] of his troops. Three squadrons of reserved[19] cavalry, Balen's own, Vere's own, and Cecil's, were all[8] that was left him, and[9] at the head of these he essayed an advance[12]. He seemed[41] the only man on the field[11] not frightened ; and me-nacing[41], conjuring, persuading the fugitives for the love of 15 fatherland, of himself and his house, of their own honour, not to disgrace themselves, urging that all was not yet lost, and beseeching them rather to die like men on the field[11] than to drown like dogs[45] in the sea, he succeeded[28] in rallying a portion of those nearest him. MOTLEY. 20

16. (*a*) SACK OF CREMONA. Huc inclinavit Antonius cingique vallum corona iussit. primo sagittis saxisque eminus certabant, maiore Flavianorum pernicie[42], in quos tela desuper librabantur; mox vallum portasque legionibus attribuit, ut dis-
5 cretus[12] labor fortes ignavosque distingueret atque ipsa contentione decoris accenderentur. proxima Bedriacensi viae tertiani septimanique sumpsere[7], dexteriora valli octava ac septima Claudiana; tertiadecumanos ad Brixianam portam impetus tulit[7]. paulum inde morae, dum ex proximis agris ligones,
10 dolabras, et alii falces scalasque convectant: tum elatis[25] super capita scutis densa testudine succedunt. Romanae utrimque artes: pondera saxorum Vitelliani provolvunt, disiectam fluitantemque testudinem lanceis contisque scrutantur, donec soluta compage scutorum exsangues aut laceros prosternerent[30]
15 multa cum strage....Acerrimum[4] tertiae septimaeque legionum certamen; et dux Antonius cum delectis auxiliaribus eodem incubuerat. obstinatos inter se cum sustinere Vitelliani nequirent et superiacta tela testudine laberentur, ipsam postremo ballistam in subeuntes propulere, quae ut[34] ad praesens
20 disiecit obruitque quos inciderat[49], ita pinnas ac summa valli ruina sua traxit; simul iuncta turris ictibus saxorum cessit, qua septimani dum nituntur[41] cuneis, tertianus securibus gladiisque portam perfregit. primum[4] inrupisse C. Volusium tertiae legionis militem inter omnes auctores constat. is in vallum
25 egressus[9], deturbatis[25] qui restiterant, conspicuus manu ac voce capta castra conclamavit; ceteri trepidis[42] iam Vitellianis seque e vallo praecipitantibus perrupere.

(*b*) Quadraginta armatorum milia inrupere, calonum lixarumque amplior numerus et in libidinem ac saevitiam cor-
30 ruptior. non dignitas, non aetas protegebat[12], quo minus stupra caedibus, caedes stupris miscerentur[12]. grandaevos senes, exacta aetate feminas, viles ad praedam, in ludibrium trahebant; ubi adulta virgo aut quis forma conspicuus incidisset, ipsos direptores in mutuam perniciem agebat[20]. dum pecuniam vel gravia
35 auro templorum dona sibi quisque trahunt, maiore aliorum vi truncabantur. Quidam obvia aspernati, verberibus tormentisque dominorum abdita scrutari, defossa eruere[41]: faces in manibus[42], quas, ubi praedam egesserant in vacuas domos et inania templa per lasciviam iaculabantur[20]: utque exercitu
40 vario linguis moribus, cui cives socii externi interessent, diversae cupidines et aliud cuique fas[11] nec quicquam inlicitum.

TAC. *Hist.* III.

(16.) *a.* SACK OF ROME, A.D. 1527. Three distinct bodies[11], one of Germans, another of Spaniards, and the last of Italians, the three different[5] nations of whom the army was composed, were appointed to this[4] service[11]; a separate attack[11] was assigned[8] to each; and the whole army advanced to support them as occasion[11] should require[42]. A thick mist concealed their[13] approach[4] until they reached almost the brink of the ditch which surrounded[29] the suburbs; having planted their ladders in a moment[34], each brigade rushed on to the assault with an impetuosity heightened by national emulation[13]. They were received at first with fortitude[13] equal to their own; the Swiss in the pope's guards fought[9] with a courage becoming men to whom the defence of the noblest city in the world was[27] entrusted. Bourbon's[10] troops, notwithstanding[14] all their valour, gained[29] no ground, and even began to give way; when[34] their leader[10], perceiving that on this critical moment the fate[45] of the day depended, leaped[9] from his horse, pressed to the front, snatched[7] a scaling-ladder from a soldier, planted it against the wall, and began to mount it, encouraging[25] his men with his voice and hand to follow him. But at that very instant[34], a musket bullet from the ramparts pierced his groin; and he soon after expired.

b. This fatal[18] event could not be concealed from the army; but instead of being disheartened by their loss, it animated them with new valour; the name of Bourbon resounded along the line, accompanied with the cry of *blood* and *revenge*[13]. The veterans[29] who defended the walls were soon overpowered by numbers; the untrained[18] body[11] of city recruits fled at the sight[13] of danger, and the enemy, with irresistible[22] violence, rushed into the town[11].

It is impossible to describe, or even to imagine the misery[13] and horror of that scene[11] which followed[4]. Whatever a city taken by storm can dread from military[13] rage, unrestrained by discipline: whatever excesses the ferocity of the Germans, the avarice of the Spaniards, or the licentiousness of the Italians could commit, these the wretched inhabitants were obliged[28] to suffer. Churches, palaces, and the houses of private persons, were plundered without distinction. No[48] age, or character, or sex was exempt from injury. Cardinals, nobles, priests, matrons, virgins, were[42] all the prey[11] of soldiers, and at the mercy[19] of men deaf to the voice of humanity. ROBERTSON.

17. (*a*) SIEGE OF ROME. Sed ante omnia obsidionis bellique mala fames utrumque exercitum urgebat[7] : Gallos pestilentia etiam ; induciae deinde cum Romanis factae, et colloquia permissu imperatorum habita : in quibus[9] cum[33] identidem Galli
5 famem objicerent, eaque necessitate ad deditionem vocarent, dicitur, avertendae ejus opinionis causa, multis locis panis de Capitolio jactatus[14] esse in hostium stationes. Sed jam[34] neque dissimulari, neque ferri ultra fames poterat. Itaque, exercitus, stationibus vigiliisque fessus[9], superatis[9] tamen humanis omni-
10 bus malis, cum famem[8] unam natura vinci non sineret, diem de die prospectans[25], ecquod auxilium ab dictatore appareret; postremo spe quoque jam, non solum cibo, deficiente, et, cum[30] stationes procederent[12], prope obruentibus[7] infirmum corpus armis, vel dedi, vel redimi se, quacumque pactione possent, jussit ; jactan-
15 tibus[9] non obscure Gallis[42], haud magna mercede se adduci posse, ut obsidionem relinquant. Tum senatus[11] habitus, tribunisque militum[7] negotium datum, ut paciscerentur. LIVY, v. 48.

(*b*) Sarta tecta acriter et cum summa fide exegerunt. Viam e foro boario [et] ad Veneris circa foros publicos, et aedem
20 Matris Magnae in Palatio faciendam[13] locaverunt. Vectigal etiam novum ex salaria annona statuerunt. Sextante sal et Romae et per totam Italiam erat ; Romae pretio eodem, pluris in foris et conciliabulis et alio alibi pretio praebendum[13] locaverunt. Lustrum conditum serius, quia per provincias dimise-
25 runt censores, ut civium Romanorum in exercitibus, quantus ubique esset, referretur numerus. Censa cum iis ducenta decem quattuor millia hominum. Condidit lustrum C. Claudius Nero. *Ib.* XXIX. 37.

18. Inde Vitellius Cremonam flexit et spectato munere Caecinae insistere Bedriacensibus campis ac vestigia recentis victoriae lustrare oculis concupivit[12]. foedum atque atrox spectaculum[9], intra quadragensimum pugnae diem[9] lacera cor-
5 pora, trunci artus, putres virorum equorumque formae, infecta tabo humus, protritis arboribus ac frugibus dira vastitas. nec minus inhumana pars viae, quam Cremonenses lauru rosaque construxerant, extructis altaribus caesisque victimis regium in morem : quae[11] laeta in praesens[9] mox perniciem ipsis
10 fecere. aderat[28] Valens et Caecina, monstrabantque pugnae locos : hinc inrupisse[44] legionum agmen, hinc equites coortos, inde circumfusas[12] auxiliorum manus : iam tribuni praefectique,

(17.) SIEGE OF PARIS, A.D. 1590. By midsummer, Paris, unquestionably the first[5] city of Europe at that day, was in extremities[11], and there[4] are few events[11] in history[13] in which our admiration is more excited[7] by the power[12] of mankind to endure almost preternatural misery, or our indignation more [5] deeply aroused[19] by the cruelty[13] with which the sublimest principles[11] of human nature may be made to serve the purpose[11] of selfish[18] ambition[13] and grovelling[18] superstition, than[4] this famous[18] leaguer.

Rarely have men at any epoch defended their fatherland[4] [10] against foreign[13] oppression[4] with more heroism[36] than that which was[7] manifested[23] by the Parisians of 1590 in resisting religious toleration[4], and in obeying a foreign and priestly despotism[13]. Men[9], women, and children cheerfully laid down their lives by thousands in order that the papal legate and the [15] king of Spain might trample upon that legitimate sovereign of France who was one[34] day to become the idol[12] of Paris and of the whole kingdom.

A census taken at the beginning of the siege had[23] showed a population of two hundred thousand souls[11], with a sufficiency [20] of provisions, it was thought, to last[28] one month. But before the terrible summer was over—so completely had the city been invested—the bushel of wheat was worth three hundred and sixty crowns. The flesh of horses, asses, dogs, cats, rats had become rare luxuries[9]. It was estimated that before July twelve [25] thousand human[11] beings in Paris had died, for want of food, within three months.   MOTLEY.

(18.) The emperor then inspected the field[11] of battle : and never was there any that exhibited a more frightful spectacle. Every thing concurred to increase the horrors of it[9] ; a lowering sky, a cold rain, a violent wind, habitations in ashes[12] ; a plain absolutely torn up and covered with fragments and ruins ; [5] all round the horizon[11] the dark[19] and funereal verdure of the North[13] ; soldiers roaming among the bodies of the slain ; wounds of a most hideous description ; noiseless bivouacs ; no songs of triumph[13], no lively narrations[13], but a general and mournful silence. Around the eagles were the officers, and a few soldiers [10] barely sufficient to guard the colours. Their clothes were[5] torn by the violence of the conflict, and stained with blood ; yet, notwithstanding all their rags, misery, and destitution, they displayed a lofty carriage[11], and even, on the appearance[11] of

sua quisque facta extollentes, falsa vera aut majora vero[11]
miscebant. volgus quoque militum clamore et gaudio de-
15 flectere[41] via, spatia certaminum recognoscere, aggerem armorum, strues corporum intueri[42] mirari ; et erant quos varia
sors rerum lacrimaeque et misericordia subiret[7]. at non Vitellius flexit oculos nec tot milia insepultorum civium exhor-
ruit : laetus[12] ultro et tam propinquae sortis ignarus instaura-
20 bat sacrum dis loci.   Tac. *Hist.* II.

19. Funeral of Germanicus. Interim adventu ejus
audito[12], intimus quisque amicorum, et plerique militares, ut
quique sub Germanico stipendia fecerant, multique etiam ignoti
vicinis e municipiis, pars officium in principem rati, plures
5 illos[13] secuti, ruere[41] ad oppidum Brundisium ; quod naviganti[13]
celerrimum fidissimumque adpulsu erat. Atque ubi primum ex
alto visa classis[42], complentur non modo portus et proxima maris,
sed moenia ac tecta, quaque longissime prospectari[12] poterat,
moerentium[25] turba, ac rogitantium[25] inter se, silentione an voce
10 aliqua egredientem[13] exciperent. Neque satis constabat[29] quid
pro tempore foret ; quum[34] classis paulatim successit, non alacri,
ut adsolet, remigio, sed cunctis ad tristitiam[11] compositis. Postquam duobus cum liberis, feralem urnam tenens[25], egressa[25] navi,
defixit oculos, idem omnium[48] gemitus, neque discerneres proxi-
15 mos, alienos, virorum foeminarumve planctus, nisi quod comi-
tatum Agrippinae longo moerore fessum, obvii[19] et recentes in
dolore anteibant[7]. Miserat duas praetorias cohortes Caesar, addito[11] ut magistratus Calabriae, Apulique, et Campani, suprema
erga memoriam filii sui munera fungerentur. Igitur tribunorum
20 centurionumque humeris cineres portabantur[29]: praecedebant in-
compta signa, versi fasces ; atque ubi colonias transgrederentur[30],
atrata plebes, trabeati equites, pro opibus loci, vestem, odores,
aliaque funerum solennia, cremabant....Consules, M. Valerius et
M. Aurelius et senatus, ac magna pars populi, viam complevere dis-
25 jecti, et ut cuique libitum flentes ; aberat quippe adulatio, guaris[42]
omnibus laetam[23] Tiberio Germanici mortem male dissimulari.

Dies, quo reliquiae tumulo Augusti inferebantur[29], modo per
silentium vastus, modo ploratibus inquies : plena urbis itinera,
conlucentes per campum Martis faces. Illic miles cum armis,
30 sine insignibus magistratus, populus per tribus, concidisse[45] rem
publicam, nihil spei reliquum, clamitabant : promptius[24] aper-
tius[36]que, quam ut meminisse imperitantium crederes.
                                            Tac. *Ann.* III.

the emperor, received him with acclamations[11] of triumph : [15] these, however, seemed[9] somewhat rare and forced ; for in this army, which was at once[17] capable[22] of discrimination[12] and enthusiasm, each individual could form a correct estimate[12] of the position of the whole. The soldiers were amazed to find[20] so many of their enemies killed, such vast numbers wounded, [20] and nevertheless so few prisoners. The[9] latter did not amount in all to eight hundred.

(19.) THE FUNERAL OF QUEEN MARY, A.D. 1691. The public[13] sorrow was great and general. For Mary's[13] blame- less life, her large charities, and her winning manners had conquered the hearts of her people. When the Commons[4] next met they sate for a time in profound silence[9]. At length [5] it was moved and resolved that an Address[11] of Condolence should be presented[20] to the King ; and then[9] the House broke up without[32] proceeding to other business[11]. The number of sad faces in the street struck every observer[11]. The mourning was more general than even the mourning for Charles the [10] Second had been....

The funeral was long remembered as the saddest and most august that Westminster had ever seen. While the Queen's remains lay in state at Whitehall, the neighbouring streets were filled[7] every day, from sunrise to sunset, by crowds which [15] made all traffic impossible. The two Houses with their maces followed the hearse, the Lords robed in scarlet and ermine, the Commons in long[19] black mantles. No preceding Sovereign had[7] ever been attended to the grave by a Parliament : for[9], till then, the Parliament had always expired with the Sovereign. The [20] whole Magistracy of the City swelled the procession. The ban- ners of England and France, Scotland and Ireland, were[7] car- ried[29] by great nobles before the corpse. The pall was borne by the chiefs of the illustrious houses of Howard, Seymour, Grey, and Stanley. On the gorgeous coffin of purple and gold were [25] laid[29] the crown and sceptre of the realm. The day was well suited to such a ceremony. The sky was dark and troubled ; and a few ghastly flakes of snow fell on the black plumes of the funeral car... Through the whole ceremony the distant booming of cannon was heard every minute from the batteries of the [30] Tower. The gentle Queen sleeps among her illustrious kindred in the southern aisle of the Chapel of Henry the Seventh.

MACAULAY.

20. (*a*) CHARACTER OF AUGUSTUS. Forma fuit[13] eximia et
per omnes aetatis gradus venustissima[12]; quamquam et omnis
lenocinii neglegens[23] et in capite comendo tam incuriosus, ut
raptim compluribus simul tonsoribus operam daret, ac modo
5 tonderet modo raderet barbam, eoque ipso tempore aut legeret
aliquid aut etiam scriberet.   Vultu erat[13] vel in sermone vel
tacitus adeo tranquillo serenoque, ut quidam e primoribus
Galliarum confessus sit inter suos, eo[8] se inhibitum ac remol-
litum, quo minus, ut destinarat, in transitu Alpium per simula-
10 tionem conloquii propius admissus, in praecipitium propelleret.
Oculos habuit claros ac[19] nitidos, quibus etiam existimari vole-
bat[29] inesse quiddam[11] divini vigoris, gaudebatque, si quis sibi
acrius contuenti[13] quasi ad fulgorem solis vultum summitteret;
sed in senecta sinistro minus[48] vidit[12]: dentes raros et exiguos
15 et scabros[19]; capillum leviter inflexum[19] et subflavum; supercilia
coniuncta; mediocres aures; nasum et a summo eminentiorem
et ab imo deductiorem [11]; colorem inter aquilum candidumque;
staturam brevem, (quam tamen Iulius Marathus, libertus et a
memoria eius[12], quinque pedum et dodrantis[51] fuisse tradit,) sed
20 quae commoditate et aequitate membrorum occuleretur, ut non-
nisi ex comparatione astantis alicuius procerioris intellegi posset.
 (*b*)   IUL. CAESAR.   Talia agentem[12] atque meditantem mors
praevenit[7].   De qua[9] prius quam dicam[30], ea quae ad formam
et habitum et cultum et mores, nec minus quae ad civilia
25 et bellica ejus studia pertineant non alienum[11] erit summatim[12]
exponere.   Fuisse traditur[14] excelsa statura, colore candido,
teretibus membris, ore paulo pleniore, nigris[19] vegetisque oculis,
valitudine prospera; nisi quod tempore extremo repente animo
linqui atque etiam per somnum exterreri[36] solebat.
30   Armorum [11] et equitandi peritissimus[12], laboris ultra[11] fidem
patiens erat. In agmine nonnumquam equo[14], saepius pedibus[14]
anteibat[12], capite detecto, seu sol[11] seu imber esset; longissimas vias incredibili celeritate confecit, expeditus, meritoria
reda, centena passuum milia in singulos dies; si flumina[30] mora-
35 rentur[12], nando traiciens vel innixus inflatis utribus, ut per-
saepe nuntios de se praevenerit[30].
 Studium et fides erga clientis ne juveni[19] quidem defuerunt[7].
Amicos[10] tanta semper facilitate indulgentiaque tractavit, ut[9]
Gaio Oppio comitanti se per silvestre iter correptoque subita
40 valitudine, deversoriolo eo, quod unum erat[5], cesserit et ipse
humi ac sub divo cubuerit[30].

SUETONIUS.

(20.) *a.* CHARACTER OF MARY QUEEN OF SCOTS. With regard[11] to the Queen's[10] person[14], all contemporary authors agree in ascribing to Mary the utmost beauty of countenance, and elegance of shape[13], of which the human form is capable[22]. Her hair was black, though, according to the fashion 5 of that age, she frequently wore borrowed[19] locks, and of different colours. Her eyes were a dark grey; her complexion was exquisitely fine; and her hands and arms remarkably delicate, both as to shape and colour. Her stature was of an height that rose[28] to the majestic. She danced[29], she walked, 10 and rode with equal grace....

To the charms of beauty, and the utmost elegance of external form, she added those accomplishments[11], which render their impression[13] irresistible. Polite, affable, insinuating, sprightly, and capable[22] of speaking and of writing with equal ease and 15 dignity. Sudden, however, and violent in all her attachments[11]; because her heart[13] was warm and unsuspicious. Impatient of contradiction[13]; because she had been accustomed from her infancy to be treated as a Queen. No stranger[12], on some occasions, to dissimulation; which, in that perfidious court where 20 she received her education[12], was reckoned among the necessary arts of government. Not insensible of flattery, or unconscious of that pleasure, with which almost every woman beholds the influence[12] of her own beauty. Formed with the qualities[11] which we love[30], not with the talents that we admire[30], she was 25 an agreeable woman, rather than an illustrious Queen.

ROBERTSON.

b. CHARLES EDWARD STUART. The person[13] of Charles was tall and well-formed; his limbs[13] athletic and active. He excelled in all manly exercises, and was inured to every kind of toil, especially long marches on foot, having applied[26] him- 30 self to field sports in Italy, and become an excellent walker[12]. His face[13] was strikingly handsome, of a perfect oval[12] and a fair complexion; his eyes light blue; his features high and noble. Contrary to the custom of the time, which prescribed[28] perukes, his own fair[18] hair usually fell in long ring- 35 lets on his neck. This goodly[18] person[14] was[7] enhanced[28] by his graceful manners; frequently condescending[25] to the most familiar kindness, yet always shielded by a[15] regal dignity, he had a peculiar talent[11] to please and to persuade, and never failed[20] to adapt his conversation to the taste[11] or to the station of those 40 whom[30] he addressed[29].

MAHON.

21. (*a*) CATO. In hoc viro tanta vis animi ingeniique fuit, ut, quocunque loco[11] natus esset, fortunam sibi ipse facturus fuisse videretur[14]. Nulla ars[11] neque privatae neque publicae rei gerendae ei defuit. Urbanas rusticasque res pariter callebat. Ad
5 summos honores alios[7] scientia iuris, alios eloquentia, alios gloria militaris provexit; huic versatile ingenium sic pariter ad omnia[11] fuit, ut natum ad id unum diceres, quodcunque ageret. In bello manu[13] fortissimus multisque insignibus clarus pugnis; idem[17], postquam ad magnos honores pervenit, summus impera-
10 tor[13]; idem in pace, si ius consuleres, peritissimus, si causa oranda esset, eloquentissimus, nec is[16] tantum, cuius lingua vivo[1] eo viguerit[10], monumentum eloquentiae nullum exstet; vivit immo vigetque eloquentia eius sacrata scriptis omnis generis. Orationes et pro se multae et pro aliis et in alios; nam non
15 solum accusando, sed etiam causam dicendo fatigavit inimicos. Simultates nimio plures et exercuerunt eum et[34] ipse exercuit eas, nec facile dixeris, utrum magis presserit eum nobilitas, an ille agitaverit nobilitatem. Asperi procul dubio animi et linguae acerbae[19] et immodice liberae fuit, sed invicti a cupiditati-
20 bus animi, rigidae innocentiae, contemptor gratiae et divitiarum. In parsimonia, in patientia laboris periculique ferrei prope corporis animique; quem[9] ne senectus quidem, quae solvit omnia, fregerit; qui sextum et octogesimum annum agens[25] causam [dixerit], ipse pro se oraverit scripseritque, nonagesimo anno
25 Ser. Galbam ad populi adduxerit iudicium.   LIVY, xxxix. 40.

(*b*) CATILINE. Lucius Catilina, nobili genere natus, magna vi et animi et corporis, sed ingenio[19] malo pravoque. Huic ab adolescentia bella intestina, caedes, rapinae, discordia civilis, grata[12] fuere; ibique juventutem suam exercuit. Corpus[14] patiens
30 inediae, vigiliae, algoris, supra quam cuique credibile est: animus audax, subdolus, varius[12], cujus rei libet simulator ac dissimulator: alieni adpetens, sui profusus, ardens in cupiditatibus: satis loquentiae, sapientiae parum[42]. Vastus animus immoderata, incredibilia, nimis alta semper cupiebat. Hunc[7], post
35 dominationem Lucii Sullae, lubido maxuma invaserat reipublicae capiundae; neque id quibus modis adsequeretur, dum sibi regnum[11] pararet, quidquam pensi habebat[29]. Agitabatur magis magisque in dies animus ferox, inopia rei familiaris, et conscientia scelerum; quae[9] utraque[5] his artibus auxerat, quas
40 supra memoravi. Incitabant[7] praeterea corrupti civitatis mores, quos pessuma[19] ac diversa inter se mala[5], luxuria atque avaritia, vexabant[7].   SALLUST *Cat.* v.

Cf. Tac. *A.* iii. 30; vi. 51; II. i. 10; iii. 75, 86; iv. 5.

(21.) *a.* DANTON. His natural endowments[12] were great for any[4] part[11] in public life, whether at the bar, or in the senate, or even in war: for the part[4] of a revolutionary leader they were of the highest order[11]. A courage[13] which nothing could quell[31]; a quickness[12] of perception at once and clearly to per- 5 ceive his own opportunity, and his adversary's error; singular fertility of resources, with the power[12] of sudden change in his course, and adaptation[12] to varied circumstances; a natural eloquence, hardy, caustic, masculine; a mighty frame[11] of body; a voice overpowering all resistance[13];—these[8] were the 10 grand qualities which Danton brought to the prodigious[15] struggle in which he was engaged.

b. PITT. At an[5] age when others are but entering upon the study[12] of state affairs, and the practice of debating, he came forth a mature politician, a finished orator, an accom- 15 plished debater. His knowledge[12] was[7] not confined to the study of the classics; with political philosophy he was more familiar than most Englishmen of his own age. Having prepared himself, too, for being called to the bar, and both attended on courts[45] of justice and frequented the Western 20 Circuit, he had more knowledge and habits[11] of business than can fall to the share of our young patricians. In private life he was singularly amiable; his spirits[13] were naturally buoyant and even playful; his affections[13] warm; his veracity scru- pulously exact; his integrity wholly without a stain; as a 25 son and a brother he was perfect, and no man was[7] more fondly beloved or more sincerely mourned by his friends.

c. ROBESPIERRE. From his earliest years he had never been known to indulge[28] in the frolics or evince[28] the gaiety of youth. Gloomy, solitary, austere, intent upon his work, 30 careless of relaxation, averse to amusement, without a con- fidant, or friend, or even companion, it is recorded[14] of him that at the College of Louis the Grand, where he was educated, he was never seen once to smile. As a boy and a youth he was re- markable for vanity[12], jealousy, dissimulation, and trick, with 35 an invincible obstinacy[12] on all subjects, a selfishness[12] hardly natural, a disposition[11] incapable of forgiving any injury, but a close concealment of his resentment till the occasion arose[30] of gratifying it. It[4] would have been difficult to bring into the tempest of the Revolution qualities[11] more likely to weather its 40 fury, and take advantage of its force. BROUGHAM.

Cf. Holden *F. C.* §§ 32, 59, 95, 124, 261, 321.

22. (*a*) AGRICOLA. Credunt plerique militaribus ingeniis subtilitatem deesse, quia castrensis jurisdictio secura et obtusior ac plura manu[13] agens calliditatem fori non exerceat[13]. Agricola naturali prudentia, quamvis inter togatos, facile[36] justeque agebat.
5 jam vero tempora curarum remissionumque divisa: ubi conventus ac judicia poscerent[30], gravis[12], intentus, severus, set saepius misericors: ubi officio[11] satis factum, nulla ultra potestatis persona: tristitiam et adrogantiam et avaritiam exuerat. nec illi, quod[5] est rarissimum[11], aut facilitas auctoritatem aut severitas
10 amorem deminuit. integritatem atque abstinentiam in tanto viro referre injuria virtutum fuerit. ne famam[11] quidem, cui[11] saepe etiam boni indulgent, ostentanda[12] virtute aut per artem quaesivit. Natus erat Gaio Caesare tertium consule idibus Iuniis: excessit sexto et quinquagesimo anno, decumo kalendas
15 Septembris Collega Priscoque consulibus[13]. quod si habitum quoque eius posteri noscere velint, decentior[24] quam sublimior fuit; nihil metus in voltu: gratia oris supererat. bonum virum facile crederes, magnum libenter. TAC. *Agricola.*

(*b*) GALBA. Hunc[16] exitum habuit Servius Galba, tribus et
20 septuaginta annis quinque principes prospera fortuna emensus" et alieno imperio felicior[12] quam suo. Vetus in familia nobilitas, magnae opes[28]: ipsi[10] medium ingenium, magis extra vitia quam cum virtutibus[18]. Famae nec[34] incuriosus[11] nec venditator: pecuniae alienae non adpetens[12], suae parcus, publicae avarus:
25 amicorum libertorumque, ubi in bonos incidisset, sine reprehensione patiens, si mali forent, usque ad culpam[20] ignarus[12]. Sed claritas natalium et metus temporum obtentui, ut quod segnitia erat, sapientia vocaretur. Dum vigebat[14] aetas, militari laude[11] apud Germanias floruit. Pro consule Africam moderate[36], iam
30 senior citeriorem Hispaniam pari iustitia continuit, maior[24] privato visus[9], dum privatus fuit[12], et omnium[40] consensu capax imperii, nisi imperasset[12]. TAC. *Hist.* I. 49.

(*c*) CLAUDIUS. Auctoritas dignitasque formae non defuit vel stanti vel sedenti ac praecipue quiescenti; (nam et prolixo
35 nec exili corpore erat, et specie canitieque pulcra, opimis cervicibus) ceterum et ingredientem destituebant poplites minus firmi, et remisso quid vel serio agentem multa dehonestabant: risus indecens, linguae titubantia, caputque cum semper, tum in quantulocumque actu vel maxime tremulum. Saevum et
40 sanguinarium natura fuisse, magnis minimisque apparuit rebus. Sed nihil aeque quam timidus fuit. SUETONIUS.

(22.) *a.* WASHINGTON. His integrity[13] was most pure, his justice the most[24] inflexible I have ever known; no motives[11] of interest or consanguinity, of friendship or hatred, being[6] able to bias his decision[12]. He was, indeed, in every sense, a wise, a good, and a great man. His temper[6] was naturally irritable 5 and high toned; but reflection and resolution[6] had obtained a firm and habitual[36] ascendancy[12] over it[9]. If ever[9], however, it[6] broke its bounds, he was[42] most tremendous in his wrath. In his expenses he was honourable, but exact; liberal in con-tributions[12] to whatever promised[20] utility[12]; but frowning[19] 10 and unyielding on all visionary projects.[11] His heart[6] was not warm in its affections[11]; but he exactly calculated[29] every man's value[12], and gave him a solid esteem[12] proportioned to it. His person[6], you know, was fine; his deportment easy, erect, and noble. Although in the circle[11] of his friends, where he might[48] 15 be unreserved with safety[36], he took[29] a free share in conver-sation, his colloquial[11] talents were not above mediocrity[12]. In public, when called on for a sudden[18] opinion, he was unready, short, and embarrassed. Yet he wrote[29] readily, rather diffusely, in an easy and correct style. 20

On the whole, his character[11] was, in its mass, perfect, in nothing bad, in a few points[11] indifferent. JEFFERSON.

b. LOUIS NAPOLEON. He had boldness of the kind[16] which is produced[7] by reflection rather than that which is the result of temperament[11]. In order to cope[28] with the extraordinary[18] 25 perils into which he now and then thrust himself[29], and to cope with them decorously, there was wanted a[15] fiery quality[11] which nature had refused to the great bulk of mankind as well as[34] to him. But it was only[9] in emergencies[11] of a really trying[12] sort, and involving[28] instant physical[14] danger, that his boldness fell short. 30

He loved to contrive and brood over plots, and[9] he had a great skill in making the preparatory arrangements[11] for bring-ing his schemes to ripeness[12]; but like most of the common herd[11] of men, he was unable to command[28] the presence[11] of mind and the flush[11] of animal spirits which are needed for the critical 35 moments of a daring adventure[13]. In short, he was a thought-ful, literary man, deliberately tasking himself[25] to venture[20] into a desperate path, and going great lengths[11] in that direction[11]; but liable to find[28] himself balked[7] in the moment[11] of trial by the sudden and chilling return[12] of his good[11] sense. 40

KINGLAKE.

N. 3

23. (*a*) Bellum scripturus sum, quod populus Romanus cum Jugurtha, rege Numidarum, gessit: primum, quia magnum et atrox[18], variaque victoria fuit: dein, quia tum[8] primum superbiae nobilitatis obviam[7] itum est ; quae[5] contentio divina et
5 humana cuncta permiscuit, eoque vecordiae processit, uti studiis civilibus bellum atque vastitas Italiae finem faceret[7]. Sed, priusquam hujuscemodi rei[11] initium expedio, pauca supra repetam[12] ; quo, ad cognoscendum[12], omnia illustria magis, magisque in aperto sint. Sallust, *Jug.* v.

10 (*b*) Initium mihi operis Servius Galba iterum Titus Vinius consules[13] erunt: nam post conditam urbem octingentos et viginti prioris aevi[2] annos multi auctores rettulerunt[7]....

Opus[8] adgredior opimum casibus, atrox proeliis, discors seditionibus, ipsa etiam pace saevom[20]. Quattuor principes ferro
15 interempti : trina bella civilia, plura externa ac plerumque permixta : prosperae in oriente, adversae in occidente res : turbatum Illyricum, Galliae nutantes, perdomita Brittania et statim missa[13]. Iam vero Italia novis cladibus vel post longam saeculorum seriem repetitis adflicta. Haustae aut obrutae
20 urbes fecundissima Campaniae ora, et urbs incendiis vastata, consumptis[12] antiquissimis delubris, ipso Capitolio civium manibus incenso[42]. Pollutae caerimoniae, magna adulteria : plenum exiliis mare, infecti caedibus scopuli.

Non tamen adeo virtutum sterile saeculum, ut non et bona
25 exempla prodiderit[6]. Comitatae profugos liberos matres, secutae maritos in exilia coniuges, propinqui audentes, constantes generi, contumax etiam adversus tormenta servorum fides; supremae clarorum virorum necessitates, ipsa necessitas fortiter tolerata et laudatis antiquorum mortibus par[18] exitus. Praeter
30 multiplices rerum humanarum casus caelo terraque prodigia et fulminum monitus et futurorum praesagia, laeta tristia, ambigua manifesta ; nec enim umquam atrocioribus populi Romani cladibus magisve iustis iudiciis adprobatum est non esse curae deis securitatem nostram[8], esse[28] ultionem.
35 Ceterum antequam destinata componam[33], repetendum[12] videtur, qualis status urbis, quae mens exercituum, quis habitus provinciarum, quid in toto terrarum orbe validum[11], quid aegrum fuerit, ut non modo casus eventusque rerum, qui plerumque fortuiti sunt[20], sed ratio etiam causaeque noscantur.

Tac. *Hist.* i. 1.

(23). *a.* Je me propose d'écrire l'histoire[12] d'une révolution mémorable, qui a profondément agité les hommes, et[5] qui les divise encore aujourd'hui. Je ne me dissimule pas les difficultés[12] de l'entreprise, car des passions que l'on croyait étouffées sous l'influence[11] du despotisme[13] militaire, viennent 5 de se réveiller. Tout à coup des hommes accablés d'ans et de travaux ont senti renaître en eux des ressentimens qui paraissaient apaisés, et nous les ont communiqués, à nous, leurs fils et leurs héritiers. Mais si nous avons à soutenir la même cause[4], nous n'avons pas à défendre leur conduite, et nous pou- 10 vons séparer la liberté de ceux qui l'ont bien ou mal servie, tandis que nous avons l'avantage[11] d'avoir[33] entendu et observé ces vieillards, qui, tout pleins encore de leurs souvenirs, tout agités de leurs impressions, nous apprennent à les comprendre.

THIERS.   15

b. I purpose[28] to write the history[11] of England[13] from the accession[13] of King James the Second down to a time[11] which is within the memory of men still living. I shall recount the errors which, in a few months, alienated a loyal gentry and priesthood[13] from the House of Stuart. I shall trace the course 20 of that revolution which terminated the long struggle between our sovereigns and their parliaments[9], and bound up together the rights of the people and the title of the reigning dynasty[11]. I shall relate how from the auspicious union[13] of order and freedom, sprang a[16] prosperity of which the annals of human 25 affairs had furnished no example; how our country, from a state[11] of ignominious vassalage, rapidly rose to the place[12] of umpire among European powers[11]; how Scotland was at length united to England; how in America the British colonies became mightier and wealthier than the realms which[5] Cortez and 30 Pizarro had added to the dominions of Charles V.; how in Asia British adventurers founded an empire not less splendid and more durable than that of Alexander. Nor will it be less my duty faithfully to record disasters[11] mingled with triumphs, and great national crimes and follies far more humiliating than 35 any[43] disaster.

The events which I propose to relate form[28] only a single act of a great[19] and eventful drama extending[20] through ages, and must be very imperfectly understood unless the plot of the preceding acts be[27] well known. I shall therefore introduce[20] 40 my narrative[11] by a slight[12] sketch of the history of our country from the earliest times.   MACAULAY.

3—2

24. (*a*) FIRE AT ROME. Interrupit[7] hos sermones nocte[39] quae pridie Quinquatrus fuit, pluribus simul locis circa forum incendium ortum. Eodem tempore septem tabernae, quae postea quinque, et argentariae, quae nunc novae appellantur, 5 arsere[12]; comprehensa postea privata aedificia (neque enim tum basilicae erant), comprehensae lautumiae forumque piscatorium et atrium regium; aedes Vestae vix defensa est tredecim maxime servorum opera, qui in publicum[11] redempti ac manumissi sunt. Nocte ac die continuatum incendium fuit, nec ulli 10 dubium erat, humana id fraude factum esse, quod pluribus simul locis, et iis diversis, ignes coorti essent. Itaque consul ex auctoritate senatus pro contione edixit, qui, quorum opera id conflatum incendium *esset*, profiteretur, praemium fore libero[20] pecuniam, servo libertatem. Eo praemio inductus Campanorum 15 Calviorum servus (Manus ei nomen erat) indicavit[12], dominos et quinque praeterea iuvenes nobiles Campanos, quorum parentes a Q. Fulvio securi percussi erant, id incendium fecisse, vulgoque facturos alia, ni comprehendantur. Comprehensi ipsi familiaeque eorum. Et primo elevabatur[29] index indiciumque : pridie 20 eum verberibus castigatum ab dominis discessisse; per iram ac levitatem[11] ex re fortuita crimen commentum; ceterum ut coram coarguebantur[29] et quaestio ex ministris facinoris foro medio haberi coepta est[29], fassi omnes, atque in dominos servosque conscios animadversum[12] est. Indici libertas data et viginti millia 25 aeris. LIVY, XXVI. 27.

(*b*) Sequitur clades[7], forte an dolo principis incertum (nam utrumque[11] auctores prodidere[7]), sed omnibus[48] quae huic urbi per violentiam ignium acciderunt gravior atque atrocior[24]. Initium in ea parte circi ortum quae Palatino Caelioque montibus 30 contigua est, ubi per tabernas, quibus[25] id[15] mercimonium inerat quo flamma alitur[10], simul coeptus[9] ignis et statim validus[20] ac vento citus longitudinem circi corripuit[9]. Neque enim domus munimentis saeptae vel templa muris cincta aut quid aliud morae interiacebat. Impetu pervagatum[9] incendium plana primum, 35 deinde in edita adsurgens, et rursus inferiora populando[42], anteiit remedia velocitate mali et obnoxia[13] urbe artis itineribus hucque et illuc flexis, atque enormibus vicis, qualis vetus Roma fuit. Ad hoc lamenta paventium feminarum, fessi aevo aut rudis pueritiae aetas, quique sibi quique aliis consulebant, dum 40 trahunt[25] invalidos aut opperiuntur[33], pars mora, pars festinans[12] cuncta impediebant. Et saepe, dum in tergum respectant[55], lateribus aut fronte circumveniebantur; vel si in proxima

(24.) *a.* GREAT FIRE OF LONDON. While[41] the war continued without[48] any decisive success on either side, a calamity
happened in London, which[5] threw the people into great consternation. Fire, breaking out in a baker's house near the
bridge, spread itself on all sides with such rapidity, that no 5
efforts could extinguish it[6], till it laid in ashes a considerable
part of the city. The inhabitants, without[32] being able to provide effectually for their relief, were reduced[28] to be spectators[12]
of their own ruin; and were pursued[7] from street to street by
the flames, which unexpectedly gathered round them. Three 10
days and nights did the fire advance; and it[8] was only by[33] the
blowing up of houses, that it was at last extinguished. The
king and duke used their utmost endeavours[12] to stop the progress of the flames; but[9] all their industry was unsuccessful.
About four hundred streets, and thirteen thousand houses, 15
were reduced to ashes[12].

The causes of this calamity were evident. The narrow
streets of London, the houses built entirely of wood, the dry
season, and a violent east wind which blew[29]; these were so
many concurring circumstances[11], which[8] rendered it easy to 20
assign the reason of the destruction that ensued[28]. But the
people[9] were[7] not satisfied with this obvious account[11].
Prompted[26] by blind rage, some ascribed the guilt to the repub-
licans, others to the catholics; though it is not easy to conceive how the burning[13] of London could serve the purposes[11] 25
of either party.   HUME.

b. The conflagration was so universal[4], and the people so
astonished, that from the beginning they hardly stirred to
quench it; so that there was nothing heard or seen but crying
out and lamentation, running[33] about like distracted creatures[11], 30
without[32] at all attempting to save even their goods. Such a
strange consternation there was upon them, as it burned[29], both
in breadth and length[36], the churches, public halls, hospitals,
monuments, and ornaments, leaping after a prodigious manner
from house to house, and street to street, at[5] great distances[12] 35
one from the other; for the heat, with a long[12] set of fair[18] and
warm weather, had even ignited the air, and prepared the
materials to conceive the fire, which devoured[29], after an in-
credible manner, houses, furniture, and every thing. Oh the
miserable[19] and calamitous spectacle! such as haply the world 40
had not seen since the foundation[13] of it. God grant my eyes

evaserant[33], illis quoque igni correptis[9], etiam quae longinqua
crediderant in eodem casu reperiebant[29]. Postremo, quid vitarent
45 quid peterent ambigui, complere vias, sterni per agros[41]; quidam
amissis[12] omnibus fortunis, diurni quoque victus *egeni*[12], alii cari-
tate suorum, quos eripere nequiverant, quamvis patente effugio[9]
interiere. Nec quisquam defendere audebat[29], crebris[42] multorum
minis restinguere prohibentium[25], et quia alii palam faces iacie-
50 bant atque esse sibi auctorem[13] vociferabantur, sive ut raptus
licentius[30] exercerent, seu iussu. Sexto demum[34] die finis incendio factus prorutis per immensum aedificiis, ut continuae vio-
lentiae campus et velut vacuum caelum occurreret.

TAC. *Ann.* XV. 38.

25. PLINY'S DEATH. Interim e Vesuvio monte pluribus
locis latissimae flammae atque incendia relucebant, quorum
fulgor et claritas tenebris noctis excitabatur[29]. Ille agrestium
trepidatione ignis relictos desertasque villas per solitudinem
5 ardere in remedium formidinis dictitabat. Tum se quieti dedit,
et quievit verissimo quidem somno. Nam meatus animae,
qui illi propter amplitudinem corporis gravior et sonantior erat,
ab iis, qui limini obversabantur, audiebatur. Sed area, ex qua
diaeta adibatur, ita jam cinere missisque pumicibus oppleta
10 surrexerat, ut, si longior in cubiculo mora esset, exitus negare-
tur. Excitatus[9] procedit, seque Pomponiano ceterisque, qui
pervigilarant, reddit. In commune consultant, an intra tecta
subsistant, an in aperto vagentur. Nam crebris vastisque
tremoribus tecta nutabant, et quasi emota sedibus suis, nunc
15 huc nunc illuc abire aut referri videbantur. Sub divo rursus,
quamquam levium exesorumque, pumicum casus metuebatur:
quod[9] tamen periculorum collatio elegit[7]. Cervicalia capitibus
imposita[9] linteis constringunt. Id munimentum adversus deci-
dentia fuit[28]. Jam dies alibi, illic nox omnibus[48] noctibus
20 nigrior densiorque: quam[7] tamen faces multae variaque lumina
solabantur[29]. Placuit egredi in litus, et e proximo adspicere,
ecquid jam mare admitteret; quod[9] adhuc vastum et adversum
permanebat. Ibi[34] super abiectum linteum recubans, semel atque
iterum frigidam poposcit, hausitque. Deinde flammae flam
25 marumque praenuntius odor sulfuris alios in fugam vertunt,
excitant illum[4]. Innixus servis duobus adsurrexit, et statim
concidit, ut ego[16] conjecto, crassiore caligine spiritu obstructo.
Ubi dies redditus (is ab eo, quem novissime viderat, tertius)
corpus inventum est integrum: habitus corporis quiescenti,
30 quam defuncto[13], similior.

PLIN. *Ep.* VI. 16.

may never behold the like[4]. The noise and cracking[13] of the impetuous flames, the shrieking of women and children, the hurry[13] of people, the fall[13] of houses and churches, was like a hideous storm, and the air all about so hot and inflamed, that at last one was not able to approach it[24]: so that they were forced[30] to stand still and let the flames burn on, which they did[28] for near two miles in length and one in breadth. The clouds of smoke were dismal, and[9] reached, upon computation[12], near fifty miles in length. Thus I left it this afternoon burning, a resemblance[12] of Sodom, or the last day. London was, but is no more.   EVELYN.

(25.) DEATH OF PLINY THE ELDER. As the shades of evening gathered[29], the brightness[13] of the flames became more striking; but to calm the panic of those around him[25], the philosopher[10] assured[29] them that they arose[28] from cottages on the slope, which the alarmed[19] rustics had abandoned to the descending[19] flakes of fire. He then took his customary[36] brief[19] night's rest[12], sleeping[25] composedly as usual[36]; but his attendants were not so easily tranquillized, and[9] as the night advanced, the continued fall of ashes within the courts of the mansion convinced[28] them that delay[13] would make escape impossible. They roused their master, together with the friend at whose house he was resting, and[9] hastily debated how to proceed[23]. By this time[34] the soil around them was rocking with repeated shocks of earthquake, which recalled the horrors of the still recent catastrophe[11]. The party quitted the treacherous[18] shelter[18] of the house-roof, and[9] sought the coast in hopes of finding[33] vessels to take them off. To protect themselves from the thickening[18] cinders they tied cushions to their heads. The sky was darkened by the ceaseless[16] shower, and[9] they groped[20] their way by torchlight[13], and by the intermitting[18] flashes from the mountain. The sea was agitated, and abandoned by every bark. Pliny, wearied[20] or perplexed, now[34] stretched himself on a piece of sail-cloth, and[9] refused to stir further, while on the bursting forth of a fiercer blast accompanied[26] with sulphureous gases, his companions, all but two body-slaves, fled in terror[12]. Some who looked back in their flight affirmed[29] that the old man[10] rose once with the help of his attendants, but immediately fell again, overpowered, as it seemed, with the deadly vapours.
MERIVALE.

26. (*a*) ERUPTION OF VESUVIUS. Praecesserat per multos dies tremor terrae minus formidolosus quia Campaniae solitus. Illa vero nocte ita invaluit ut non moveri[31] omnia sed verti crederentur. Inrumpit cubiculum meum mater: surgebam,
5 invicem, si quiesceret, excitaturus[12]. Residimus in area domus, quae mare a tectis modico spatio dividebat[29]. Dubito constantiam vocare an inprudentiam debeam; agebam enim duodevicensimum annum: posco[44] librum Titi Livi et quasi per otium lego adque etiam, ut coeperam, excerpo. Ecce, amicus avunculi, qui
10 nuper ad eum ex Hispania venerat, ut me et matrem sedentes, me vero etiam legentem[31] videt, illius patientiam, securitatem meam corripit: nihilo segnius ego intentus in librum. Iam[34] hora diei prima, et adhuc dubius et quasi languidus dies[41]. Iam quassatis circumiacentibus tectis[9], quamquam in aperto loco,
15 angusto tamen, magnus et certus ruinae metus. Tum demum excedere oppido visum: sequitur vulgus attonitum, [11]quodque[5] in pavore simile prudentiae alienum consilium suo praefert ingentique agmine abeuntis premit et impellit. Egressi[33] tecta consistimus. Multa[8] ibi miranda[11], multas formidines patimur.
20 Nam vehicula quae produci jusseramus, quamquam in planissimo campo, in contrarias partes agebantur ac ne lapidibus quidem fulta in eodem vestigio quiescebant[29]. Praeterea mare in se resorberi[31] et tremore terrae quasi repelli videbamus. Certe processerat litus multaque animalia maris siccis arenis
25 detinebat[7]. Ab altero latere nubes atra et horrenda[19] ignei spiritus tortis vibratisque discursibus rupta in longas flammarum figuras dehiscebat: fulguribus illae et[34] similes et maiores[24] erant. Tum mater orare[41], hortari, jubere quoquo modo fugerem; posse[44] enim juvenem, se et annis et corpore gravem[9]
30 bene morituram, si mihi causa mortis non fuisset[27]. Ego[17] contra[28], salvum me nisi una non futurum: dein manum ejus amplexus, addere gradum cogo. Paret aegre incusatque se quod me moretur[33]. Jam cinis, adhuc tamen rarus: respicio; densa caligo tergis imminebat, quae nos torrentis modo infusa
35 terrae sequebatur[25]. 'Deflectamus', inquam[28], 'dum videmus ne in via strati comitantium[25] turba in tenebris opteramur'. Vix consideramus[34], et nox, non qualis inlunis aut nubila, sed qualis in locis[11] clausis lumine extincto. Audires ululatus feminarum, infantum quiritatus, clamores virorum: alii parentes, alii liberos,.
40 alii conjuges vocibus requirebant, vocibus noscitabant[41]: hi suum casum, illi suorum miserabantur: erant qui metu mortis mortem precarentur: multi ad deos manus tollere, plures nus-

(26.) EARTHQUAKE OF LISBON. It was[n] on the morning of this fatal[18] day, between the hours[13] of nine and ten, that I was set down in my apartment, just finishing[4] a letter, when the papers and table I was writing on began[41] to tremble with a[15] gentle motion, which rather surprised me, as I could not[5] perceive a breath of wind stirring[28]. Whilst I was[41] reflecting with myself what this could be owing to, the house I was in shook with such violence, that the upper stories immediately fell, and though my apartment (which was the first floor) did not then share[28] the same fate, yet everything was thrown[10] out of its place, in such a manner that it was with no small difficulty I kept[28] my feet, and[9] expected nothing less than to be soon crushed to death, as the walls continued[28] rocking to and fro in a frightful manner, opening[41] in several places; large stones falling down[25] on every side from the cracks, and[15] the ends of most of the rafters starting[41] out from the roof. To add[28] to this terrifying scene[11], the sky in a moment became so gloomy that I could now distinguish no particular object[11]; it was[41] an Egyptian darkness indeed, such as might be felt; owing[14], no doubt, to the prodigious clouds of dust[20] and lime raised from so[35] violent a concussion, and, as some reported, to sulphureous exhalations, but this I cannot affirm; however, it is certain I found[28] myself almost choked for near ten minutes.

I had still presence[12] of mind enough left[23] to put on a[25] pair[11] of shoes and a coat, the first[5] that came in my way, which was everything[23] I saved, and in this dress I hurried down stairs[11], and[9] made directly to that end of the street which opens to the Tagus.

In the midst of our devotions[12], the second great[18] shock[30] came on, little less violent than the[15] first, and[9] completed the ruin[12] of those buildings which had been already much shattered. You may judge of the force[12] of this shock, when I inform[28] you it was so violent that I could scarce keep on my knees; but it was[7] attended[20] with some circumstances[35] still more dreadful than the former. On a sudden I heard a general outcry, "the sea is coming in[44], we shall be all lost." Upon this, turning[25] my eyes towards the river, which in that place is near four miles broad, I could perceive it heaving and swelling[31] in a most unaccountable manner, as no[40] wind was stirring[20]. In an instant there appeared, at some small distance, a large body of water, rising[31] as it were like

quam jam deos ullos, aeternamque illam[15] et novissimam[19]
noctem mundo interpretabantur[41]. Paulum reluxit; quod[9] non
45 dies nobis sed adventantis ignis indicium videbatur. Et ignis
quidem longius substitit, tenebrae rursus, cinis rursus multus
et gravis[12]. Hunc identidem adsurgentes excutiebamus: operti
alioqui adque etiam oblisi pondere essemus. Tandem illa[15]
caligo tenuata quasi in fumum nebulamve discessit: mox dies
50 verus, sol etiam effulsit, luridus tamen, qualis esse, cum deficit[12],
solet[36]. Occursabant trepidantibus adhuc oculis mutata omnia
altoque cinere, tamquam nive, obducta. Regressi Misenum,
curatis[9] utcumque corporibus suspensam[15] dubiamque noctem
spe ac metu exegimus. PLIN. *Ep.* VI. 20.

55 (*b*) Varie itaque quatitur[12], et mira eduntur opera, alibi
prostratis moenibus, alibi hiatu profundo haustis, alibi egestis
molibus, alibi emissis amnibus nonnumquam etiam ignibus
calidisve fontibus, aliubi averso fluminum cursu. Praecedit[7]
vero comitaturque terribilis sonus, alias murmuri similis, alias
60 mugitibus aut clamori humano armorumve pulsantium fragori,
pro qualitate materiae excipientis[25] formaque vel cavernarum
vel cuniculi per quem meet, exilius grassante in angusto[11],
eodem rauco in recurvis, resultante in duris, fervente in umidis,
fluctuante in stagnantibus, furente contra solida[11]. Itaque et
65 sine motu saepe editur sonus. Nec simplici modo quatitur
umquam, sed tremit vibratque[12]. Hiatus vero alias remanet
ostendens quae sorbuit, alias occultat ore conpresso[25] rursusque
ita inducto solo ut nulla vestigia exstent, urbibus plerumque
devoratis[33] agrorumque tractu hausto.
70 Tutissimum est cum vibrat[12] crispante aedificiorum crepitu
et cum intumescit adsurgens alternoque motu residit; innoxium
et cum concurrentia tecta contrario ictu arietant, quoniam alter
motus alteri renititur. Undantis[13] inclinatio et fluctus more
quaedam[11] volutatio infesta est, aut cum in unam partem totus
75 se motus impellit.
Fiunt simul cum terrae motu et inundationes maris eodem
videlicet spiritu infusi[9] aut terrae residentis[25] sinu recepti[2].
Maximus terrae memoria mortalium exstitit motus Tiberi
Caesaris principatu, XII. urbibus Asiae una nocte prostratis[20],
80 creberrimus Punico bello intra eundem annum septiens ac
quinquagiens nuntiatus[20] Romam, quo[9] quidem anno ad Tra-
simennum lacum dimicantes[25] maximum motum neque Poeni
sensere[7] nec Romani. PLIN. *N. H.* II.

a mountain. It[9] came on foaming[25] and roaring, and rushed towards the shore with such impetuosity[30], that we all immediately ran[45] for our lives as fast as possible; many were actually swept away, and the rest above their waist in water at a good distance from the banks. For my[17] own part, I had the narrowest escape[12], and should certainly have been lost, had I not grasped a large beam that lay[29] on the ground, till the water returned[30] to its channel, which it did[28] almost at the same instant, with equal rapidity. As there now appeared[29] at least as much danger from the sea as the land, and I scarce knew whither to retire for shelter[12], I took a sudden[18] resolution of returning back, with my clothes all dripping, to the area of St Paul's.

The new scenes[11] of horror[5] I met with here exceed all description[12]; nothing[41] could be heard but sighs and groans; I did not meet with a soul in the passage who was[30] not bewailing the death[13] of his nearest relations and dearest friends, or the loss[13] of all his substance; I could hardly take a single step, without[32] treading on the dead or the dying: in some places lay[29] coaches, with their masters, horses and riders *almost* crushed in[12] pieces; here mothers with infants in their arms: there ladies richly dressed, priests, friars, gentlemen, mechanics, either in the same condition, or just expiring; some had their backs or thighs broken, others vast stones on their breasts; some lay[29] almost buried in the rubbish, and, crying out in vain to the passengers[25] for succour, were left to perish with the rest.

As soon[34] as it grew dark, another scene presented[28] itself little less shocking than those already described: the whole city appeared[29] in a blaze, which was so bright that I could easily see to read by it. It may be said without exaggeration[12], it was on fire at least in a hundred different places at once, and thus continued[28] burning for six days together, without[32] intermission, or the least attempt being made to stop its progress.

It went[28] on consuming everything the earthquake had spared[28], and the people were so dejected and terrified, that few or none had[28] courage enough to venture[28] down to save any part of their substance[12]; every one had his eyes turned towards the flames, and stood[29] looking on with silent grief, which was only interrupted[7] by the cries and shrieks of women and children calling on the saints and angels for succour.

DAVY.

27. M. T. C. C. CURIONI S. D. — Epistolarum genera multa esse non ignoras: sed unum illud[16] certissimum, cujus causâ inventa res ipsa est, ut certiores faceremus absentes, si quid esset, quod eos scire, aut nostrâ aut ipsorum interesset.
5 Hujus generis literas a me profecto non expetis. Tuarum enim rerum domesticarum habes et scriptores et nuntios. In meis autem rebus nihil est sane novi. Reliqua sunt epistolarum genera duo, quae me magnopere[7] delectant; unum familiare et jocosum, alterum severum et grave. Utro me minus deceat
10 uti, non intelligo. Jocerne tecum per literas? civem (mehercule) non puto esse, qui temporibus his ridere possit. An gravius aliquid scribam? quid est, quod possit graviter a Cicerone scribi ad Curionem, nisi de re publicâ? Atque in hoc genere haec mea causa est, ut neque ea, quae sentio, nec quae
15 non[12] sentio, velim scribere. Quamobrem, quoniam mihi nullum scribendi argumentum relictum est, utar eâ clausulâ, qua[33] soleo; teque ad studium summae laudis cohortabor.

28. (*a*) Epistolam hanc convicio efflagitârunt[7] codicilli tui: nam res quidem ipsa, et is dies[18] quo tu es profectus, nihil mihi ad scribendum argumenti sane dabat[38]. Sed, quemadmodum, coram cum sumus, sermo nobis deesse non solet[36], sic epistolae
5 nostrae debent[48] interdum hallucinari....Reliquis diebus, si quid erit[27], quod te scire opus sit, aut etiam si nihil erit, tamen scribam quotidie aliquid. Prid. Idus neque tibi, neque Pomponio, deero[28]. CICERO.

(*b*) C. PLINIUS SABINO SUO S.—Facis iucunde quod[33] non
10 solum plurimas epistulas meas verum etiam longissimas flagitas; in quibus parcior fui, partim quia tuas occupationes verebar[33], partim quia ipse multum distringebar[29] plerumque frigidis negotiis, quae simul et avocant animum et comminuunt. Praeterea nec materia plura[12] scribendi dabatur[29]. Neque enim
15 eadem nostra conditio quae M. Tulli, ad cuius exemplum nos vocas. Illi enim et copiosissimum ingenium et ingenio qua varietas rerum qua magnitudo largissime suppetebat[7]. Nos quam[5] angustis terminis claudamur etiam tacente[32] me perspicis, nisi forte volumus scholasticas tibi adque, ut ita dicam,
20 umbraticas litteras mittere. Sed nihil minus aptum arbitramur, cum arma vestra, cum castra, cum denique cornua tubas sudorem pulverem soles cogitamus. Habes, ut puto, iustam excusationem, quam[9] tamen dubito an tibi probari velim. Est enim[11] summi amoris negare veniam brevibus epistulis ami-
25 corum, quamvis scias illis constare rationem. Vale.

(27.) Rien ne se ressemble moins que le style épistolaire de Cicéron et celui[16] de Pline, que le style de madame de Sévigné et celui de M. de Voltaire. Lequel faut-il imiter? Ni l'un ni l'autre, si l'on veut être quelque chose; car on n'a véritablement un style que lorsqu'on a celui de son caractère [5] propre et de la tournure naturelle de son esprit, modifié par le sentiment qu'on éprouve en écrivant.

Les lettres n'ont pour objet que de communiquer ses pensées et ses sentiments à des personnes absentes; elles sont[7] dictées par l'amitié, la confiance, la politesse[9]. C'est une[15] con- [10] versation par écrit: aussi le ton des lettres ne doit différer de celui[16] de la conversation ordinaire que par un peu plus de choix[12] dans les objets et de correction[13] dans le style.

Le naturel et l'aisance[12] forment donc le caractère[11] essentiel du style épistolaire: la recherche d'esprit d'élégance ou de [15] correction y est insupportable[22].   Suard.

(28.) William Cowper to Rev. W. Unwin.—My dear Friend, you like[37] to hear[37] from me—This is a very good reason why I should write—but I have[38] nothing to say—This seems equally a good reason why I should not—Yet if you[46] had alighted from your horse at our door this morning, and at this [5] present writing, being five o'clock in the afternoon, had found[28] occasion to say to me—"Mr Cowper[39], you have not spoke since I came in, have you resolved never to speak again?" it would be but a poor[12] reply, if in answer to the summons[13], I should plead inability[12] as my best and only excuse[12]. And this, by the [10] way, suggests to me a seasonable piece[11] of instruction, and reminds me of what I am very apt to forget, when I have any epistolary[11] business in hand; that a letter may be written upon anything or nothing just as that anything or nothing happens[27] to occur. A man that has a journey before him twenty miles [15] in length, which he is to perform on foot, will not hesitate, and doubt, whether he shall set out or not, because he does not readily conceive how he shall ever reach the end of it; for he knows, that by the simple operation[11] of moving[33] one foot forward first, and then the other, he shall be sure to accomplish it. So [20] it is in the present case, and so it is in every similar case.

A letter is written as a conversation is maintained[7], or a journey performed, not by preconcerted or premeditated means but merely by maintaining a progress[12]. If a man may talk without[32] thinking, why may he not write upon the same terms? [25]

29. (*a*) Cicero Attico S.—Accepi ab Isidoro literas, et postea datas[13] binas. Ex proximis cognovi[38] praedia non venisse. Videbis ergo, ut sustentetur per te. De Frustinati, sim odo futuri sumus, erit mihi res opportuna.

5 Meas literas quod[33] requiris, impedior inopiâ rerum, quas nullas habeo literis dignas; quippe cui nec, quae[12] accidunt, nec, quae[12] aguntur, ullo modo probentur. Utinam coram tecum olim potius, quam per epistolas! Hic tua, ut possum, tueor apud hos: caetera Celer. Ipse fugi adhuc omne munus, eo ma-
10 gis, quod ita nihil poterat agi, ut mihi et meis rebus aptum esset.

Quid sit gestum novi, quaeris: ex Isidoro scire poteris: reliqua non videntur esse difficiliora. Tu id, velim, quod scis me maxime velle, cures, ut scribis[37], ut facis. Me[7] conficit sol-licitudo, ex qua etiam summa infirmitas corporis: quâ levata,
15 ero una cum eo, qui negotium gerit, estque in spe magna. Brutus amicus in causa versatur acriter.

Hactenus fuit, quod caute à me scribi posset. Vale. Idi-bus Jun. ex castris.

(*b*) Cicero Attico S.—Ego[16] etsi tamdiu requiesco, quamdiu
20 aut ad te scribo, aut tuas literas lego; tamen et ipse egeo argu-mento epistolarum, et tibi idem accidere certo scio. Quae enim soluto animo familiariter scribi solent[36], temporibus his exclu-duntur: quae autem sunt horum temporum, ea jam contrivi-mus. Sed tamen, ne me totum aegritudini dedam, sumsi mihi
25 quasdam tanquam θέσεις quae et politicae sunt, et temporum horum; ut et abducam animum ab querelis, et in eo ipso[11], de quo agitur, exercear. Eae sunt huiusmodi: εἰ μενετέον ἐν τῇ πατρίδι τυραννουμένῃ; τυραννουμένης δ᾽ αὐτῆς εἰ παντὶ τρόπῳ τυραννίδος κατάλυσιν πραγματευτέον;...
30 In his ego me consultationibus exercens[25], et disserens in utramque partem, tum Graece, tum Latine, et abduco parumper animum a molestiis, et του προυργου τι delibero. Sed vereor, ne tibi ἄκαιρος sim. Si enim recte ambulaverit[27] is qui hanc epistolam tulit, in ipsum tuum diem incidit[36].

30. C. Plinius Fabio Iusto Suo S.—Olim[8] mihi nullas epistulas mittis. Nihil est, inquis[28], quod scribam. At hoc ipsum scribe nihil esse quod scribas, vel solum illud[16] unde in-cipere priores solebant 'si vales, bene est; ego valeo.' Hoc
5 mihi sufficit; est enim maximum. Ludere[12] me putas? serio peto. Fac sciam quid agas, quod[9] sine sollicitudine summa nescire[12] non possum. Vale.

(29.) My dear Friend, A dearth of materials, a conscious-ness[12] that my subjects[11] are for the most part, and must be unin-teresting[22] and unimportant, but above all, a poverty of animal spirits[11], that makes writing[33] much a great fatigue to me, have occasioned my choice[12] of smaller paper[4]. Acquiesce[23] in the just- 5 ness[19] of these reasons for the present; and if ever the times should[29] mend with me, I[17] sincerely promise to amend with them.

Homer says on a certain[34] occasion, that Jupiter, when he was wanted[29] at home, was gone to partake[28] of an entertain-ment[28] provided for him by the Æthiopians. If by Jupiter we 10 understand the weather, or the season, as the ancients frequently did[28], we may say, that our English Jupiter has been absent on account of some[12] such invitation: during the whole month of June he left[28] us to experience[28] almost the rigours[13] of winter. This[34] fine day[38], however, affords[28] us some hope that the feast is 15 ended, and that we shall enjoy his company without the inter-ference[11] of his Æthiopian friends again.

I have[38] bought a great dictionary, and want nothing but Latin authors, to furnish[28] me with the use of it[4]. Had I pur-chased them[4] first, I had begun at the right[45] end[9]. But I 20 could not afford it. I beseech you admire my prudence.

Yours affectionately, WILLIAM COWPER.

Mr Pope to Dr Swift.

I find, though I have less experience[12] than you, the truth[12] of what you told me some time ago, that increase[12] of years makes men more talkative but less writative; to that degree[11], 25 that I now write no letters but of plain business, or plain how-d'yes, to those few[7] I am forced to correspond with either out of necessity or love, and I grow laconick even beyond la-conicism[13]; for sometimes I return only yes, or no, to ques-tionary or petitionary epistles of half a yard long. You and 30 lord Bolingbroke are[8] the only men to whom I write, and always in folio. You are indeed almost the only men I know, who either can write in this age, or whose writings will reach the next; others are mere mortals.

A Monsr. Monsr. Hunter.

(30.) The French lady wrote[47] to her husband, "*J'écris, par-ceque je n'ai rien à faire ; je finis, parceque je n'ai rien à dire.*" I have, however, much better excuses: I[17] have had time enough and much to say, but yet I have been able to write nothing. If you knew what it was to have a thumping heart and a jumping 5 imagination, you would pity your affectionate friend, L. H.

31. C. Plinius Domitio Apollinari Suo S.—Amavi[29] curam et sollicitudinem tuam, quod[33], cum audisses[33] me aestate Tuscos meos petiturum, ne facerem suasisti, dum[25] putas insalubres. Est sane gravis et pestilens ora Tuscorum quae per
5 litus extenditur : sed hi procul a mari recesserunt, quin etiam Appennino, saluberrimo[18] montium, subiacent. Adque adeo ut omnem pro me metum ponas, accipe temperiem caeli, regionis situm, villae amoenitatem. Caelum est hieme frigidum et gelidum; myrtos oleas, quaeque alia[5] adsiduo tepore laetantur,
10 aspernatur ac respuit; laurum tamen patitur atque etiam nitidissimam[13] profert, interdum, sed non saepius quam sub urbe nostra necat. Aestatis mira clementia : semper aër spiritu aliquo movetur; frequentius tamen auras quam ventos habet[28]. Regionis[11] forma pulcherrima. Imaginare amphitheatrum ali-
15 quod[11] inmensum et quale sola rerum natura possit effingere; lata et diffusa planities montibus cingitur, montes summa sui parte procera nemora[19] et antiqua habent[28]. Inde caeduae silvae cum ipso monte descendunt. Sub his per latus omne vineae porriguntur unamque faciem longe lateque contexunt[25] ; quarum[9]
20 a fine imoque quasi margine arbusta nascuntur. Prata florida et gemmea[19] trifolium aliasque herbas teneras semper et molles[19] et quasi novas alunt, cuncta enim perennibus rivis nutriuntur. Magnam capies voluptatem, si hunc regionis situm ex monte prospexeris[27]. Neque enim terras[8] tibi sed formam aliquam ad
25 eximiam pulchritudinem pictam[12] videberis cernere : ea[8] varietate, ea[16] descriptione, quocumque inciderint oculi, reficientur.

32. Italia dehinc[28] primique eius Ligures, mox[20] Etruria, Umbria, Latium, ibi Tiberina ostia et Roma terrarum caput, xvi. m. pass. intervallo a mari. Volscum postea litus et Campaniae, Picentinum inde ac Lucanum Bruttiumque. Nec
5 ignoro ingrati ac segnis animi[13] existimari posse merito, si obiter atque in transcursu ad hunc modum dicatur terra omnium terrarum alumna eadem[17] et parens; sed quid agam? tanta[8] nobilitas omnium locorum, tanta rerum singularum populorumque claritas tenet. Urbs Roma vel sola in ea quo
10 tandem narrari debet opere? Qualiter Campaniae ora per se felixque illa ac beata amoenitas, ut palam sit uno in loco gaudentis opus esse naturae? Iam vero tota ea vitalis ac perennis salubritas, caeli temperies, tam fertiles campi, tam aprici colles, tot montium adflatus, tanta frugum vitiumque et olearum fer-
15 tilitas, tot lacus, tot amnium fontiumque ubertas totam eam perfundens.   Plin. *N. H.* iii.

(31.) Italy is such an exhausted subject[11], that[6], I dare say, you would easily forgive my[83] saying nothing of it. I[4] am nevertheless lately returned from an island, where I passed three or four months, which, were it set out in its true colours[11], might, methinks, amuse you agreeably enough for a minute or two. The island[10] Inarime is an epitome[12] of the whole earth, containing[25] within the compass[11] of eighteen miles, a wonderful variety of hills, vales, ragged rocks, fruitful plains, and barren mountains, all thrown together in a most romantic confusion[12]. The[7] air is in the hottest season constantly refreshed by cool breezes from the sea. The vales produce excellent wheat, but are mostly covered with vineyards, intermixed with fruit-trees. The hills are the greater part covered to the top with vines, some with chestnut-groves. The fields in the northern side are divided[7] by hedge-rows of myrtle. Several fountains and rivulets add to the beauty of this landscape[11], which is[7] likewise set off by the variety of some barren spots[11] and naked rocks. The inhabitants of this delicious[18] isle, as they are without riches and honours, so they are[28] without the vices and follies that attend them: and[9] were they but as much strangers to revenge as they are to avarice and ambition, they might in fact answer the poetical notions[12] of the golden age. But they have got, as an alloy[12] to their happiness, an ill habit[12] of murdering one another on slight offences. BISHOP BERKELEY TO POPE.

(32.) We now came to a short rocky pass, from which you descend into the valley of Campana, the most enchanting spot[11] I have ever seen[5]; it is[9] like a[15] boundless garden, covered entirely with plants and vegetation as far as the eye can reach. On one side are the blue outlines[13] of the sea, on the other an undulating[13] range of hills above which snowy peaks project[28]; and at a great distance Vesuvius and the islands, bathed in blue vapours, start up on the level surface; large avenues of trees intersect the vast space, and a verdant growth forces its way from under every stone. Everywhere you see grotesque aloes and cactuses, and the fragrance and vegetation are[6] quite unparalleled. The pleasure[5] we enjoy in England through men, we here enjoy through nature; and as there is no corner there, however small, of which some one has not taken possession[12] in order to cultivate and adorn it, so here there is no spot[11] which Nature has not appropriated[28], bringing[25] forth on it flowers and herbs, and all that is beautiful. MENDELSSOHN.

33. Mane lectulo continetur, hora secunda calceos poscit, ambulat milia passuum tria nec minus animum quam corpus exercet[12]. Si adsunt amici, honestissimi sermones explicantur: si non, liber legitur; interdum etiam praesentibus[12] amicis, si
5 tamen illi non gravantur. Deinde considit, et liber rursus aut sermo libro potior[12]: mox vehiculum ascendit, adsumit uxorem singularis[11] exempli vel aliquem amicorum, ut me proxime. Peractis septem milibus passuum iterum ambulat mille, iterum residit vel se cubiculo ac stilo reddit. Ubi hora balinei nun-
10 tiata est (est autem hieme nona, aestate octava), in sole, si caret vento, ambulat nudus. Deinde movetur pila vehementer[36] et diu: nam hoc quoque exercitationis genere pugnat cum senectute. Lotus[20] accubat et paulisper cibum differt: interim audit legentem[13] remissius aliquid[12] et dulcius. Per hoc omne
15 tempus liberum[12] est amicis vel eadem facere vel alia, si malint. Adponitur cena non minus nitida quam frugi in argento puro et antiquo: sunt in usu et Corinthia, quibus delectatur nec ad-ficitur[33]. Frequenter comoedis[13] cena distinguitur, ut voluptates quoque studiis condiantur[12]. Sumit aliquid de nocte et aestate:
20 nemini hoc longum est[28]; tanta[8] comitate convivium trahitur. Inde illi post septimum et septuagensimum annum aurium oculorum[14] vigor integer, inde agile et vividum[13] corpus solaque ex senectute prudentia. PLINY.

34. C. PLINIUS FUSCO SUO S.—Quaeris quemadmodum in Tuscis diem aestate disponam. Evigilo cum libuit[27], plerum-que circa horam primam, saepe ante, tardius raro: clausae fenestrae manent. Mire enim silentio et tenebris ab iis[12] quae
5 avocant abductus[6], et liber et mihi relictus[9], non oculos animo sed animum oculis sequor, qui eadem quae mens vident, quo-tiens non vident alia. Cogito, si quid in manibus, cogito ad verbum scribenti[25] emendantique similis, nunc pauciora nunc plura, ut vel difficile[36] vel facile componi tenerive potuerunt.
10 Notarium voco et die admisso quae formaveram[27] dicto: abit rursusque revocatur rursusque dimittitur. Ubi hora quarta vel quinta (neque enim certum dimensumque tempus), ut dies suasit[27], in xystum me vel cryptoporticum confero, reliqua me-ditor et dicto. Vehiculum ascendo. Ibi quoque idem quod
15 ambulans aut iacens[25]. Durat intentio mutatione ipsa refecta: paulum redormio, dein ambulo, mox orationem Graecam Lati-namve clare et intente, non tam vocis causa quam stomachi lego: pariter tamen et illa firmatur[12]. Iterum ambulo, ungor,

(33.) In this season I rise not at four in the morning but a little before eight; at nine, I am called from my study to breakfast, which I always perform alone, in the English style. Our mornings are usually passed[7] in separate studies; we never approach each other's door without a previous message, or [5] thrice knocking[32], and my apartment is already sacred and formidable to strangers. I dress at half-past one, and at two (an early hour[11], to which I am not perfectly reconciled,) we sit down to dinner. After dinner, and the departure[12] of our company, one, two, or three friends, we read together some amusing [10] book, or play at chess, or retire to our rooms, or make visits[12], or go to the coffee-house. Between six and seven the assemblies begin, and[9] I am oppressed only with their number and variety. Between nine and ten we withdraw[28] to our bread and cheese, and friendly converse, which sends[28] us to bed at eleven; but [15] these sober hours are too often interrupted[7] by private or numerous suppers, which I have not the courage to resist, though I practise a laudable abstinence at the best furnished tables. Such[16] is the skeleton of my life. GIBBON.

(34.) *a.* During your stay[13] in London, my hermitage, such as it is, is at your service[11], and you will be expected[6] in it[9]. I am a single man, turned of seventy; but as far from melancholy[13] as a man need be. Hour of dinner, six; tea, between nine and ten; bed, a quarter before eleven. Dinner and tea in society[13]; [5] breakfast, my guests, whoever they are, have at their own hour[11], and by themselves; my breakfast, of which a newspaper, read to me to save my weak eyes, forms an indispensable part, I take by myself. Wine I drink none, being, in that particular[11], of the persuasion of Jonadab the son of Rechab. At dinner, [10] soup as constantly as if I were a Frenchman, an article[11] of my religion[5] learnt in France: meat, one or two sorts, as it may happen; ditto sweet things, of which, with the soup, the principal part of my dinner is composed. BENTHAM.

b. Your notions[12] of friendship are new to me: I believe [15] every man is born with his *quantum;* and he cannot give to one without[32] robbing another. I very well know to whom I[4] would give the first places in my friendship, but[9] they are not in the way; I am condemned[9] to another scene[11], and therefore I distribute it in penny-worths to those about me, and who [20] displease me least; and[9] should do the same to my fellow-

exerceor, lavor[12]. Cenanti[12] mihi, si cum uxore vel paucis, liber
20 legitur: post cenam comoedus aut lyristes[13]: mox cum meis
ambulo, quorum in numero sunt eruditi. Ita variis sermonibus
vespera extenditur, et quamquam longissimus[20] dies cito conditur.
Non numquam ex hoc ordine aliqua[12] mutantur. Nam si diu
iacui vel ambulavi[12], post somnum demum lectionemque non
25 vehiculo sed, quod[5] brevius[11], quia velocius, equo gestor. Inter-
veniunt amici ex proximis oppidis partemque diei ad se trahunt
interdumque lasso mihi opportuna interpellatione subveniunt.

35.   Peropportune mihi redditae sunt litterae tuae, quibus
flagitabas[33] ut tibi aliquid ex scriptis meis mitterem, cum ego id
ipsum destinassem[38]. Addidisti ergo calcaria sponte currenti[13].
Petiturus sum enim ut rursus vaces sermoni quem apud muni-
5 cipes meos habui[28] bibliothecam dedicaturus[20]. Memini quidem
te iam quaedam[12] adnotasse, sed generaliter: ideo nunc rogo ut
non tantum universitati eius attendas, verum etiam particulas
qua soles lima persequaris. Erit enim et post emendationem
liberum[12] nobis vel publicare vel continere. Quin immo fortasse
10 hanc ipsam cunctationem nostram in alterutram sententiam
emendationis ratio deducet, quae[9] aut indignum editione, dum
saepius retractat[33], inveniet aut dignum, dum id ipsum experi-
tur[12], efficiet. Quamquam huius cunctationis meae causae non
tam in scriptis quam in ipso materiae genere[11] consistunt[28]. Est
15 enim paulo quasi gloriosius et elatius[11]. Onerabit[12] hoc modes-
tiam nostram, etiamsi stilus[11] ipse pressus demissusque fuerit,
propterea quod cogimur cum de munificentia parentum nostro-
rum tum de nostra disputare. Anceps hic et lubricus locus
est, etiam cum illi necessitas lenocinatur.

PLINY.

36.   Tristissimus[11] haec tibi scribo, Fundani nostri filia
minore defuncta[9], qua puella[5] nihil umquam festivius, amabilius,
nec modo longiore vita sed prope immortalitate dignius vidi.
Nondum annos quattuordecim impleverat, et iam illi anilis
5 prudentia, matronalis gravitas erat, et tamen suavitas puellaris
cum virginali verecundia. Ut illa patris cervicibus inhaerebat!
ut nos amicos paternos et amanter et modeste complectebatur!
ut nutrices, ut paedagogos, ut praeceptores pro suo quemque
officio diligebat! quam studiose, quam intellegenter lectitabat!

prisoners if I were[29] condemned to jail. I[4] would describe to
you my way of living, if any method could be called so in this
country. I choose companions[4] out of those of least consequence[12] and most compliance[12]: I read the most trifling[5] 25
books I can find; and whenever I write, it is upon the most
trifling subjects[11]; but riding, walking, and sleeping, take up
eighteen of the twenty-four hours. I procrastinate[28] more than
I did twenty years ago; and have several things to finish, which
I put off to twenty years hence; *Hæc est vita solutorum, &c.* 30
SWIFT.

(35.) I send for your edification[12], a Defence of Usury and
some other enormities. Abuse it[9] and keep it, or abuse it[9] and
print it, as to your wisdom may seem meet. Don't let Trail
see it or hear it (the blasphemous 14th letter I mean) till he
has[29] submitted to have his hands tied behind him, for fear of 5
mischief. Douglas's phlegm[13] might be[7] trusted, but he is
Attorney-general by this time[34], and has not time. Don't let
any very flagrant absurdities[12] go for want[12] of correction or
erasure: false or dubious law I don't so much care about,
provided you correct it or clear it up in a note. What I send 10
you at large is only the middle; the condemned head and tail
I send you only the contents of: somewhat of their history[11] you
will find in margin of said contents. The chapter on Blackstone
I give you full power over. Sam, as often as he considered it
in the abstract[11], was for suppressing it, because Blackstone is 15
dead, and it is[30] harping on the old string, &c.; but as often as he
heard it read over, which he did two or three times, he laughed
so heartily at the parody that he could not bear the thoughts of
parting[33] with it[28]. You see there is nothing at all ill-natured in
it, and[9] as it adds a considerable strength, I think, to the 20
argument, I should be rather sorry it were out. BENTHAM.

(36.) My dearest friend, After too long a silence I was
sitting down to write, when, only yesterday morning (such is
now the irregular[19] slowness of the English post[39]), I was suddenly
struck, indeed struck to the heart, by the fatal intelligence[12]
from sir Henry Clinton. Alas! what is life, and what are our 5
hopes and projects! When I embraced her at your departure[12]
from Lausanne, could I imagine that it was for the last time?
when I postponed to another summer my journey to England,
could I apprehend that I never, never should see her again?

10 ut parce custoditeque[36] ludebat! Qua illa temperantia, qua patientia, qua etiam constantia novissimam valetudinem tulit!
Medicis obsequebatur[29], sororem, patrem adhortabatur, ipsam-
que se destitutam corporis viribus vigore animi sustinebat[2P].
Duravit hic illi usque ad extremum nec aut spatio valetudinis
15 aut metu mortis infractus[32] est. O triste plane acerbumque
funus! o morte ipsa mortis tempus indignius! iam destinata
erat egregio iuveni, iam electus nuptiarum dies, iam nos vocati.
Quod gaudium quo maerore mutatum[12] est! Non possum ex-
primere verbis quantum animo vulnus acceperim, cum audivi
20 Fundanum ipsum praecipientem[31], quod in vestes margarita
gemmas fuerat erogaturus, hoc in tus et unguenta et odores
impenderetur. Est quidem ille eruditus et sapiens, sed nunc
omnia quae audiit saepe quae dixit aspernatur expulsisque
virtutibus aliis pietatis est totus. Ignosces, laudabis etiam, si
25 cogitaveris[27] quid amiserit. Amisit enim filiam quae non minus
mores eius quam os vultumque referebat[29] totumque patrem
mira similitudine exscripserat[29].   Pliny.

37. (*a*) Serv. Sulpicius M. T. Ciceroni S. D.—Posteaquam
mihi renuntiatum[12] est de obitu Tulliae[2], filiae tuae, sane quam
pro eo ac debui graviter molesteque tuli, communemque eam
calamitatem existimavi. Qui[9] si istic affuissem, neque tibi
5 defuissem, coramque meum dolorem tibi declarassem. Etsi
genus[11] hoc consolationis miserum atque acerbum est, tamen,
quae in praesentia in mentem mihi venerunt, decrevi brevi ad
te perscribere; non quo ea te fugere existimem, sed quod
forsitan dolore impeditus, minus ea perspicias.
10   Quid est, quod tanto opere te[7] commoveat tuus dolor in-
testinus? Cogita, quemadmodum adhuc fortuna nobiscum
egerit; ea[11] nobis erepta esse, quae hominibus non minus quam
liberi cara esse debent, patriam, honestatem, dignitatem,
honores omnes. Hoc uno incommodo addito[12], quid ad dolorem
15 adiungi potuit? aut qui[8] non in illis rebus exercitatus animus
callere iam debet, atque omnia minoris existimare? An illius[b]
vicem, credo, doles? Quoties in eam cogitationem necesse est
et tu veneris, et[34] nos saepe incidimus hisce temporibus, non
pessime[35] cum iis esse actum, quibus sine dolore licitum est
20 mortem cum vita commutare?...
    Quod si quis etiam inferis sensus est; qui illius in te amor[2]
fuit, pietasque in omnes suos, hoc certe illa te facere non vult.

I always hoped[27] that she would spin her feeble thread to a long [10] duration[11], and that her delicate frame[11] would survive (as is often the case[12]) many constitutions[13] of a stouter appearance[12]. In four days! in your absence[18], in that of her children! But she is now at rest[12]; and if there be a future life, her mild virtues have surely[20] entitled her to the reward of pure and perfect felicity. [15] It is for[8] you that I feel, and[9] I can judge of your sentiments by comparing them with my own. [4]I have lost, it is true, an amiable an affectionate friend whom I had known and loved above three-and-twenty years, and whom I often styled by the endearing name of sister. But you are deprived of the com- [20] panion of your life, the wife of your choice[12], and the mother of your children; poor children! The only consolation in these melancholy trials[11] to which human life is exposed, the only one at least in which I have any confidence[12], is the presence[12] of a real friend; and of that, as far as it[27] depends[28] on myself, you [25] shall not be destitute. GIBBON.

(37.) *a.* *Robert Earl of Leicester to his daughter.*
Oxford, Oct. 10, 1643.
I know it is no purpose[12] to advise[33] you not to grieve; that is not my intention[12]; for such a loss as yours cannot be[7] received indifferently; but though your affection to him whom you [5] loved so dearly, and your reason in valuing[33] his merit[12] did expose you to the danger[11] of that sorrow which now oppresseth you; yet if you consult with that affection, and with that reason, I am persuaded that you will see cause to moderate that sorrow; for[9] your affection to that worthy person[11] may tell [10] you, that even to it you cannot justify yourself, if you lament his being[33] raised to a degree[11] of happiness, far beyond any that he did or could enjoy upon the earth. And your reason will assure you, that beside the vanity[13] of bemoaning[33] that which hath[30] no remedy, you offend him whom you loved, if you hurt [15] that person whom he loved. Remember how apprehensive he was of your dangers, and how sorry for anything that troubled you: imagine that he sees how you afflict and hurt yourself; you will then believe that he may censure you, if you pursue[29] not his desires in being[33] careful of yourself, who was so dear [20] unto him. But he sees you not; he knows not what you do; well, what then? Will[49] you do anything that would displease him if he knew it, because he is where he doth not know it? I am sure that was never in your thoughts[12]; for the rules[11]

Da hoc illi mortuae ; da ceteris amicis ac familiaribus, qui tuo[2]
dolore moerent : da patriae, ut si qua in re opus sit, opera et
25 consilio tuo uti possit.

(*b*) M. Cicero S. D. Titio.—Etsi unus[8] ex omnibus
minime sum ad te consolandum[12] accommodatus, quod tantum
ex tuis molestiis cepi doloris, ut consolatione ipse egerem, tamen,
quum longius a summi luctus acerbitate meus abesset dolor
30 quam tuus, statui nostrae necessitudinis esse meaeque in te
benevolentiae non tacere tanto in tuo maerore tam diu, sed
adhibere aliquam modicam consolationem quae levare dolorem
tuum posset, si minus sanare potuisset[20].   Est autem consolatio
pervulgata quidem illa maxime, quam semper in ore atque in
35 animo habere debemus, homines nos ut esse meminerimus ea
lege natos, ut omnibus telis[45] fortunae proposita sit vita nostra.
Quod si tuum[3] te desiderium movet aut si tuarum[8] rerum cogi-
tatione maeres, non facile exhauriri tibi istum dolorem posse
universum puto : sin illa te res[11] cruciat, quae magis amoris est,
40 ut eorum, qui occiderunt, miserias lugeas[12], ut ea non dicam[31],
quae saepissime et legi et audivi, nihil mali esse in morte, in
qua[9] si resideat sensus, immortalitas illa potius quam mors
ducenda sit, sin sit amissus, nulla videri miseria debeat quae
non sentiatur, hoc tamen non dubitans confirmare possum, ea[16]
45 misceri, parari, impendere rei publicae, quae[9] qui reliquerit,
nullo modo mihi quidem deceptus esse videatur....His ego litteris si quid profecissem[38], existimabam optandum quiddam me
esse adsecutum : sin minus forte valuissent, officio tamen
esse functum viri benevolentissimi atque amicissimi, quem me
50 tibi et fuisse semper existimes velim et futurum esse confidas.

(*c*) C. Plinius Gemino Suo S.—Grave vulnus Macrinus
noster accepit. Amisit uxorem singularis exempli, etiam si
olim fuisset. Vixit cum hac triginta novem annis sine iurgio,
sine offensa. Quam illa reverentiam marito suo praestitit, cum
55 ipsa summam mereretur[25] ! quot quantasque virtutes ex diversis
aetatibus sumptas collegit et miscuit[12] ! Habet quidem Macrinus
grande solacium quod tantum bonum tam diu tenuit[33] : sed hinc
magis exacerbatur quod amisit[33]. Nam[8] fruendis[12] voluptatibus
crescit carendi[12] dolor. Ero ergo suspensus pro homine ami-
60 cissimo, dum admittere avocamenta et cicatricem pati possit,
quam[9] nihil aeque ac necessitas ipsa et dies longa[13] et satietas
doloris inducit. Vale.

of your actions[19] were, and must be, virtue, and affection to [25] your husband, not the consideration[12] of his ignorance or know. ledge[12] of what you do.

b.   *Robert Southey to C. Biddlecombe, Esq.*

Bath, May 6, 1798.

Your letter, my dear friend, has deeply affected me. I [30] knew[27] nothing of your loss[12]; if I had[46], I would immediately have written—not to[31] have intruded on you with idle conso- lations, but at least to say[37] that we think of you in your afflic- tion[12]. I know not how to address[28] you; to say much were impertinence[12]—and yet the silence[13] of a friend is unkind. [35] These things make one tremble. God bless you. God com- fort you. There is at least this mercy[11] in affliction, that it compels us to the only source[11] of consolation.

I will write again soon, and often—anything that but for a moment engages your attention[11] now must be relief[12]. I [40] write[30] on the immediate receipt[12] of your letter—Edith knows[38] not yet your loss, but she will feel with you[9]. Once more, God bless you.   Yours most affectionately,

R. SOUTHEY.

c.   *To Dr Swift.*   [45]

Dec. 5, 1732.

It is not a time[12] to complain that you have not answered me two letters, it is not indeed a time to think of myself, when one[5] of the nearest and longest[12] ties I have ever had, is broken[7] all on a sudden, by the unexpected death of poor Mr [50] Gay. An inflammatory fever hurried him out of this life in three days[9]. He died[9] last night at nine o'clock, not deprived of his senses entirely at last, and possessing them perfectly till within five hours. He asked of you a few hours before, when in acute torment[12] by the inflammation in his bowels and [55] breast.—Good God! how often are we to die before we go quite off this stage? In[9] every friend we lose a part of ourselves, and the best part. God keep those we have left!

Adieu. I can add nothing to what you will feel, and diminish nothing from it. Yet write to me, and soon. Believe[9] [60] no man living loves you better, I believe no man ever did, than   A. POPE.

Dr Arbuthnot, whose humanity you know, heartily com- mends[38] himself to you. Once more adieu, and write to one who is truly disconsolate.   [65]

38. (*a*) Tullius S. P. D. Terentiae et Tulliolae et Ciceroni Suis.—Brundisio profecti sumus a. d. v. Kalendas Maias : per Macedoniam Cyzicum petebamus[38]. O me perditum ! o adflictum ! quid nunc rogem te, ut venias, mulierem aegram
5 et corpore et animo confectam ? Non rogem ? sine te igitur sim[26] ? Opinor, sic agam : si est spes nostri reditus, eam confirmes et rem[11] adiuves : sin, ut ego metuo, transactum est, quoquo modo potes, ad me fac venias. Unum hoc scito : si te habebo[27], non mihi videbor plane perisse. Sed quid Tulliola mea fiet ? Iam
10 id vos videte : mihi deest consilium....Quod reliquum est, sustenta te, mea Terentia, ut potes, honestissime. Viximus : floruimus : non vitium[8] nostrum, sed virtus nostra nos adflixit. Peccatum est nullum, nisi quod[33] non una animam cum ornamentis amisimus. Cura, quod potes, ut valeas, et sic existimes,
15 me vehementius tua miseria quam mea commoveri. Mea Terentia, fidissima atque optima uxor, et mea carissima filiola et spes reliqua nostra, Cicero, valete. Pridie Kalendas Maias Brundisio.

Obsecro te, mea vita, quod ad sumptum attinet, sine alios,
20 qui possunt, si modo volunt, sustinere et valetudinem istam infirmam, si me amas, noli vexare. Nam mihi ante oculos dies noctesque versaris : omnes labores te excipere[31] video : timeo ut sustineas. Sed video in te esse omnia. Qua re ut id, quod speras et quod agis, consequamur, servi valetudini. Longius,
25 quoniam ita vobis placet, non discedam, sed velim quam saepissime litteras mittatis, praesertim, si quid est[26] firmius quod speremus[12]. Valete mea desideria, valete.

(*b*) C. Plinius Calpurniae Suae S.—Numquam sum magis de occupationibus meis questus, quae me non sunt passae
30 aut proficiscentem[12] te valitudinis causa in Campaniam prosequi aut profectam[12] e vestigio subsequi. Equidem etiam fortem[20] te non sine cura desiderarem[12] ; est enim suspensum[11] et anxium[11] de eo quem ardentissime diligas interdum nihil scire : nunc vero me cum absentiae tum infirmitatis tuae ratio incerta et varia
35 sollicitudine exterret. Vereor omnia, imaginor omnia, quaeque[5] natura metuentium est, ea maxime mihi quae maxime abominor fingo. Quo inpensius rogo ut timori meo cotidie singulis vel etiam binis epistulis consulas. Ero enim securior, dum lego[25], statimque timebo, cum legero[20]. Vale.

(38.) *a.* *The Bishop of Rochester to Mrs Morice.*

Montpelier, Sept. 3, 1720.

My dear heart,

I have so much to say to you, that I can hardly say any thing to you till I see you[27]. My heart is full; but it is in vain to begin upon paper what I can never end. I have a thousand desires to see you, which are checked by a thousand fears, lest any ill accident should happen to you in the journey. God preserve you in every step of it[9], and send you safe hither! And I will endeavour, by his blessing and assistance[12], to send you well back again, and to accompany you in the journey, as far as the law of England will suffer me. I stay here only to receive and take care of you, and I live only to help towards lengthening[33] your life, and rendering[33] it, if I can[27], more agreeable to you: for I see not of what use I am, or can be, in other respects[11]. I shall be impatient till I hear[27] you are safely landed, and as impatient after that till you are[27] safely arrived in your winter quarters.

Adieu, my dear heart, till I see you[27]! and till then satisfy[28] yourself, that, whatever uneasiness[12] your journey may give you, my expectation[12] of you, and concern[12] for you, will give me more. I am[36] got to another page, and must do violence to myself to stop here—but I will[46]—and abruptly bid you, my dear heart, adieu, till I bid[27] you welcome to Montpelier.

A line, under your own hand, pray, by the post[39] that first sets[27] out after you land[27] at Bordeaux.

b. *The Countess of Leicester to her husband.*

My dearest heart[30], the apprehension[12] of your going to Hamburgh brought me much trouble[12], till I was[29] told that it would be absolutely left to your choice; and offered to you rather as a compliment[11], than pressed on you as a necessity[11]. Wherefore, in that particular[11] I am now reasonably well satisfied; yet will I not desist from the performance[12] of all that may[49] defend you from that journey: for I[16] am more adverse to it than you can be. You tell[37] me that I do not care for news, but I desire much more than you do afford me; for it is[9] very long since you told me any thing of your opinion[12] concerning the success of your business, which I long extremely to hear; and any thing else that belongs to you I covet with an excessive greediness. Wherefore, my dearest, be a little more liberal in those informations[12], and be assured, that your pains are bestowed for

39. (*a*) C. PLINIUS MAXIMO SUO S.—Nuper me[7] cuiusdam[16] amici languor admonuit optimos esse nos, dum infirmi[12] sumus. Quem[8] enim infirmum[12] aut avaritia aut libido sollicitat[7]? Non amoribus servit[12], non adpetit honores, opes neglegit et quantu-
5 lumcumque ut relicturus[9] satis habet. Tunc deos, tunc hominem esse se meminit, invidet nemini. neminem miratur, neminem despicit ac ne sermonibus quidem malignis aut attendit aut alitur: balinea[8] imaginatur et fontes. Haec summa curarum, summa votorum, mollemque in posterum et pinguem, si con-
10 tingat evadere, hoc est innoxiam beatamque destinat vitam. Possum ergo quod[11] plurimis verbis, plurimis etiam voluminibus[13] philosophi docere conantur ipse breviter tibi mihique praeci-pere, ut tales esse sani[20] perseveremus quales nos futuros pro-fitemur infirmi[12]. Vale.

15 (*b*) Quod[9] me recordantem[25] fragilitatis humanae mise-ratio[11] subit[7]. Quid enim tam circumcisum, tam breve quam hominis vita longissima? Tam angustis[8] terminis tantae multitudinis vivacitas ipsa concluditur, ut mihi non venia solum dignae verum etiam laude videantur illae regiae lacrimae.
20 Nam ferunt[47] Xerxen, cum inmensum exercitum oculis obisset[33], inlacrimasse, quod[11] tot milibus tam brevis immineret[7] oc-casus[30]. Sed tanto magis hoc quidquid est temporis futilis et caduci, si non datur factis[11] (nam horum materia in aliena manu[28]), certe studiis proferamus, et quatenus nobis denegatur
25 diu vivere, relinquamus aliquid quo nos vixisse testemur. Scio stimulis non egere; me tamen tui caritas evocat ut cur-rentem[13] quoque instigem, sicut tu soles me. Ἀγαθὴ δ᾽ ἔρις, cum invicem se mutuis exhortationibus amici ad amorem im-mortalitatis exacuunt. Vale.

PLINY.

40. Ante omnia ne sit vitiosus sermo nutricibus; quas[9], si fieri posset, sapientes Chrysippus optavit, certe, quantum res pateretur[30], optimas eligi voluit. Et morum quidem in his haud dubie prior ratio est: recte tamen etiam loquantur. Has[8] pri-

her[4] satisfaction, who would not refuse to give her life for your service[12].

Penshurst, 28th December, 1636.

My sister is yet here, and all your children are[30] well. 45

July 15, 1712.

(39.) POPE TO STEELE.—You formerly observed[23] to me, that nothing made a more ridiculous figure[11] in a man's life, than the disparity[12] we often find[26] in him sick and well : sickness is a sort[11] of early old age : it teaches us a diffidence[12] in our earthly state[11], 5 and inspires us with the thoughts of a future, better than a thousand volumes[13] of philosophers and divines. Youth, at the very best, is but a betrayer[12] of human life in a gentler and smoother manner[36] than age : it is like[9] a stream that[8] nourishes a plant upon a bank, and causes it to flourish and blossom[19] to 10 the sight[11], but at the same time[17] is undermining it at the root in secret[4]. My[2] youth has dealt more fairly and openly with me ; it[9] has afforded several prospects[11] of my danger, and given me an advantage[11] not very common to young men, that the attractions of the world have not dazzled me very much. When a smart 15 fit[11] of sickness tells me this empty tenement[18] of my body will fall in a little time, I am even as unconcerned as was that honest Hibernian[47], who being[25] in bed in the great storm some years ago, and told the house would tumble over his head, made answer, What care I for the house[44] ! I am only a lodger. 20 I fancy[4] it is the best time to die when one is in the best humour ; and so excessively weak as I now am, I may say with[36] conscience, that I am not at all uneasy at the thought[12], that many men, whom I never had any esteem for, are likely to enjoy this world after me. When I reflect what an incon- 25 siderable little atom every single man is, with respect to the whole creation, methinks it is a shame[12] to be concerned at the removal[12] of such a trivial animal as I am. The morning after my exit[12], the sun will rise as bright as ever, the flowers smell as sweet, the plants spring as green, the world will proceed in 30 its own course, people will laugh as heartily, and marry as fast, as they were used to do.

London, Sept. 15, 1752.

(40.) Dear Dayrolles, In the first place I make my compliments[39] to my god-son, who, I hope, sucks and sleeps heartily, which is all that can yet be desired, or expected from

5 mum audiet puer, harum verba effingere imitando conabitur.
Et natura tenacissimi[12] sumus eorum, quae rudibus annis per-
cepimus : ut sapor, quo nova[12] imbuas, durat ; nec lanarum
colores, quibus simplex ille candor mutatus est, elui possunt.

Si tamen non continget, quales maxime velim nutrices,
10 pueros habere ; paedagogus at unus certo sit assiduus, dicendi
non imperitus, qui, si qua erunt ab his praesente[12] alumno dicta
vitiose[12], corrigat protinus, nec insidere illi sinat. A Graeco
sermone puerum incipere malo : quia Latinum, qui pluribus
in usu est, vel nobis nolentibus perbibet ; simul quia disciplinis
15 quoque Graecis prius instituendus est, unde nostrae fluxerunt[12].
Non tamen hoc adeo superstitiose velim fieri, ut diu tantum
loquatur Graece aut discat, sicut plerisque moris est.　　Hinc
enim accidunt et oris plurima vitia in peregrinum sonum corrupti[12], et sermonis ; cui[9] quum Graecae figurae assidua consue-
20 tudine haeserunt, in diversa quoque loquendi ratione perti-
nacissime durant.　　Non longe itaque Latina subsequi debent,
et cito pariter ire.　　Ita[47] fiet[28], ut, quum aequali cura linguam
utramque tueri coeperimus[33], neutra alteri officiat.

Quidam literis instituendos, qui minores septem annis
25 essent, non putaverunt, quod[11] illa primum aetas[9] et intellectum
disciplinarum capere et laborem pati posset[30].　　Melius autem
qui nullum tempus vacare cura volunt, ut Chrysippus.　　Nam
is[16], quamvis nutricibus triennium dederit, tamen ab illis quoque
iam informandam quam optimis institutis mentem infantium
30 iudicat.　　Cur autem non pertineat ad literas aetas, quae ad
mores iam pertinet ?　　Quid melius alioqui facient, ex quo loqui
poterunt[27] ?　　Faciant enim aliquid necesse est.　　Non ergo perdamus primum statim tempus ; atque eo minus, quod initia
literarum sola memoria constant, quae non modo iam est[28] in
35 parvis, sed tum etiam tenacissima[12] est.　　　　QUINTILIAN.

41.　CICERO ATTICO S.—Avere te certo scio, quum scire,
quid hic agatur, tum mea a me[11] scire.

Armatis hominibus, ante diem tertium Nonas Novembres,
expulsi sunt fabri de areâ nostrâ ; disturbata porticus Catuli,
5 quae, ex senatûs-consulto, consulum locatione reficiebatur, et
ad tectum paene pervenerat.　　Quinti fratris domus primo fracta
coniectu lapidum ex areâ nostrâ, deinde inflammata iussu
Clodii, inspectante Urbe, coniectis ignibus, magna querela et
gemitu, non dicam bonorum, qui nescio an nulli sint, sed plane

him. Though you, like a prudent father, I find[20], carry your 5
thoughts a great deal farther, and are already forming the plan
of his education[12], you have still time to consider of it, but yet
not so much as people commonly think ; for I am very sure,
that children are capable of a certain degree[11] of education[12] long
before they are commonly thought to be so[40]. At a year and 10
a half old I am persuaded that a child might be made to com-
prehend the injustice[12] of torturing flies and strangling birds;
whereas, they are commonly encouraged in both, and their
hearts hardened by habit. There is another thing, which may
be taught him very early, and save him trouble and you 15
expense, I mean languages. You have certainly some French
servants, men or maids, in your house[9]. Let them be chiefly
about him, when he is six or seven months older, and speak
nothing but French to him, while you and madame Dayrolles
speak nothing to him but English ; by which means those two 20
languages will be equally familiar to him. By the time that he
is three years old, he will be too heavy and too active for a
maid to carry, or to follow him ; and one of your footmen
must necessarily attend him. Let that footman be a Saxon,
who speaks nothing but German, and who will, of course, teach 25
him German without any trouble[36]. Some silly people will, I
am sure, tell you, that you will confound the poor child so with
these different languages, that he will jumble them all together
and[9] speak no one well ; and this will be true for five or six
years ; but then he will separate them of himself, and speak 30
them all perfectly.......My compliments to madame Dayrolles.
Adieu, mon cher enfant. LORD CHESTERFIELD.

Tuesday Night, June, 1780.

(41.) My dear Shackleton,
I feel[39] as I ought for your friendly solicitude[12] about me and
this family. Yesterday our furniture was entirely replaced,
and my wife, for the first time since the beginning[12] of this 5
strange tumult, lay at home. During that week* of havoc and
destruction, we were under the roof[11] of my worthy and valuable
friend General Burgoyne, who did everything that could be
done to make her situation[11] comfortable to her. You will hear
with satisfaction[12] that she went through the whole with no 10
small degree[11] of fortitude. On Monday se'nnight, about nine
o'clock, I received undoubted intelligence[11] that, immediately
after the destruction[12] of Savile House, mine was to suffer the

10 hominum omnium.　Ille vehemens ruere[41] ; post hunc furorem, nihil nisi caedem inimicorum cogitare ; vicatim ambire ; servis aperte spem libertatis ostendere : videt[41], si omnes, quos vult, palam occiderit[27], nihilo suam causam difficiliorem, quam adhuc sit, in iudicio futuram.　Itaque, ante diem tertium Idus

15 Novembres, cum Sacra via descenderem, insecutus est me cum suis.　Clamor, lapides, fustes, gladii, haec improvisa omnia.　Discessimus in vestibulum Tettii Damionis.　Qui erant mecum, facile operas aditu prohibuerunt.　Ipse occidi potuit[43] : sed ego diaeta curari incipio ; chirurgiae taedet.

20 Milonis domum, pridie Idus Novemb. expugnare et incendere ita conatus est, ut palam hora V cum scutis homines, eductis gladiis, alios cum accensis facibus, adduxerit.　Ipse domum P. Sullae pro castris sibi ad eam impugnationem sumserat.　Tum ex Anniana Milonis domo Q. Flaccus eduxit viros

25 acres ; occidit homines ex omni latrocinio Clodiano notissimos : ipsum cupivit ; sed ille se in interiora aedium.

　　　Ante diem XII Cal. Decemb. Milo media nocte cum magna manu in Campum venit.　Clodius, cum haberet fugitivorum delectas copias, in Campum ire non est ausus.

30　　　Ante diem VIII Cal. haec ego scribebam, hora noctis nona. Milo Campum iam tenebat[38]...

　　　Nos animo duntaxat vigemus : re familiari comminuti sumus.　Quinti fratris tamen liberalitati, pro facultatibus nostris, ne omnino exhaustus esset, illo recusante, subsidiis ami-

35 corum respondemus.　Quid consilii de omni nostro statu capiamus, te absente, nescimus.　Quare appropera.

　　　42.　(*a*)　C. PLINIUS MAURICO SUO S.—Sollicitas me in Formianum.　Veniam[46] ea[15] conditione ne quid contra commodum tuum facias[28] ; qua pactione invicem mihi caveo.　Neque enim mare[a] et litus sed te, otium, libertatem sequor : alioqui satius

5 est in urbe remanere.　Oportet enim omnia aut ad alienum arbitrium aut ad suum facere : mei certe stomachi haec natura est ut nihil nisi totum et merum velit.　Vale.　　　PLINY.

　　　(*b*)　C. PLINIUS CATILIO SEVERO SUO S.—Veniam[28] ad cenam, sed iam nunc paciscor sit expedita, sit parca, Socraticis

10 tantum sermonibus abundet, in his quoque teneat modum. Vale.

same fate[13]. I instantly came[9] and removed such papers as I thought of most importance. In about an hour after, sixteen [15] soldiers, without my knowledge or desire[12], took possession[12] of the house. Government[13] had, it seems, been apprised[28] of the design, and obligingly afforded[26] me this protection. The next day I had my books and furniture removed, and the guards dismissed. I thought, in the then[3] scarcity[12] of troops, they [20] might be better employed than in looking after[33] my paltry remains[12].

For four nights I kept watch at Lord Rockingham's, or Sir George Savile's, whose houses were garrisoned[7] by a strong body[11] of soldiers, together with numbers[12] of true friends of the [25] first rank, who were willing to share their danger. Savile-house, Rockingham-house, Devonshire-house to be turned into garrisons[31]! *O tempora!* We have all served the country for several years—some of us for near thirty—with fidelity, labour, and affection; and we are obliged to put ourselves under military [30] protection[11] for our houses and our persons[14]. The bell rings[30], and I have[38] filled my time and paper with a mere account of this house; but it is[8] what you[17] will first inquire about[30], though of the least concern[12] to others[4]. God bless you;—remember me[39] to your worthy host. We can hardly think of leaving[30] town;— [35] there is much to be done to repair the ruins[13] of our country and its reputation, as well as to console the number of families ruined by wickedness, masking[25] itself under the colour[11] of religious zeal[11].* Adieu, my dear friend,—our best regards to your daughter[39].   Yours ever,   EDM. BURKE.   40

(42.)   *a.*   My dear Dickens,

I accept[28] your obliging[19] invitation conditionally[36]. If I am[27] invited[7] by any man of greater genius than yourself, or one by whose works I have been more completely interested[20], I will repudiate you, and[9] dine with the more splendid phe- 5 nomenon of the two.   Ever yours sincerely[39].

            Green Street, April 8th, 1810[53].

b.   I wish I may be able to come, but I doubt. Will[47] you come to a philosophical breakfast on Saturday,—ten o'clock[52] precisely? Nothing taken for granted! Everything (except [20] the Thirty-nine Articles) called in question[12]—real philosophers!   Affectionately yours,   SYDNEY SMITH.

       * The Gordon Riots.

43. C. PLIN. ROMANO.—Post longum tempus epistulas tuas, sed tres pariter recepi, omnes elegantissimas, amantissimas, et quales a te venire, oportebat[49]; quarum[9] una iniungis mihi iucundissimum ministerium ut ad Plotinam, sanctissimam femi-
5 nam[2] litterae tuae perferantur: perferentur[46]. Altera epistula nuntias multa te nunc dictare nunc scribere quibus nos tibi repraesentes: gratias ago; agerem[46] magis, si me illa ipsa quae scribis aut dictas legere voluisses. Polliceris in fine, cum certius de vitae nostrae ordinatione aliquid audieris[27], futurum
10 te fugitivum[45] rei familiaris statimque ad nos advolaturum, qui[9] iam tibi compedes nectimus, quas perfringere nullo modo possis[30]. Tertia epistula continebat[38] esse tibi redditam orationem pro Clario eamque visam uberiorem quam dicente me, audiente te, fuerit. Est uberior[46]: multa enim postea inserui.
15 Adicis alias te litteras curiosius scriptas misisse: an acceperim quaeris: non accepi[46] et accipere gestio. Proinde prima quaque occasione mitte, adpositis quidem usuris[51], quas ego (num parcius possum?) centesimas computabo. Vale.

44. (*a*) C. PLINIUS CALPURNIO FLACCO SUO S.—Accepi[37] pulcherrimos turdos, cum quibus parem calculum ponere nec urbis copiis ex Laurentino nec maris[11] tam turbidis[20] tempestatibus possum. Recipies ergo epistulas steriles[19] et simpliciter ingratas
5 ac ne illam[15] quidem sollertiam Diomedis in permutando munere imitantes. Sed, quae facilitas tua, hoc magis dabis[20] veniam quod se non mereri fatentur[33]. Vale.

b. CICERO ATTICO S.—Tandem a Cicerone tabellarius; et (mehercule) literae πεπινωμένως scriptae: quod ipsum προκοπην
10 aliquam significaret: itemque caeteri praeclara[11] scribunt[37]. Leonidas tamen retinet suum illud "Adhuc:" summis vero laudibus Herodes[40]. Quid quaeris[39]? vel verba mihi dari facile patior in hoc; meque libenter praebeo credulum.

Narro tibi[39]; haec loca venusta sunt, abdita certe, et, si
15 quid scribere velis, ab arbitris libera: sed, nescio quomodo, οικος φιλος. Itaque me[7] referunt pedes in Tusculanum. Tu (quaeso) fac sciam, ubi Brutum nostrum, et quo die, videre possim.

c. Obsecro te, quid est hoc? Formiani, qui apud me coenabant[38], Plancum se, aiebant, hunc Buthrotium, pridie quam
20 hoc scribebam, id est IV. Nonas, vidisse demissum, sine phaleris: servulos autem dicere, cum et agripetas ejectos a Buthrotiis. Macte! Sed (amabo te[39]) perscribe mihi totum negotium.

June 3, 1787[53].

(43.) Dear Sir,

It is no encouragement[12] to be good[4], when it is so profitable to do evil: and I[17] shall[48] grow wicked upon principle, and ungrateful by system[19]. If I thought that not answering[33] one letter 5 would always procure me two such, I would be as silent as ingratitude, bad taste, and an unfeeling heart[13], can cause the most undeserving to be. I did[4], indeed[34], receive your first[37] obliging letter, and intended, in the true spirit[11] of a Bristol trader, to have sent you some of my worthless beads and bits 10 of glass, in exchange for your ivory and gold dust; but a very tedious[19], nervous headache[12] has made me less than ever qualified[28] to traffic with you in this dishonest way[11]. I am now better[33], and would not have named being sick at all, if there were[8] any other apology in the world that would have justified 15 my not writing[33]....

I am become a perfect outlaw from all civil society[13] and regular life. I spend almost my whole time in my little garden. From 'morn to noon, from noon to dewy eve,' I am employed[28] in raising dejected pinks, and reforming disorderly honey- 20 suckles. Yours, dear Sir, very faithfully,

HANNAH MORE.

(44.) *a.* Dearest Gee,

Nothing could exceed the beauty of the grapes[37], except the beauty of the pine-apple. How well you understand the clergy[40]!

I am living, young and lively as I am, in the most profound 5 solitude. I saw a crow[4] yesterday, and had a distant view[20] of a rabbit to-day. I have ceased to trouble myself about[4] company[11]. If anybody thinks it worth while to turn aside to the Valley of Flowers, I am most happy[23] to see them; but I have ceased[28] to lay plots, and to toil for visitors. I save myself by 10 this much disappointment[12].

b. Dear Dickens,

Excellent! nothing can[40] be better! You[17] must settle[40] it with the Americans as you can[27], but I[17] have nothing to do with that. I have only to certify[28] that the number is full of wit, 15 humour, and power[11] of description.

I am[38] slowly recovering from an attack[11] of gout in the knee, and am very sorry to have missed[20] you.

SYDNEY SMITH.

5—2

45. (*a*) Cicero Bruto S.—Breves tuae literae : breves dico? immo nullae. Tribusne versiculis his temporibus Brutus⁴ ad me³¹? nihil scripsissem potius. Et requiris meas. Quis unquam ad te tuorum sine meis venit? Quae autem epistola non ⁵ pondus habuit? Quae si ad te perlatae³⁹ non sunt, ne domesticas quidem tuas perlatas arbitror. Ciceroni scribis³⁷ te longiorem daturum epistolam³⁹. Recte id quidem : sed haec quoque debuit⁴⁹ esse plenior. Ego autem, cum ad me de Ciceronis abs te³ discessu scripsisses, statim extrusi tabellarios, literasque ad ¹⁰ Ciceronem ; ut, etiam si in Italiam venisset, ad te rediret. Nihil enim mihi jucundius, nihil illi honestius. Quamquam aliquoties ei scripseram, sacerdotum comitia, mea summa contentione, in alterum annum esse rejecta : quod at te etiam scripseram. Sed videlicet, cum illam pusillam epistolam tuam ¹⁵ ad me dabas, nondum erat tibi id notum. Quare, omni studio a te, mi Brute, contendo, ut Ciceronem meum ne dimittas tecumque deducas.

(*b*) C. Plinius Paulino. — Irascor, nec liquet mihi an debeam, sed irascor. Scis quam sit amor iniquus interdum, ²⁰ inpotens saepe, μικραίτιος semper. Haec tamen causa magna est, nescio an iusta : sed ego¹⁷, tamquam non minus iusta quam magna sit, graviter irascor quod a te tam diu litterae nullae. Exorare me potes uno modo, si nunc saltem plurimas et longissimas miseris. Haec⁸ mihi sola excusatio vera, ceterae falsae ²⁵ videbuntur. Non sum auditurus 'non eram Romae' vel 'occupatior eram.' Illud enim nec di sinant⁴⁰, ut 'infirmior.' Ipse ad villam partim studiis partim desidia fruor, quorum utrumque ex otio nascitur. Vale.

46. Curius M. Ciceroni Suo S.— S. V. B.³⁹ Sum enim χρήσει μὲν tuus, κτήσει δὲ Attici nostri¹⁶ : ergo fructus est tuus, mancipium illius : quod quidem si inter senes coëmptionales venale proscripserit²⁷, egerit non multum. At illa nostra praedi- ⁵ catio quanti est, nos, quod simus, quod habeamus, quod homines existimemur³³, id omne abs te habere! Qua re, Cicero mi, persevera constanter nos conservare et Sulpicii successori nos de meliore nota⁴⁷ commenda, quo facilius tuis praeceptis obtemperare possimus teque ad ver lubentes videre et nostra refigere ¹⁰ deportareque tuto possimus. Sed, amice magne, noli⁴⁰ hanc epistolam Attico ostendere : sine eum errare¹² et putare me virum bonum esse nec solere³⁶ duo parietes de eadem fidelia dealbare⁴⁵. Ergo, patrone mi, bene vale Trionemque meum saluta nostris verbis³⁹. Dat. a. d. IV. Kal. Novembr.

Lyons, Sept. 18, 1739[53].

(45.) Savez vous bien[30], mon cher ami, que je vous hais, que
je vous déteste ? voila des termes un peu fortes ; and that[5] will
save me, upon a just computation[12], a page of paper and six
drops of ink ; which, if I confined myself to reproaches of a
more moderate[11] nature, I should be obliged to employ[28] in using[33]
you according to your deserts. What ! to let[31] any body reside
three months at Rheims, and write but once to them ? Please[39]
to consult Tully de Amicit. page 5, line 25, and you will find
it said in express terms, " Ad amicum inter Remos relegatum
mense uno quinquies scriptum esto ;" nothing more plain, or
less liable to false interpretations[13]. Now[34] because, I suppose,
it will give you pain to know we are in being[28], I take this
opportunity[28] to tell[48] you that we are at the ancient and cele-
brated Lugdunum, a city situated[5] upon the confluence of the
Rhone and Saone (Arar, I should[49] say), two people, who[5], though
of tempers[13] extremely unlike, think fit to join hands here, and[9]
make a little party[12] to travel to the Mediterranean in company[11];
the lady[10] comes gliding along through the fruitful plains of
Burgundy ; the gentleman[10] runs all rough and roaring down
from the mountains of Switzerland to meet her ; and with all
her soft airs[12] she likes him never the worse ; she[17] goes through
the middle of the city in state[12], and he passes incog. without
the walls, but[9] waits for her a little below.   GRAY.

(46.) Lucy, Lucy, my dear child[39], don't tear your frock ;
tearing[33] frocks is not of itself a proof[12] of genius ; but write as
your mother writes, act as your mother acts ; be frank, loyal,
affectionate, simple, honest ; and then integrity[13] or laceration
of frock is of little import.

And Lucy, dear child, mind your arithmetic. You[47] know,
in the first sum of yours[5] I ever saw, there was a mistake. You
had carried two and you ought[49], dear Lucy, to have carried but
one. Is this a trifle ? What[47] would life be without arithmetic,
but a scene[11] of horrors ?

You are going to Boulogne, the city of debts[13], peopled by
men who never understood arithmetic ; by the time you return[27], I shall probably have received my first paralytic stroke,
and shall have lost all recollection[12] of you ; therefore I now give
you my parting[18] advice[12]. Don't marry anybody who has[30]
not a tolerable understanding and a thousand a year, and God
bless[39] you, dear child.   SYDNEY SMITH.

47. (*a*) Cicero Attico.—Undecimo die postquam a te discesseram[33], hoc literularum exaravi, egrediens e villa ante lucem : atque eo die cogitabam[38] in Anagnino, postero autem in Tusculano ; ibi unum diem. V. Calend. igitur ad constitutum :
5 atque utinam continuo ad complexum meae Tulliae, ad osculum Atticae, possim currere ! quod quidem ipsum scribe, quaeso, ad me ; ut, dum consisto[41] in Tusculano, sciam, quid garriat : sin rusticatur, quid scribat ad te : eique interea aut scribe salutem, aut nuntia[39], itemque Piliae : et tamen, etsi continuo congres-
10 suri sumus, scribes[40] ad me, si quid habebis[27]. Cum complicarem hanc epistolam, noctuabundus ad me venit cum epistola tua tabellarius : qua lecta[9], de Atticae febricula scilicet valde dolui. Reliqua, quae exspectabam, ex tuis literis cognovi omnia.

b. Ego me[17] spero Athenis fore[27] mense Septembri. Tu-
15 orum[4] itinerum tempora scire sane[34] velim. Ευηθειαν Sempronii Rufi cognovi ex epistola tua Corcyraea. Quid quaeris ? invideo potentiae Vestorii. Cupiebam[38] etiam nunc plura garrire ; sed lucet ; urget turba : festinat Philogenes. Valebis igitur ; et valere Piliam et Caeciliam nostram jubebis literis. Salvebis a
20 meo Cicerone[30].

48. C. Plinius Curio.—Officium consulatus iniunxit mihi ut[11] rei publicae nomine principi gratias agerem. Quod[5] ego in senatu cum ad rationem et loci et temporis ex more fecissem[33], bono civi convenientissimum credidi eadem illa spa-
5 tiosius et uberius volumine amplecti. Cepi autem non medio-crem voluptatem quod, hunc librum cum amicis recitare volu-issem[33], non per codicillos, non per libellos, sed 'si commodum' et 'si valde vacaret' admoniti (numquam porro aut valde vacat Romae aut commodum est audire recitantem[13]), foedissimis in-
10 super tempestatibus, per biduum convenerunt, cumque modestia mea finem recitationi facere voluisset, ut adicerem tertium diem exegerunt. Mihi[4] hunc honorem habitum putem an studiis? studiis malo, quae[5] prope extincta refoventur. Ad cui materiae[6] hanc sedulitatem praestiterunt ? nempe quam in senatu quoque,
15 ubi perpeti necesse erat, gravari tamen vel puncto temporis solebamus[36], eandem nunc et qui recitare et qui audire triduo velint inveniuntur. Ego cum studium audientium tum iudicium mire probavi : animadverti enim severissima[11] quaeque vel maxime satisfacere. Habes acta mea tridui ; quibus cognitis
20 volui tantum te voluptatis absentem et studiorum nomine et meo capere, quantum praesens percipere potuisses[49]. Vale.

(47.) *a.* My dear Friend,

Come when you will, or when you can[27], you[47] cannot come[43] at a wrong time, but we shall expect[40] you on the day mentioned. I scratch[30] this between dinner and tea ; a time[5] when I cannot write much without[35] disordering my noddle, and bringing a flush into my face. You will excuse me therefore, if through respect for the two important[18] considerations[11] of health and beauty, I conclude myself, Ever yours, WILLIAM COWPER.

Oct. 31, 1779.

b. I wrote my last letter merely to inform[30] you, that I had nothing to say[37], in answer to which you have said nothing. I admire the propriety[12] of your conduct[11], though I[17] am a loser[12] by it. I will[47] endeavour to say something now, and shall hope for something[17] in return.

I have been[7] well entertained[28] with Johnson's biography, for which I thank you[37] : with one exception I think he has acquitted[28] himself with his usual[36] good sense. His treatment[12] of Milton is unmerciful to the last degree....

I could talk a good while longer, but I have no room[38] ; our love attends you[39]. Yours affectionately, WM. COWPER.

We are sorry[37] for little William's illness. We are sorry too for Mr ———'s dangerous condition. But he that is well prepared for the great journey cannot enter on it too[24] soon for himself, though his friends will weep at his departure[13].

(48.) My lectures are gone to the dogs[45], and are utterly forgotten. I knew nothing of moral philosophy[4], but I was thoroughly aware[20] that I wanted £200 to furnish my house. The success[12], however, was prodigious ; all Albemarle-street blocked up with carriages, and such an uproar as I never remember to have been excited by any other literary imposture[7]. Every week[53] I had a new theory[11] about conception and perception, and supported by a natural manner a torrent of words, and an impudence scarcely creditable in this prudent[18] age. Still, in justice[12] to myself, I must say there were some[17] good things in them. But good and bad are all gone[4]. I think the University[13] uses[28] you and us very ill, in keeping[33] you so strictly at Cambridge. If Jupiter could[49] desert Olympus for twelve days to feast with the harmless Ethiopians, why may[49] not the Vice-Chancellor commit the graduating[18], matriculating world for a little time to the inferior deities, and[9] thunder and lighten at the tables of the metropolis ? Our kind regards to Mrs Whewell[39].

SYDNEY SMITH.

49. (*a*) CICERO TREBATIO.—Nisi ante Roma profectus
esses, nunc eam certe relinqueres. Quis enim tot interregnis
jure consultum desiderat ? Sed heus tu, quid agis ? ecquid fit ?
Video enim te iam iocari per litteras. Haec signa meliora sunt
5 quam in meo Tusculano. Sed quid sit scire cupio. Consuli
quidem te a Caesare scribis[37], sed ego tibi ab illo[17] consuli
mallem.

Audi, Testa mi : utrum[8] superbiorem[35] te pecunia facit an
quod te imperator consulit[33] ? Moriar[39], ni, quae tua gloria est,
10 puto te malle a Caesare consuli quam inaurari. Si vero utrumque est, quis te feret praeter me, qui omnia ferre possum ?
Sed, ut ad rem redeam, te istic invitum non esse vehementer
gaudeo, et, ut illud erat molestum, sic hoc est iucundum. Tantum metuo, ne artificium tuum tibi parum prosit. Nam, ut
15 audio, istic

> *non ex iure manum consertum, sed mage ferro*
> *rem repetunt.*

Sed, ut ego quoque te aliquid admoneam de vestris cautionibus,
Treviros vites censeo : audio capitales esse : mallem auro, aere,
20 argento essent.

(*b*) Accepi a te aliquot epistolas uno tempore, quas tu diversis temporibus dederas[39]. Sic habeto[39], non tibi maiori esse
curae, ut iste tuus a me[3] discessus quam fructuosissimus tibi sit,
quam mihi. Itaque, quoniam vestrae cautiones infirmae sunt,
25 Graeculam tibi misi cautionem chirographi mei. Sed, ut ad
epistolas tuas redeam, caetera belle, illud[16] miror : quis solet
eodem exemplo plures dare, qui sua manu[14] scribit ? Nam quod[33]
in palimpsesto[40], laudo equidem parcimoniam. Sed miror quid
in illa chartula fuerit, quod delere malueris quam haec non
30 scribere, nisi forte tuas formulas. Non enim puto te meas
epistolas delere, ut reponas tuas. An hoc significas, nihil fieri,
frigere te, ne chartam quidem tibi suppeditare ? Iam[34] ista tua
culpa est, qui[33] verecundiam tecum extuleris et non hic nobiscum
reliqueris[27]. Tu, si intervallum longius erit[27] mearum litterarum,
35 ne sis admiratus : eram[30] enim abfuturus mense Aprili. Cura
ut valeas. VI. Idus April. de Pomptino[53].

Epistolam tuam, quam accepi ab L. Arruntio, conscidi in-
nocentem[30] : nihil enim habebat quod non vel in connectione recte
legi posset. Sed et[31] Arruntius ita te mandasse aiebat et tu
40 ascripseras. Verum illud esto. Nihil. te ad me postea scrip-
sisse demiror, praesertim tam novis rebus.   CICERO.

(49.) *a.* My dear Manning,—The general scope[11] of your letter afforded no indications of insanity, but some particular points[11] raised a scruple[29]. For God's sake don't think any more of "Independent Tartary." Think what a sad pity[12] it would be to bury such[35] parts in heathen countries, among nasty 5 unconversable, Tartar-people! Some say, they are Cannibals; and[34] then, conceive[31] a Tartar-fellow eating my friend, and[9] adding the cool malignity of mustard and vinegar! I am afraid 'tis the[13] reading[33] of Chaucer has misled you; his foolish stories about Cambuscan, and the ring, and the horse of brass. 10 Believe me[39], there are no[48] such things. The Tartars, really[34], are a cold, insipid set. You'll be sadly moped[4] (if you are[27] not eaten) among them. Pray *try* and cure yourself. Take hellebore. Shave yourself oftener. Accustom yourself to write familiar letters, on common subjects[11], to your friends in 15 England, such as are of a moderate understanding[12]. I supped last night[52] with[50] Rickman, and met a merry captain, who pleases himself vastly with once having[33] made a pun at Otaheite in the O. language. Rickman is a man "absolute in all numbers." I think I may one day bring you acquainted, 20 if you do[27] not go to Tartary first; for you'll never come back. Have a care, my dear friend, of Anthropophagi! their[9] stomachs are always craving. 'Tis terrible to be weighed out at fivepence a-pound; to sit at a table not as a guest, but as a meat. God bless you: do[39] come to England. Air and exercise may[49] 25 do great things. Your sincere friend, C. LAMB.

b. Dear Miss H.,—Mary has such[31] an invincible reluctance to any[17] epistolary[18] exertion, that I am[38] sparing her a mortification by taking[33] the pen from her. The plain truth[12] is, she writes such a mean detestable hand, that she is ashamed of the 30 formation of her letters. There is an[15] essential poverty and abjectness in the frame of them[9]. They look like begging[22] letters[9]. And then she is sure[36] to omit a most substantial word in the second draught[39], (for she never ventures an epistle without a foul copy[39] first,) which is obliged to be interlined[7]; 35 which spoils the neatest epistle, you know[39]. Her figures, 1, 2, 3, 4, &c., where she has occasion[12] to express numerals[11], as in the date[12], (25th April, 1823,) are not figures, but[34] figurantes; and[9] the combined posse[10] go staggering up and down shamelessly, as drunkards in the daytime. It is no better[40] when she 40 rules her paper. Her lines[9] are not less erring than her words.

C. LAMB.

50. (*a*) CICERO VARRONI.—Περὶ δυνατῶν me scito[39] κατὰ Διό-
δωρον κρίνειν. Quapropter, si venturus es, scito necesse esse te
venire: sin autem non es, τῶν ἀδυνάτων est te venire[33]. Nunc
vide utra te κρίσις magis delectet, Chrysippi an haec, quam
5 noster Diodotus non[28] concoquebat. Sed de his etiam rebus,
ociosi quum erimus[37], loquemur: hoc etiam κατὰ Χρύσιππον
δυνατὸν est. De Coctio mihi gratum est: nam id etiam Attico
mandaram. Tu si minus ad nos[28], nos accurremus ad te. Si
hortum in bibliotheca habes, deerit nihil.

10 *b.* MARCUS Q. FRATRI S.—Calamo et atramento temperato,
charta etiam dentata, res agetur[28]. Scribis[37] enim, te meas
literas superiores vix legere potuisse: in quo[5] nihil eorum, mi
frater, fuit, quae putas: neque enim occupatus eram, neque
perturbatus, nec iratus alicui: sed hoc facio semper, ut, quicum-
15 que calamus in manus meas venerit, eo sic utar, tamquam bono.

51. (*a*) Q. CICERO S. P. D. TIRONI SUO.—Verberavi te
cogitationis tacito dumtaxat convicio, quod fasciculus alter
ad me iam siue tuis[50] litteris perlatus est. Non potes effugere
huius culpae poenam te patrono[13]. Marcus[4] est adhibendus;
5 is[16]que diu[3] et multis lucubrationibus commentata oratione vide
ut probare possit te non peccasse. Plane te rogo, sicut olim[48]
matrem nostrum facere memini, quae lagenas etiam inanes
obsignabat, ne dicerentur[14] inanes aliquae fuisse, quae furtim
essent[30] exsiccatae, sic tu, etiam si quod scribas non habe-
10 bis[27], scribito tamen, ne furtum cessationis quaesivisse videaris.
Valde enim mi semper et vera et dulcia tuis epistolis nun-
ciantur[12]. Ama nos et vale.

(*b*) CICERO S. D. M. MARIO.—A. d. IX. Kal. in Cumanum
veni cum Libone tuo vel nostro potius: in Pompeianum sta-
15 tim[40] cogito, sed faciam ante te certiorem[39]. Te quum semper
valere cupio tum certe, dum hic sumus. Vides enim, quanto
post[8] una futuri simus. Qua re, si quod constitutum cum
podagra habes, fac[39] ut in alium diem differas. Cura igitur ut
valeas et me hoc biduo aut triduo[53] exspecta.

20 *c.* Dii immortales? quam me conturbatum[12] tenuit[7] epistolae tuae prior pagina! quid autem iste in domo tuâ[3] casus
armorum? sed hunc quidem nimbum[45] cito[35] transiisse laetor.
Hoc tempore, quod scriberem, nihil erat[38]; eoque minus, quod
dubitabam, tu has ipsas literas essesne accepturus: erat enim
25 incertum, visurusne te esset tabellarius. Ego tuas literas vehementer exspecto. CICERO.

(50.) *a.* My dear fellow,—For me to come to Cambridge
now is one of heaven's[13] impossibilities. Metaphysicians tell us,
even it can work nothing which implies a contradiction. But
for you[17] to come to London instead!—muse upon it, revolve it,
cast it about in your mind, think upon it. Excuse the paper ; 5
it is all I have.

   b. *Ecquid meditatur Archimedes ?* What is Euclid doing ?
What hath happened[39] to learned Trismegist ? Doth he take
it in ill part, that his humble friend did not comply[28] with his
courteous invitation[12]? Let it suffice[39], I could not come. Are 10
impossibilities nothing?—be they abstractions of the intellect?
—or not (rather) most sharp and mortifying realities[12]? Observe the superscription[12] of this letter. In adapting[33] the size
of the letters, which constitute *your* name and Mr *Crisp's* name[11]
respectively[4], I had an eye[12] to your different stations in life. 15
'Tis truly[34] curious, and must be soothing to an *aristocrat.* I
wonder it has never been[7] hit on before my time[11].

C. LAMB.

May 10, 1790.

(51.) My dear Mrs. Frog,
   You have by this time, I presume[28], heard[37] from the Doctor,
whom I desired to present[28] to you our best affections, and to
tell[46] you that we are well. He sent an urchin, expecting that 5
he would find you at Bucklands, charged with divers articles[11],
and among others with letters, or at least with a letter, which I
mention, that if the boy should be lost, together with the dis-
patches, past all possibility of recovery[12], you may yet know that
the Doctor stands acquitted of not writing[33]. That[47] he is utterly 10
lost (that is to say, the boy, for the Doctor being the last antecedent, as the grammarians say, you might[49] otherwise suppose
that he was intended) is the more probable, because he was
never four miles from his home before, having only travelled[26]
at the side of a plough team; and when the Doctor gave him 15
his directions[12] to Bucklands, he asked, very naturally, if that
place[11] was in England. So what has become[39] of him Heaven
knows!...

   I cannot learn from any creature whether the Turnpike
Bill is alive or dead;—so ignorant am I, and by such igno- 20
ramuses surrounded[7]. But if I know little else, this at least I
know, that I love you, and Mr Frog; that I long for your
return, and that I am,   Ever yours,   WM. COWPER.

52. (*a*) Tullius Tironi Suo S. P. D. et Cicero et Q.
Frater et Q. F.—Varie sum adfectus tuis litteris: valde
priore pagina perturbatus, paullum altera recreatus. Qua re
nunc quidem non dubito quin, quoad[30] plane valeas, te neque
5 navigationi neque viae committas. Satis te mature videro, si
plane confirmatum videro[27]...Sic habeto[30], mi Tiro, neminem esse
qui me amet quin idem[17] te amet, et quum[34] tua et mea maxime
interest te valere, tum multis est curae. Adhuc, dum mihi
nullo loco deesse vis[12], numquam te confirmare potuisti. Nunc
10 te nihil impedit: omnia depone, corpori[14] servi. Quantam diligentiam in valetudinem tuam contuleris[27], tanti me fieri a te
iudicabo. Vale, mi Tiro, vale, vale et salve. Lepta tibi
salutem dicit et omnes. Vale. VII. Idus Novembr. Leucade[30].

(*b*) Sollicitat[7], ita vivam[30], me tua, mi Tiro, valetudo, sed
15 confido, si diligentiam quam instituisti adhibueris[27], cito te fir-
mum fore. Libros compone: indicem, quum Metrodoro lube-
bit[27], quoniam eius arbitratu vivendum est. Cum olitore[40], ut
videtur. Tu potes Kalendis spectare gladiatores[13], postridie
redire, et ita censeo. Verum, ut videbitur[27]. Cura te, si me
20 amas, diligenter. Vale.

(*c*) Tullius S.P.D. Tironi.—Quid igitur[30]? non sic oportet?
Equidem censeo sic: addendum etiam 'suo.' Sed, si placet,
invidia vitetur: quam[5] quidem ego[17] saepe contempsi. Si me
amas, quod quidem aut facis[46] aut perbelle simulas, indulge vale-
25 tudini tuae, cui[9] quidem tu adhuc, dum mihi deservis[33], servisti
non satis. Fac bellus revertare: non modo te, sed etiam Tusculanum nostrum plus amem. Horologium mittam et libros,
si erit sudum. Sed tu nullosne tecum libellos? an pangis aliquid Sophocleum? Fac opus appareat. Cura te diligenter.
30 Vale.   Cicero.

53. M. Cicero S. D. Volumnio.—Quod[33] sine praenomine
familiariter, ut debebas[49], ad me epistolam misisti, primum addu-
bitavi num a Volumnio[2] senatore esset, quocum mihi est magnus
usus, deinde εὐτραπελία litterarum fecit, ut intelligerem tuas
5 esse. Quibus[5] in litteris omnia mihi periucunda fuerunt praeter
illud, quod parum diligenter possessio salinarum mearum a te[13]
procuratore defenditur. Ais enim, ut ego discesserim, omnia
omnium dicta, in his etiam Sestiana, in me conferri. Quid?
tu id pateris? non me defendis? non resistis? Equidem spera-

A Paris, vendredi 11 juin 1677.

(52.) Il me semble que pourvu que je n'eusse mal qu'à poitrine, et vous qu'à la tête, nous ne ferions qu'en rire; mais votre[4] poitrine me tient fort au cœur, et vous[17] êtes en peine de ma tête; hé bien! je lui ferai, pour l'amour[12] de vous, plus 5 d'honneur qu'elle ne mérite; et, par la même raison, mettez bien, je vous supplie[39], votre petite poitrine dans du coton. Je suis fâchée que vous m'ayez écrit une si grande lettre en arrivant[33] à Melun; c'était[8] du repos qu'il vous fallait d'abord. Songez à vous, ma chère enfant; songez à me venir achever votre 10 visite. Votre santé[13] est plus propre à exécuter ce project que votre langueur; et comme vous voulez que mon cœur et ma tête soient libres, ne croyez pas que cela puisse être, si votre mal augmente[27]. Si vous voulez donc me faire tout le plus grand bien que[5] je puisse desirer, mettez toute votre application[12] 15 à sortir de cet état. Adieu, ma très-chère; je me trouve toute nue, toute seule, de ne plus vous avoir. Il ne faut regarder que la Providence dans cette séparation : on n'y comprendrait rien autrement; mais c'est peut-être par-là que Dieu veut vous redonner votre santé. Je le crois, je l'espère, vous nous en avez quasi répondu; donnez-y donc tous vos soins, je vous en conjure. 20

Mme DE SEVIGNE.

Kensington, 22nd November, 1850.

(53.) My dear William Allingham,—For I think we know and regard[28] one another by this time sufficiently to drop the "Sir;" and by-and-by, I hope, we will drop all addressing[33] whatsoever inside our letters, like two friends talking[23] who are 5 sure of one another's affection[11]—an admirable ancient custom still observed[28] in some countries, and[9] which[5] I have long wished to see introduced[20] into this. I should have thanked you immediately both for your congratulations and your poem, which of course[31] is also welcome[39], but I wanted to say what I could not 10 say till now; nor, indeed, can I say even that as precisely as I wish till I have[27] had another talk[12] with my fellows in the *Journal.* This[16] much, however, forthwith, that you must be paid for your verses, and will (that[5] is a sine-qua-non), and that I want you very much to try your hand at some prose 15 tales—also, of course, to be paid for[50]. Do you feel inclined[23] to this? and do you think you could send me a specimen before the month is out?

Pray[39] try for me if you can[27], and believe me, ever affectionately yours,

LEIGH HUNT. 20

10 bam ita notata me reliquisse genera[11] dictorum meorum, ut
cognosci sua sponte possent. Sed quoniam tanta faex est in
urbe, ut nihil tam[24] sit ἀκύθηρον quod non alicui venustum esse
videatur pugna, si me amas, nisi acuta ἀμφιβολία, nisi elegans
ὑπερβολή, nisi παράγραμμα bellum, nisi ridiculum παρὰ προσ-
15 δοκίαν, nisi caetera, quae sunt a me in secundo libro DE
ORATORE per Antonii personam disputata de ridiculis ἔντεχνα
et arguta apparebunt[27], ut sacramento contendas mea non esse.
Nam de iudiciis quod quereris[12], multo laboro minus. Trahantur
per me[39] pedibus omnes rei, sit vel Selius tam eloquens, ut possit
20 probare se liberum: non laboro[3]. Urbanitatis[34] possessionem,
amabo[39], quibusvis interdictis defendamus: in qua te unum
metuo, contemno caeteros.

54. Cicero Paeto.—Dupliciter delectatus sum tuis litteris,
et quod ipse risi et quod te intellexi[38] iam posse ridere. Me
autem a te, ut scurram velitem, malis oneratum[27] esse non
moleste tuli. Illud[16] doleo, in ista loca venire me, ut consti-
5 tueram, non potuisse: habuisses enim non hospitem, sed con-
tubernalem. At quem virum! non eum, quem tu es solitus[36]
promulside conficere. Integram famem ad ovum adfero: itaque
usque ad assum vitulinum opera perducitur. Illa mea[11], quem
solebas antea laudare, "O hominem facilem! o hospitem non
10 gravem!" abierunt. Proinde te para: cum homine et edaci tibi
res[45] est et qui iam aliquid intelligat: ὀψιμαθεῖς autem homines
scis quam insolentes sint. Dediscendae tibi sunt sportellae et
artolagani tui. Nos iam etiam artis tantum habemus, ut Ver-
rium tuum et Camillum—qua munditia homines[13]! qua ele-
15 gantia!—vocare saepius audeamus. Sed vide audaciam: etiam
Hirtio cenam dedi, sine pavone tamen. Haec igitur est nunc
vita[11] nostra: mane salutamus[39] domi et[34] bonos viros multos,
sed tristes[19], et hos laetos victores, qui me quidem perofficiose et
peramanter[36] observant[12]. Ubi salutatio defluxit[45], litteris me
20 involvo[45], aut scribo aut lego. Veniunt etiam qui me audiunt[12]
quasi doctum hominem, quia paullo sum quam ipsi doctior.
Inde corpori[14] omne tempus datur. Patriam eluxi iam et gravius[36] et diutius quam ulla mater unicum filium. Sed cura,
si me amas, ut valeas, ne ego te iacente bona tua comedim.
25 Statui enim tibi ne aegroto quidem parcere.

(53.) *b.* Not a sentence, not a syllable of Trismegistus shall be lost through my neglect[12]. I am his word-banker, his storekeeper of puns and syllogisms. You cannot conceive the strange joy which I felt at the receipt[13] of a letter from Paris. It seemed to give me a learned[18] importance, which placed me above 5 all who had not Parisian correspondents[11]. Believe[39] that I shall carefully husband every scrap, which will save you the trouble of memory[12], when you come back[27]... Your letter was just what a letter should be[49], crammed, and very funny. Every part[13] of it[9] pleased me till you came to Paris; then[34] your 10 philosophical indolence, or indifference, stung me. You cannot stir from your rooms till you know the language[43]! Are men all tongue and ear? Have these creatures, that you and I profess to know something about, no[48] faces, gestures, gabble, no folly, no absurdity, no similitude nor dissimilitude 15 to English? LAMB.

Mons. de Coulanges à Madame de Sévigné.

À Saint-Martin, le 16 février 1696.

(54.) Mais pourquoi ne pas écrire[40] quelquefois *in-folio*, quand on trouve un beau[19] et bon papier, qui vous y invite[30]? J'ai reçu ici, ma très-aimable gouvernante, la grande et la petite 5 lettre que vous avez bien[29] voulu m'écrire en même jour pour répondre à toutes les miennes; et je suis[7] toujours charmé de votre style et de votre bon et loyal commerce. Il y a tantôt quinze jours que[8] je suis ici auprès de cet adorable cardinal; et il y a tantôt quinze jours que je suis l'homme du monde le plus 10 heureux; bonne compagnie[13]; par-tout de grands feux, bonne symphonie, table bien servie, vins délicieux; enfin, Madame, voici le pays de cocagne au pied de la lettre[45]. Les officiers même de cette maison ont une[15] rage de toujours apprendre[33] quoiqu'ils soient maîtres passés; en sorte qu'ils nous feront 15 crever à la fin; ils possédaient au suprême degré tous les ragoûts les plus exquis de France et d'Italie: les voilà devenus apprentifs sous le meilleur officier de cuisine d'Angleterre, pour être bientôt en ragoûts anglais beaucoup plus savants que lui; nous ne savons donc plus où nous en sommes; tous nos ragoûts 20 parlent des langues différentes; mais[9] ils se font si bien entendre que nous les mangeons, sous quelque figure et dans quelque sauce qu'ils se présentent. Vous voyez bien, Madame, que ce seul article[11] de la bonne chère demandait un *in-folio*.

55. Cicero S. D. L. Papirio Paeto.—Accepi tuas litteras plenissimas[18] suavitatis, ex quibus intellexi[38] probari tibi meum consilium, quod, ut Dionysius tyrannus, quum Syracusis pulsus esset[33], Corinthi dicitur ludum aperuisse, sic ego sublatis[12] iudi-
5 ciis, amisso[33] regno forensi, ludum quasi habere coeperim[33]. Quid quaeris[39]? me[7] quoque delectat consilium: multa enim consequor: primum, id quod maxime nunc opus est, munio me ad haec tempora. Sequitur illud[16]: ipse melior fio: primum valetudine, quam intermissis[12] exercitationibus amiseram: deinde ipsa
10 illa, si qua fuit in me, facultas orationis, nisi me ad has exercitationes rettulissem, exaruisset. Extremum illud est, quod tu nescio an primum putes: plures iam pavones confeci quam tu pullos columbinos. Tu[4] istic te Hateriano iure delectas, ego me hic Hirtiano. Veni igitur, si vir es, et disce a me προλεγομέ-
15 vας, quas quaeris: etsi sus Minervam[45]. Sed quoniam, ut video, aestimationes tuas vendere non potes neque ollam denariorum implere, Romam tibi remigrandum est, Satius est hic cruditate quam istic fame[40]. Video te bona perdidisse: spero idem istuc[46] familiares tuos. Actum[45] igitur de te est, nisi pro-
20 vides. Potes mulo isto, quem[5] tibi reliquum dicis esse, quoniam cantherium comedisti, Romam pervehi. Sella tibi erit in ludo tamquam hypodidascalo proxima: eam pulvinus sequetur.

56. Cicero S. D. Paeto.—Accubueram[38] hora nona[52], quum ad te harum [litterarum] exemplum in codicillis exaravi. Dices, ubi? apud[34] Volumnium Eutrapelum et quidem supra me Atticus, infra Verrius, familiares tui. Miraris tam exhilaratam
5 esse servitutem. nostram? Quid ergo faciam? te consulo, qui philosophum audis. Augar[43]? excruciemne me? quid adsequar? Deinde quem ad finem? Vivas, inquis[28], in litteris. An quidquam me aliud agere censes? aut possem vivere, nisi in litteris viverem[46]? Sed est earum etiam non satietas, sed quidam[15]
10 modus. Convivio[4] delector[8]: ibi loquor, quod in solum[45], ut dicitur, et gemitum in risus[11] maximos transfero. An tu id melius, qui etiam in philosophum irriseris? quum ille, si quis quid quaereret, dixisset, cenam te quaerere a mane dixeris. Ille[15] baro te putabat quaesiturum, unum caelum esset an innumera-
15 bilia. Quid ad te? At hercule cena num quid ad te, ibi praesertim? Sic igitur vivitur: cotidie aliquid legitur aut scribitur: dein, ne amicis nihil[26] tribuamus, epulamur una non modo non contra legem, si ulla nunc lex est, sed etiam intra legem et quidem aliquanto. Qua re nihil est quod adventum nostrum
20 extimescas. Non multi cibi[4] hospitem accipies, multi[34] ioci.

55. My dear Arthur,—I was much pleased with your kind letter[37]. So[9] you approve, I see, of my last venture in retiring[33] from the Bar and stumping the country as a lecturer. To tell the truth, I like it myself; it has a good many advantages— first, increased influence[12], the thing I most want just now: next, 5 better health[12]; for want of practice, means want of exercise, and my natural flow of eloquence would have been quite dried up, had it not found a vent for itself in these new channels[45]: lastly, what you, of course, would put first, with improved appetite, improved dinners also; instead of dining[33] like you 10 on a chop at the Cock, I now feast like a turkey-cock, study- ing digestion instead of Digests. You had better follow my example[13], especially as, you know, you haven't a chance of a brief[13]—far better to die of apoplexy than starvation[12]. Come while you can; it's all up with you if you wait. That last 15 sovereign in your purse which[5] you talk of, will just pay for your ticket. You shall have one of the front seats at all my lectures, cushion included[9].

56. My dear friend,—I write[38] this hurried scrawl just before dinner to catch the 6 o'clock post. "And where pray?" At[50] my friend Vincent's, where I am staying with two or three friends of yours. "Indeed!" you will say, "enjoying yourself at such a time as this?" Well what am I to do, my 5 good fellow? You're a philosopher[9],—I put it to you. Am I to afflict and torment myself? What for? What good shall I get by *that?*" "Devote myself to literature then?" Can you imagine me doing anything else? In fact could I have lived[29] till now, except in such pursuits? Still, there is such a thing 10 as having enough, if not too much, even of literature. Now in a dinner there is something I like. *There,* you may say what you like, chatter any nonsense, and all my sighs turn into loud guffaws. However, what has this got to do with *you?* How can *you* be expected to care about such sublunary things as 15 dinners?—especially where you now are. Such then is my course of life—a little reading[33] or writing in the morning: a little dinner in the evening; neither to excess. So you needn't be afraid of my promised visit. You will find me more of a gabbler than a gobbler; more fond of cracking jokes than wal- 20 nuts. Yours ever,

C. H. R.

57.　C. Plinius Tacito Suo S.—Proxime cum in patria
mea fui, venit ad me salutandum municipis mei filius praetexta-
tus.　Huic ego 'studes?' inquam.　Respondit 'etiam.'　'Ubi?'
'Mediolani.'　'Cur non hic?'　Et pater eius (erat enim una atque
5 etiam ipse adduxerat puerum) 'quia nullos hic praeceptores
habemus.'　'Quare nullos? nam vehementer intererat vestra,
qui patres estis,' et opportune conplures patres audiebant,
'liberos vestros hic potissimum discere.　Ubi enim aut iucun-
dius morarentur quam in patria aut pudicius continerentur
10 quam sub oculis parentum aut minore sumptu quam domi?
Quantulum est ergo collata pecunia conducere praeceptores,
quodque nunc in habitationes, in viatica, in ea quae peregre
emuntur inpenditis adicere mercedibus?　Atque adeo ego, qui
nondum liberos habeo, paratus sum pro re publica nostra, quasi
15 pro filia vel parente, tertiam partem eius quod conferre vobis
placebit dare.　Proinde consentite, conspirate maioremque animum ex meo sumite, qui cupio esse quam plurimum quod debeam
conferre.　Nihil honestius praestare liberis vestris, nihil gratius
patriae potestis.　Educentur hic qui hic nascuntur statimque
20 ab infantia natale solum amare frequentare consuescant.　Atque
utinam tam claros praeceptores inducatis ut finitimis oppidis
studia hinc petantur, utque nunc liberi vestri aliena in loca, ita
mox alieni in hunc locum confluant!'　　　　　Pliny iv. 13.

58.　C. Plinius Septicio Claro Suo S.—Heus tu promittis
ad cenam nec venis! Dicetur ius: ad assem inpendium reddes,
nec id modicum.　Paratae erant lactucae singulae, cochleae
ternae, ova bina, alica cum mulso et nive (nam hanc quoque
5 computabis, immo hanc in primis, quae periit in ferculo),
olivae, betacei, cucurbitae, bulbi, alia mille non minus lauta.
Audisses comoedos vel lectorem vel lyristen vel, quae mea
liberalitas, omnes.　Ad tu apud nescio quem ostrea, vulvas,
echinos, Gaditanas maluisti.　Dabis poenas, non dico quas.
10 Dure fecisti: invidisti, nescio an tibi, certe mihi, sed tamen et
tibi. Quantum nos lusissemus, risissemus, studuissemus! Potes
apparatius cenare apud multos, nusquam hilarius simplicius in-
cautius.　In summa, experire, et nisi postea te aliis potius ex-
cusaveris, mihi semper excusa.　Vale.　　　　　Pliny i. 15.

(57.) Being lately at Como, a young lad, son to one of my neighbours, made me a visit. I asked him whether he went to school, and where? he told me he did, and at Milan. "And why not here?" "Because" (said his father, who came with him) "we have no masters." "No!" said I, "surely it concerns you who 5 are fathers (and very opportunely several of the company were so) that your sons should receive their education here, rather than anywhere else. Upon what very easy terms might you, by a general contribution, procure proper masters, if you would only apply towards the raising a salary for them, the extra- 10 ordinary expense it costs you for your sons' journey, lodgings, &c. Though I have no children myself, I will willingly advance a third part of any sum you shall think proper to raise for this purpose. I would take upon myself the whole expense, were I not apprehensive that my benefaction might hereafter be abused 15 and perverted to private ends. The single means to prevent this mischief is, to leave the choice of the masters entirely in the breast of the parents, who will be so much the more careful to determine properly, as they shall be obliged to share the expense of maintaining them. Let my example then encourage 20 you to unite heartily in this useful design; and may you be able to procure professors of such distinguished abilities, that the neigh- bouring towns shall be glad to draw their learning from hence; and as you now send your children to strangers for education, may strangers in their turn flock hither for their instruction." 25

(58.) What does this mean, Sir? Engage to dine and break your engagement? But you shall pay for it: I'll have the law of you. You shall pay for the dinner that you missed, to wit, consommee aux œufs, two chops apiece, one lettuce ditto, cucumber, cheese, and a hundred other dainties equally 5 sumptuous, especially some ice for your wine which above all I shall charge to your account, as a rarity that would not keep. You should likewise have been entertained either with a private penny reading, a rubber of whist, or some music, as you liked best; or (such was my liberality) with all three. But the 10 salmon and port of some Lord or other, were, it seems, more to your taste. Ah, well, you may dine, I confess, at many places more splendidly; but you will find nowhere, believe me, more unconstrained cheerfulness, simplicity and freedom: only make the experiment; and if you do not ever afterwards prefer 15 my table to any other, never favour me with your company again.

59. C. Plinius Acilio Suo S.—Rem atrocem nec tantum epistula dignam Largius Macedo, vir praetorius, a servis suis passus est, superbus alioqui dominus et saevus et qui servisse patrem suum parum, immo nimium meminisset. Lavabatur in
5 villa Formiana: repente eum servi circumsistunt: alius fauces invadit, alius os verberat, alius pectus et ventrem atque etiam, foedum dictu, oculos contundit; et cum exanimem putarent, abiciunt in fervens pavimentum, ut experirentur an viveret. Ille, sive quia non sentiebat, sive quia se non sentire simulabat, immo-
10 bilis et extentus fidem peractae mortis implevit. Tum demum quasi aestu solutus effertur, excipiunt servi fideliores, concubinae cum ululatu et clamore concurrunt. Ita et vocibus excitatus et recreatus loci frigore sublatis oculis agitatoque corpore vivere se, et iam tutum erat, confitetur. Diffugiunt servi; quorum
15 magna pars conprehensa est, ceteri requiruntur. Ipse paucis diebus aegre focilatus non sine ultionis solacio decessit, ita vivus vindicatus ut occisi solent. Vides quot periculis, quot contumeliis, quot ludibriis simus obnoxii; nec est quod quisquam possit esse securus, quia sit remissus et mitis: non enim iudicio
20 domini sed scelere perimuntur. Verum haec hactenus. Quid praeterea novi? quid? nihil; alioqui subiungerem: nam et charta adhuc superest et dies feriatus patitur plura contexi.

Pliny iii. 14.

60. C. Plinius Suetonio Tranquillo Suo S.—Scribis te perterritum somnio vereri ne quid adversi in actione patiaris, rogas ut dilationem petam et pauculos dies, certe proximum, excusem. Difficile est, sed experiar: καὶ γάρ τ' ὄναρ ἐκ Διός ἐστιν.
5 Refert tamen eventura soleas an contraria somniare. Mihi reputanti somnium meum istud quod times tu egregiam actionem portendere videtur. Susceperam causam Iuni Pastoris, cum mihi quiescenti visa est socrus mea advoluta genibus ne agerem obsecrare. Egi tamen λογισάμενος illud
10   εἷς οἰωνὸς ἄριστος ἀμύνασθαι περὶ πάτρης.
Nam mihi patria et si quid carius fides videbatur. Prospere cessit, atque adeo illa actio mihi aures hominum, illa ianuam famae patefecit. Proinde dispice an tu quoque sub hoc exemplo somnium istud in bonum vertas, aut si tutius putas illud
15 cautissimi cuiusque praeceptum 'quod dubitas ne feceris,' id ipsum rescribe. Ego aliquam stropham inveniam agamque causam tuam, ut ipsam agere tu, cum voles, possis. Vale.

Pliny i. 18.

(59.) A horrid barbarity has lately been committed upon a person of high rank by his own servants. They surrounded him as he was bathing, beat him about the face and head, trampled upon his breast, and when they imagined they had thus completed their intentions, they threw him upon the burn- 5 ing pavement of the hot bath, to try if there was any remaining life left in him. He lay there stretched out, and motionless, either as really senseless, or counterfeiting to be so; upon which they concluded him actually dead. In this condition they brought him out, pretending that he had fainted away by the 10 heat of the bath. Some of his more trusty servants received him, and the alarm spread through the family. The noise of their cries, together with the fresh air, brought him a little to himself, and he gave signs (as he now safely might) that he was not quite dead. The murderers immediately made their escape; 15 but the greater part of them are taken, and they are in pursuit of the rest. By proper application he was, with great difficulty, kept alive for a few days, and then expired; having however the satisfaction before he died of seeing just vengeance inflicted on his assassins. So much for this piece of news: and now 20 you will ask, "Is this all?" In truth it is; otherwise, you should have it; for my paper and my time too (as it is holiday with me) will allow me to add more.

(60.) I gather from your letter that you are extremely terrified with a dream, apprehending that it threatens some ill success to you in the case which you have undertaken; and therefore desire that I would get it adjourned for a few days, or at least to the next. I will use all my interest for that 5 purpose, for "dreams descend from Jove."

In the meanwhile it is very material for you to recollect whether your dreams generally represent things as they afterwards fall out, or quite the reverse. The truth is, as an eminent critic has observed with great good sense, there seems to 10 be as much temerity in never giving credit to dreams, as there is superstition in always doing so. The true medium between these two extremes, is, to treat them as we would a known liar; we are sure he most usually relates falsehoods, however, nothing hinders but he may sometimes speak truth. Consider then 15 whether your dream may not portend success. Or after all, perhaps, you will think it more safe to pursue this cautious maxim: "Never do a thing of which you are in doubt:" if so, write me word.

INDEX.

Grammatical notes are referred to by sections. The other references are to the pages of the extracts.

CAMBRIDGE: PRINTED BY C. J. CLAY, M.A. AT THE UNIVERSITY PRESS.